The Dea

Sarah Ward is a critically acclaimed crime and gothic thriller writer. Her book, A Patient Fury, was an Observer book of the month and The Quickening, written as Rhiannon Ward, was a Radio Times book of the year. Sarah is a former Vice-Chair of the Crime Writers Association, Trustee of Gwyl Crime Cymru Festival and an RLF Fellow at Sheffield University.

Also by Sarah Ward

A Mallory Dawson Crime Thriller

The Birthday Girl
The Sixth Lie
The Vanishing Act
The Death Lesson

Carla James Crime Thrillers

Death Rites
Quiet Bones

THE
DEATH
LESSON

SARAH WARD

First published in the United Kingdom in 2025 by

Canelo, an imprint of
Canelo Digital Publishing Limited,
20 Vauxhall Bridge Road,
London SW1V 2SA
United Kingdom

A Penguin Random House Company
The authorised representative in the EEA is Dorling Kindersley Verlag GmbH.
Arnulfstr. 124, 80636 Munich, Germany

A CIP catalogue record for this book is available from the British Library.

Print ISBN 978 1 83598 145 0
Ebook ISBN 978 1 83598 144 3

Cover design by Andrew Smith

Cover images © Shutterstock

Printed and bound in Great Britain by Clays Ltd, Elcograf S.p.A.

Look for more great books at
www.canelo.co | www.dk.com

To Judith Butler

1

Pippa placed her anxiety medication in the top of the chest of drawers, jamming a pile of knickers on top of the box to hide its hateful presence. She had no idea how secure her room would be. The door had a sturdy-looking lock on it but she'd been told that the space plus the en-suite bathroom would be cleaned once a week by Mrs Jones, the staff cleaner. Perhaps Mrs Jones would be the non-curious type, loath to rifle through the belongings of teaching colleagues. Then again, perhaps she was exactly the sort to do that. Pippa winced at the thought of her medical condition becoming the topic of conversation in this hothouse setting. She pulled her emergency ration from the bottom of her suitcase and looked for a place to stash it. A bottle of brandy probably wasn't top of most teachers' essential supplies list, but Pippa had long learnt that things could be made more palatable with a nip of the strong stuff. In the end, she decided to leave it on the table by the bed. If someone complained, she could always say she'd brought it as a present for someone.

Pippa turned to survey the room, which was sparse but tastefully furnished. Everything about the decor suggested discreet wealth. The single oak-framed bed was covered in thick white sheets topped with a woollen Welsh blanket, the type she'd seen in vintage shops going for around two hundred quid. There was a narrow wardrobe to match the chest of drawers and a large desk with an office-style chair improbably covered in William Morris fabric. Someone had thought to put a bowl of fruit on the table in the corner. The room was charming but completely unfamiliar, and Pippa experienced a pang of longing for her old digs in the attic of a Victorian terrace in Cardiff. She suspected she would never ever feel at home here.

She closed her eyes and listened to the sound of girls singing the evening prayer across the frosty quadrangle. The music was unfamiliar but moving. On her arrival, Dr Rhys had told her that staff were expected to attend Sunday services, but given she had just arrived Pippa could miss choral evensong just this once. She now wished she'd gone along as a means of orientating herself in her new workplace, which was a world away from the Cardiff comprehensive where she'd been temping as a maths and geography teacher. When her agency had called to say a job had suddenly come up in a private boarding school, she'd assumed they'd called the wrong person. There was nothing on her CV that would catch the eye of a place as exclusive as Penbryn Hall, but she'd been told that Dr Rhys had seen her résumé and wanted to interview her.

Pippa glanced down at the bed and contemplated the pile of clothes she'd bought herself once she'd secured the position. Dr Rhys – Pippa couldn't yet bring herself to call her new boss Lowri – had said she preferred her staff to wear navy, black or brown, which more or less corresponded to Pippa's own preferences, but she'd still gone to Marks and Spencer in town to buy some thick jumpers and lined trousers ready for the draughty days ahead. She saw now she'd be sweltering in the classrooms if this heated room was anything to go by. Penbryn Hall, it seemed, liked its students to be cosseted from the wild winds that swept across the Cors Caron nature reserve to the north.

The interview to get this position had gone well, but the only morsel of information Pippa had managed to glean about her presence here was that her predecessor had been taken ill suddenly and an immediate replacement was needed. Dr Rhys had given this information willingly at the interview, almost as an aside, but Pippa was convinced that if a better teacher of mathematics had been available, then they would have been a preferred choice. But Dr Rhys had assured her that Pippa, with her first-class degree from Cardiff University and willingness to live in the wilds of West Wales among predominantly female staff and students, had been by far the best candidate. When it came down to it, Lowri Rhys preferred academic achievement over any other accomplishments or social advantages.

After depositing her clothes in the wardrobe, Pippa was at a loss for what to do. She grabbed her quilted coat and decided to explore the grounds until the service finished. Aware that she'd be plunged into the cold once she left the stifling heat of the building, she pushed her wool beret into the coat pocket and wound a scarf around her neck. Her footsteps echoed along the wooden floor as she made her way along the corridor and down the steps to the staff accommodation. She could hear hushed voices in the distance – not everyone, it appeared, was required to go to chapel. Perhaps it was catering staff preparing supper for the girls. Pippa had been told she'd be eating in the staff dining room that evening and she'd memorised directions to the place in readiness for her meal.

At the bottom of the staircase, she pulled open the huge arched door and stepped out into the night. The moon was nearly full and shone brightly above the horizon. A perfect late autumn evening with a hint of winter still to come. This far from the city, the stars lit up the sky, leaving Pippa to stare for a moment in wonder. Only the cold made her push onwards and she walked across the grass, with just a touch of frost glistening on its stems. In the centre of the quadrangle was a fountain, well kept with its marble nymph unblemished by age. In the basin, the pool of water was beginning to freeze. She would need to come down in the morning to see if it was turned on in winter.

Pippa turned her back on the marbled nymph and glanced up at the Edwardian mansion that housed the girls' school. Once she'd received the offer of the job, she'd done some research into the history of the institution. The house had once belonged to the Cadwallader family, who had made their money from slate quarries to the north, but the house and land had been sold off in the 1950s, the first buyer turning it into an upmarket hotel before finally selling the property to the trustees of Penbryn Hall school. It was a bleak-looking building in this light, its grey stone glittering in the sparse landscape. When she'd arrived earlier in the day, the low autumn sun had made it feel more welcoming. Not now.

A gust of wind swept across the lawn taking Pippa by surprise. She pulled her coat around her and made her way back towards the main building. Her room held no attraction, and although Dr Rhys had told her to relax after dinner, Pippa had no intention of fretting in her room all evening. She watched as the chapel door swung open and a gaggle of girls streamed out, their voices kept low as they hurried across the courtyard to the warmth of the building opposite. There were lots of them, all identically dressed in grey coats and skirts with felt hats. The website

4

had emphasised a relaxed approach to school uniform, so perhaps this was their Sunday garb worn to attend chapel. Among the girls, two adults came out under the light, teachers clearly talking to a group of girls and laughing. Pippa felt some of the tension inside her dissipate. Perhaps it would be all right. There was a sense of bonhomie and shared purpose in their laughter. Surely it couldn't be too hard for her to join in with that.

She was about to step forward and join the gathering when she saw a figure emerge from the chapel porch. There was something about the way she stooped before lifting up the hood of her coat that felt familiar and Pippa was surprised to feel a knot of fear in her stomach. What did her body recognise before her brain caught up? She hesitated, caution keeping her rooted to the spot as she watched the woman straighten and pull on her gloves. The porch light shone onto her partially hidden face, and one glance at the profile was enough for Pippa to freeze.

'Christ. Oh, no. Christ.'

The terror that had started in her abdomen rushed through the rest of her and she felt her legs begin to tremble. What was this monster doing here? Pippa glanced around, hoping that someone else recognised the danger they were in, but the girls carried on streaming out, glad to be away from the church and hurrying towards a warm meal. The woman glanced briefly across the courtyard in Pippa's direction, perhaps aware that she was being scrutinised. Pippa withdrew into the shadows, breathing deeply and wondering what the hell she was going to do. Because it was imperative that she got as far away from this place as possible.

2

WESTERN MAIL

12 November

DEATH OF A TEACHER AT EXCLUSIVE SCHOOL

Staff and students at Penbryn Hall near Tregaron were shocked last night by the death of maths teacher Pippa Evans. Pippa, who had only arrived at the school that term, was found deceased in woodland on the school grounds. She had been dead some hours, discovered by teachers who had mounted a search for their missing colleague after she exhibited worrying behaviour.

Penbryn Hall is home to one hundred and fifty students from the wealthiest families around the world, including European royalty. The school issued a statement, saying that everyone was shocked by the death of Pippa, who had been a member of staff for just under a week. Police say that, while they are treating the death as unexplained, they're not looking for anyone else in relation to the incident.

3

Mallory Dawson stood in the foyer of the police station at Carmarthen, intrigued by the unexpected summons. Things had been getting a bit bleak on the employment front and, not for the first time, Mallory had been reassessing her life choices. September had been a warm month, and she'd been basking in memories of her summer near the beach at the caravan park and a week with Harri and the kids in Spain. In fact, the week in Spain had been more kids than Harri. Both her son, Toby, and Harri's children, Ben and Ellie, had acted like self-appointed guardians, watching over any budding romance between their parents like hawks. Mallory had felt inhibited and self-conscious, and she was sure Harri felt the same. Kids. Still, it had been a lovely month.

October and November, however, had been a shock. The weather had plunged and the thin walls of the caravan had clarified for Mallory why people didn't stay in the holiday park all year round. Thoughts of her meagre finances, consisting mainly of her police disability pension, were keeping her awake at night and she was scouring the internet for jobs in the area. Since her arrival in Wales, she'd worked as a hotel night manager, gift shop assistant and, more rewardingly, a civilian investigator at Dyfed Powys Police. It was strictly on an as-and-when contract because of budgetary constraints and meant Mallory had no guarantee of regular work.

Harri, of course, knew her situation and had promised to call if any positions came up in CID. He clearly liked having an ex-copper on call, and Mallory had found herself hoping that West Wales would be the scene of a crime that needed her own expertise. And finally, here she was, kicking her heels in this dull foyer which smelt of carpet freshener, wondering why Harri wanted to see her. Before setting off from her bitterly cold caravan, she'd scoured the news sites and, as far as she was aware, there had been no serious crime in the last forty-eight hours. Perhaps a cold case team needed her help. This was marginally less exciting for her as Mallory preferred the buzz of a live investigation rather than poring over dusty files – an image she liked even if everything was computerised these days – looking for mistakes made by long-retired officers.

The receptionist turned her head at the sound coming from the double doors in the corner. She must have better hearing than Mallory because, on cue, they swung open and Harri came out wearing a rumpled suit where at least, for once, the jacket matched the trousers. He was distracted, making an effort to smile while he picked up Mallory's temporary pass.

'I'm sorry about the short notice,' he murmured to her. 'This has just landed on my plate and I've not had time to draw a breath yet.'

Mallory had been summoned by DS Siân Lewis, who had told her on the phone that she had no idea why Mallory was needed. Siân had sounded a little put out – not an unusual stance. Mallory wasn't sure if it was personal or whether Siân didn't like civilian investigators interfering with proper policing. Nevertheless, it was interesting that Harri hadn't chosen to share details of her visit with his team, and it added to the air of mystery about the reason Mallory was here.

'Can't you at least give me a clue what's going on?' Mallory asked Harri as she put the lanyard around her neck.

'It might as well wait now until we get inside the office. The request has come from on high. The super has come up with a plan and you're needed.'

'A plan for what?'

Harri shook his head as they went into the lift. 'Wait, Mallory.'

The doors opened onto the third floor, a space where Mallory had never been before. It was better decorated than either the offices or interview rooms below, a comfortable place away from the day-to-day hubbub of street policing. Harri opened the door and led her into a room. On one side, looking out of a window, stood a woman dressed in a tailored suit that looked like it was made of the most exquisite mohair. She turned and Mallory tried not to stare. She was a woman in her fifties, with a timeless face, her alabaster skin and pale blue eyes worthy of a pre-Raphaelite painting. Her most striking feature, however, was her pale blonde hair that was pinned back in a style once worn by the film actress-turned-princess Grace Kelly.

The woman looked at Harri, taking her cue from him. 'Mallory, I'd like you to meet Dr Lowri Rhys.' His eyes held a warning as if he knew the name would mean nothing to her but it should.

Mallory smiled and held out her hand. 'Good to meet you.'

She knew at once she was under scrutiny from Lowri. The woman had cast a glance over Mallory's choice of clothes – the cream roll-neck woollen jumper and black fitted jacket and trousers should surely pass muster.

'Shall we sit down,' said Harri pulling out a chair for Mallory. She could see a discussion had already taken place – two china mugs, not the usual paper cups, held the remnants of coffee poured from the glass cafetière. This was an honoured guest.

'I can see,' Lowri said, 'that my name means nothing to you and that, I think, will be to your advantage, if you decide to help us.'

Help, thought Mallory. That's a new one. She saw Harri was avoiding her eye and wondered what was coming next.

'Perhaps I should explain who I am,' continued Lowri. 'I'm the head of Penbryn Hall, a private boarding school near Tregaron. I believe you live in Ceredigion.'

Mallory nodded. 'I do, near New Quay.' No mention of the caravan park.

'Well, Penbryn Hall is about half an hour away from you. It's a girls' school with over a hundred and fifty pupils ranging from ages fourteen to eighteen.'

'I see.' Mallory suspected Lowri had a problem with one of these students who had done something which was or bordered on illegal and she was going to sort it out. Well, that was OK. Her teenage son Toby had taught her everything she needed to know about the vagaries of teenage life. Even if they no longer lived together, Toby's uneasy relationship with food and his refusal to discuss his issues meant he was often on Mallory's mind.

'In addition to the students, I have an academic staff of forty hand-picked by myself, plus another twenty non-teaching personnel.'

'Women only?' asked Mallory.

Harri coughed. 'That's not allowed, Mallory. Sex is a protected characteristic and you can't discriminate against applicants.'

'The current ratio of women to men is two to one. As Harri says, we don't discriminate but we have far fewer male applicants than female. I personally like my students to see women in science and maths positions. They act as good role models for the students but, nevertheless, I recruit men or women based on who is best for the role.'

'Does everyone live in the school?' asked Mallory trying to envisage a place where over two hundred people rubbed shoulders without respite.

'We have day pupils but, given our remote location, they're a small percentage of our students. They currently number sixty taken from the surrounding areas. I person-ally prefer our teachers to live on the premises – it fosters a collegiate atmosphere – but as we've sought to diversify our curriculum, it's occasionally easier to bring people in from, say, Aberystwyth, on short-term contacts. Our jiujitsu teacher lives off the premises, for example.'

'I see.' Mallory didn't, and wished the woman would get to the point. 'And there's been some trouble?'

Lowri glanced at Harri. 'Trouble is a good word. Most of my staff have been with me for years. Penbryn is an exclusive school and I can afford the best, which means people are disinclined to leave. However, at the beginning of term, one of my maths teachers was diagnosed with cancer. She's started a treatment of chemotherapy before surgery and has gone to live with family. It left me a teacher short in the subject and I took an unusual route, for me at least, of contacting an agency to look for suitable candidates.'

'Can't have been easy after term started,' said Mallory. 'Even with higher wages on offer, most teachers would have a contract with their existing schools.'

'Exactly, especially as I have stringent requirements about academic excellence. However, I did find someone – a Philippa Evans, Pippa. She had a first-class honours degree from Cardiff University and because a travel trip overran, she hadn't secured a permanent role by the start of term.'

'*Had* a first-class degree?' asked Mallory, picking up on the tense.

Lowri pursed her lips. 'Philippa, or Pippa as she preferred to be known, was found dead within a week of her appointment. She died by taking an overdose of citalopram, a drug used to treat low moods and panic attacks. She took a blister pack of the medication along with half a bottle of brandy and lay down in a remote corner of the school grounds.'

Mallory frowned, the details of the tragedy coming back to her. 'I saw the article in a newspaper which stated it was suicide.'

'I've subsequently discovered that Pippa was prescribed the drugs for anxiety, so it's entirely possible that she took her own life.'

'What do the local investigators say?' asked Mallory.

Harri stirred. 'Ceredigion Basic Command Unit agree that it's most likely suicide but they're still keeping an open mind while they continue their investigations.'

'OK,' said Mallory. So the issue wasn't a student but a new teacher, already under strain, who had decided to die by their own hand. 'So where do I come into things?'

'The problem…' said Lowri, chewing her lip, her composure slipping for the first time. 'The problem is that I think that someone else might have been a factor in Pippa deciding to end her life.'

4

So here was the reason that Mallory had been brought up to this floor in order to meet Lowri Rhys. She wasn't sure why there was a need for secrecy. If Lowri wanted Pippa's death looked at with a fresh pair of eyes, Mallory would need access to the police files and personnel working on the case, which would make her a visible member of the team. Something was off.

'Do you mean she was killed?' Mallory looked at Harri. 'The article I read quoted a police source to say they weren't looking for anyone else in relation to the incident. You and I know that's police speak for suicide.'

'I've spoken to the investigative team, as has the super-intendent,' said Harri. 'There's no evidence whatsoever that there was foul play. It's nigh on impossible to force someone to take pills and alcohol, although the patholo-gist thinks Pippa died of exposure. Her nervous system will have been depressed following the overdose and the cold weather finished her off.'

Mallory winced. She found suicide difficult to confront and a mentally struggling woman dying of the cold was a little close to home. Harri hadn't noticed her discomfort as he counted off other reasons to support the likelihood of suicide.

'As an investigator, I'd support the initial findings. First, Pippa was only at Penbryn Hall for a week and it's pretty hard to make deadly enemies in that time, although not impossible. In addition, the school and the grounds are secure and there was no evidence that security was breached.'

'Right. Is there anything in her background that would support suicide?' asked Mallory. 'A broken love affair, for example.' She noticed Lowri had sat back in her seat as Mallory quizzed Harri. A woman happy to let others lead when appropriate.

'There are two old boyfriends,' said Harri, 'but according to friends, the break-ups had been amicable and she'd been single for a year. No evidence of a presence on dating apps or other digital media.'

'OK. And what about her state of mind?'

'She had been treated by her GP for anxiety for over four years. Unfortunately, given pressures on the health service here, no follow-up appointment was made so we're not sure if the medication worked or not, but she was definitely taking the pills which she reordered regularly through a repeat prescription.'

'Is it toxic?' asked Mallory. 'Do you have to take a lot of the medication to die?'

Harri made a face. 'An overdose of around a thousand mg, which is what they think Pippa took, can induce cardiac arrest and the brandy will have increased the drug's toxicity. Prescription medication is frequently used for suicide, which is why it's shocking there were no follow-up appointments to check on Pippa's mental health.'

'I see.' Given the facts available, a presumption of suicide was sensible in Mallory's opinion. 'So why do you think someone else might have been responsible for the victim's death?' she asked Lowri.

The woman plucked at her skirt. 'Let's call her Pippa shall we? I'd only known her for a week but I'm struggling with terms such as victim. It dehumanises her.'

'It also allows us to remain objective,' said Mallory, 'but I'll use Pippa if you prefer.'

Lowri nodded. 'Thank you. I think it's important to stress that I'm not usually prone to flights of fancy, and I also like to think I'm happy to let professionals do their jobs. Something, however, about the proposed scenario isn't making sense to me.'

Mallory leant forward, intrigued. Lowri Rhys, she saw, looked worried.

'When I interviewed Pippa for the job, I was struck by how capable she was. She wasn't privately educated but that makes no difference to me. Instead, she was super bright and articulate, which I do value in my staff. I also saw that when she taught a class while under observation by myself, she had a natural rapport with the students. I hired her on the spot, subject to satisfactory references.'

'Which were presumably fine,' said Mallory.

'They were excellent and the only thing that would have given me cause to hesitate was that she didn't seem to remain at any of her previous schools for long. It suggested a restless personality but given I was looking for a temporary replacement for eight or so months, it was hardly an issue. I couldn't offer her a long-term contract.'

'Did she know of the school?' asked Harri. 'Was there any hesitation in accepting the post, for example.'

'None whatsoever. Once she'd got over the surprise at being interviewed, she became animated about the subject she was teaching. Maths was clearly her passion.'

'So what happened?' said Mallory.

Lowri sighed and looked towards the window, giving the impression she'd rather be back looking out over Llan-gunnor. 'It's difficult to say what exactly went wrong. I have to say upfront, her teaching remained exemplary. Once staff are employed, I rarely do an observed lesson, but because of Pippa's behaviour outside the classroom I did sit in on a class on the third day. She was as excellent as I'd hoped, good humoured and intellectually stimulating.'

'So what was the problem outside lessons?'

Lowri shrugged, clearly irritated that her judgement of character had been slightly off. 'She absolutely refused to mix with any of the other teachers. She never came near the staff room, and when approached by colleagues hoping to make her feel welcome, she shrank back from them and said she had teaching prep to do. My deputy, Jonathan Mellor, came to me, as the staff were talking about her behaviour.'

'What did you do?'

'I checked with the agency, who contacted her old school, and they confirmed that Pippa had mixed as normal with teachers and used the staff room.'

'Had her use of anti-anxiety medication come up at any point?'

'Of course not. As part of the employment package, permanent staff get medical insurance and they therefore have to complete a health questionnaire. Pippa remained employed by her agency so the only screening was for work references and, of course, an enhanced DBS check.'

'Did you challenge Pippa on her behaviour?' asked Mallory. 'She must have been surprised to see you observe her teaching for a second time.'

'It's possible she thought that was normal for Penbryn. I'm afraid I didn't get to speak to Pippa about her conduct before she died. I decided – given it was her first week and that the school would have been a significant change for her – that it was better to let her settle and speak to her the following week.'

'Which was too late.'

'Exactly. She took her own life before I had the chance for a meeting. However—' Lowri paused, looking uncomfortable. 'Could I have a glass of water?'

She was stalling, thought Mallory. Whatever she was about to say, Lowri wasn't looking forward to it.

'What I did discover was that Pippa spent a significant amount of time in the school library. Although she had a desk in the accommodation we provided – it's a small room with an en-suite bathroom – she liked to use one of the library tables for marking. That's not unusual in itself as we use one of the nicest rooms in the school to house our book collection. It's a room underneath the clock tower with views across the Ceredigion countryside.'

'So it's clearly somewhere that Pippa felt comfortable,' said Mallory.

'Exactly. It also appears that Emiah, our librarian, was one of the few members of staff that Pippa was happy to engage with.'

'Emiah isn't teaching staff?' asked Mallory.

'She's not. Do you think that makes a difference?'

'I've no idea. I don't know what you're asking of me yet.'

Harri shot her a warning glance which made Mallory fume. She was usually good at sussing out the balance of power in a group, and here, it sat firmly with Lowri Rhys, who'd decided to ignore Mallory's outburst.

'After Pippa's death, I asked Emiah if she'd noticed anything unusual about her behaviour, and she mentioned that Pippa had been making use of the library for research, but had specifically asked that her requests weren't logged in the system. All staff are given an ID pass for security which also acts as a library card. Pippa requested that no trace was left about what she was researching – whether it was computer files, or even word of mouth.'

'And what was she researching?' asked Mallory.

'We don't know.' Lowri's voice bristled with irritation. 'She was very good at not leaving a trail. I've spoken to Emiah, of course, and all she can tell me was that Pippa spent a lot of time by the section we call spirituality and women's studies. Many of our girls are interested in women's rights and we've spent a lot of money keeping that particular area as up to date as possible.'

'Spirituality and women's rights?' Mallory, Harri saw, stifled a bemused laugh. 'Do you have any idea what she might have been looking at?'

'None whatsoever.'

Mallory frowned, wondering for the first time if Lowri was being entirely truthful. 'So just based on a hunch that Pippa was looking into something, you think she was killed.'

Lowri wasn't deterred by Mallory's tone. 'I've spent a long time thinking about this. When Pippa came to the school she was naturally nervous but keen to join us. My deputy, Jonathan, met her on arrival and he has confirmed she was excited to get teaching. She also said hello to two members of staff who were passing without any hesitation.'

'And yet that changed soon afterwards.'

'Exactly. Within less than twelve hours, she had completely withdrawn into herself. She didn't eat with us that evening nor did she come down to breakfast.'

'What did she survive on then?'

'There's tea and coffee available in one of the rooms all day for staff and students. There's also cake, which you pay for using an honesty box. I suspect she was existing on cake and tea.'

Not a diet to help your mental health, thought Mallory. 'What time did she arrive?'

'Around three. Dinner, which she didn't attend, is between seven and eight thirty.'

'So you think something happened between three and seven.'

'I do and I want to know what. I run this school as a tight ship and if there's something wrong within Penbryn, I have no intention of turning a blind eye.'

'I see,' said Mallory, looking at Harri, wondering what the hell she was doing here. Lowri's instincts were probably right given Pippa's odd behaviour but there was an adequate investigative team on the ground working out of Aberystwyth. What did they want with her?

Harri kept his expression neutral. 'I trust Dr Rhys's instinct on this, as does Superintendent Morris. I've been asked to take over as the lead in the investigation into Pippa's death, just to review all the processes so far.'

'And you want an assistant?' That sounded OK. Working to unravel an unexplained death would give her respite from thinking about the cold caravan and her uncertain future.

'Not an assistant as such,' Harri said, watching Mallory. 'I was thinking of an undercover role.'

Mallory groaned. 'Don't tell me. I'll be employed as a member of security staff and do a bit of snooping on the side. I'll tell you now, it won't work, as I'll be an outsider and, what's more, people aren't stupid.'

'Agreed,' said Lowri crisply. 'I've already thought this through and the only way to ease you in successfully would be for you to take over Pippa's position. How good is your maths?'

5

Angharad removed the skin from the orange in one go, starting at the top and letting the peel coil underneath the fruit until she'd finished. She could see Branwen opposite staring at her in lurid fascination – the minutiae was everything inside this house and it was easy to become obsessed by other people's little quirks. From the kitchen, Angharad could hear the clatter of pans. Their new recruit was proving to be a clumsy housemaid. Her parents said she was bright and they wanted her to go to university but it was hard to see any evidence of academic excellence in the lumpen girl who glared at everyone from beneath her long fringe.

The house was bitterly cold, which was how they liked it. They had chosen both this narrow terrace and the farmhouse they intended to move to partly because of their size – there needed to be enough bedrooms for everyone – but also because both properties lacked basic comforts such as central heating and double-glazed windows. The group also rejected any form of modern appliances, which is why they needed a local girl willing to do the heavy cleaning.

Really they should all be sitting down together but Luned, the oldest resident, had been forced to go to hospital because of an accident that had been highly preventable. Someone had been too heavy handed and now explanations would be needed. They were fortunate that Kigva, so experienced in PR, would be attending A and E with Luned. Kigva could be counted on to keep a lid on things, but the worry was who else had seen what happened.

Angharad's reverie was shattered by the sound of breaking crockery in the kitchen at the far end of the house. She rose from the table, taking a candle to light her way through the hall. She made her way towards the dull glow of the kitchen lamp. Although the house had power, they preferred to light the place with candles but allowed electricity to charge their laptops and cook meals.

As she passed through the hallway, she could hear the tap tap of Sister Ceridwen's hammer. She was making the clogs they wore with their habits – wooden soled and sturdy. Ceridwen had rushed her dinner as Sister Branwen's shoes had ripped while she was putting the chickens in for the night. A replacement pair would be ready before the evening was out. Ceridwen would make sure of it.

Angharad entered the kitchen where the girl stood in mute misery, her back to the ancient ceramic sink. The maid's attire that she wore – long black skirt and blouse and an old-fashioned pinny tied round her waist – was slovenly on her. The skirt's hem was coming loose and the collar of her blouse had a stain of food on it.

'What did you break?' asked Angharad, reaching for the object in the corner of the room.

'One of the serving dishes,' said the girl, her face pale. 'It slipped out of my hand because it was so greasy.'

'You need to take more care,' said Angharad. 'I warned you what would happen if there were any breakages. Can I see your hands?'

'No.' The girl had spirit but Angharad had also spotted the flash of fear in her eyes.

'It's for your own good. It will be over in a second. Give me your hands.'

The girl hesitated and presented her arms, her hands still soapy with washing-up suds.

Bringing the switch high up into the air, Angharad brought it smartly down across the girl's palms.

'Pippa, I forgive you.'

6

Mallory had never been so terrified in her life. Well, perhaps that was an exaggeration – when she'd sustained her injury in the line of duty, she'd assumed as she lay bleeding on the pavement that she was going to die. That had been terrifying but among the horror had been the knowledge that there was nothing she could do. As the paramedics had worked on her, she'd submitted herself to the gods and been surprised to find they ruled in her favour. Here, she knew that her success or failure was completely down to her.

Fourteen faces regarded her with interest as Mallory stood in front of the interactive whiteboard trying to stop her hands trembling. When Lowri had asked her how her maths was, she'd already known that Mallory had studied the subject at university. Harri must have damn well told her. However, that had been nearly twenty years earlier and she'd certainly never taken any courses on how to teach the subject. Lowri had said she was rejigging timetables so that Mallory would be teaching year nine and lower sixth so that, although exam preparation would be involved, the actual exams wouldn't be impacted by a few weeks of Mallory's teaching.

Mallory had tried to play the safeguarding card. She knew what procedures had been introduced in the state sector as Toby had told her of a scandal involving a teacher and pupil at his London comprehensive. She was sure she'd read of similar incidents in private schools, with boarders particularly vulnerable. A school as well known as Penbryn Hall must surely have measures in place to stop non-qualified people mixing with students. Lowri had waved away objections. Mallory had been vetted for her police job, which was good enough for her, and she was sure her maths could cope with whatever the students threw at her.

Mallory forced herself to concentrate on the algebra on the board. She'd mugged up the previous evening and had been relieved to see that the module wasn't that hard. How she'd cope by staying one lesson ahead of her class, she wasn't sure, but for the moment she was happy that the girls seemed bright and focused.

After setting an exercise, Mallory walked up and down taking stock of the classroom. It was far removed from Mallory's own education, which was no surprise and helped her imagine what Pippa must have felt in this over-awing setting. The high vaulted ceiling gave the space the feel of a drawing room and even the tables were polished oak. The girls had laptops – they were allowed them in the sixth form – and were completing the exercises online. Mallory leant over one red-headed girl to look at the screen and was surprised to see her name in the Google chat bar.

'Checking up on me, Lucy?' said Mallory. Good luck with that. It had been agreed by Lowri and Harri that Mallory would keep the surname Dawson. The techies in Carmarthen had already checked that the name didn't throw up any references to Mallory's meagre online presence.

The girl started. 'I… I'm sorry. It's just I was wondering if you were a friend of Miss Evans.'

Mallory wasn't sure if she believed the explanation but it was an excellent opportunity to bring up Pippa without it sounding forced.

'That's my predecessor isn't it?' asked Mallory feigning ignorance.

'She died,' said the girl sitting next to Lucy. She had a strong athletic figure and Mallory had already discovered that Molly Jessop played for the Welsh under-18s football team.

The class had stopped and were listening to the conversation. At seventeen, Mallory had been like these girls, curious and gossipy.

'I was sorry to hear that,' she said. 'Why did you think I might be a friend of Miss Evans?'

'You look a bit like her,' said Lucy. 'She had dark hair like you and was thin.'

Mallory frowned. The connection felt tenuous and she guessed she had just been checked out by an over-curious student. 'Did you have a lesson with her the week she was here?'

Mallory felt on unsteady ground. She'd been given permission by Lowri to question staff about Pippa's death but not to speak to any students without her permission. However, this conversation felt natural and she was loath to move on.

'She taught us once,' said Molly. 'We liked her but she had strange habits. She liked darkness, for example. She kept the blinds down as she said the light hurt her eyes.'

Mallory looked at the window, where the wooden slats had been pulled to the top. 'Maybe she was sensitive to the sunlight,' she said. 'The sun is low in the sky during this time of year. Anything else?'

'She asked us about discipline here. Wanted to know how strict it was.' The voice came from a girl in the corner, painfully thin, who reminded Mallory of her son Toby. Mallory checked the classroom plan she'd made with each student's name. Isabella. She'd need to keep an eye on Isabella while she was here and perhaps speak to Lowri about her weight.

Mallory smiled and the girl lowered her head so her fringe was covering her face. 'And is it strict?'

'A bit,' said Lucy, 'but we don't mind. It's not scary strict or anything.'

Mallory nodded. 'You all have support, don't you? I believe there is a school counsellor you can talk to if you're affected by Miss Evans's death.'

For these girls, Mallory had to remember that Pippa's death would have ramifications even if they'd only shared one class with their teacher. A sea of heads nodded. 'You can also talk to me. I'll be teaching you maths this time each week but you can come and find me if anything's on your mind.'

She'd lost their interest, Mallory saw. They wanted to talk about Pippa and her death, not their own feelings. In a school like this, there would be plenty of pastoral support and she didn't especially need to add herself into the mix. Nevertheless, Mallory thought it important to plant the seed of communication among this group. Who knew where it would lead?

One girl, she saw, kept her eyes on Mallory. Her gaze was neither curious nor hostile but held a question.

'Is everything all right, um...' Mallory checked her sheet. 'Livvy.'

'I've finished, miss.'

'Oh.' Mallory crossed the room and looked at the girl's working online. Shit. This was what she'd been afraid of. Finding someone whose capability was well beyond her own. Even a quick glance showed Mallory that every answer was correct.

'I always finish quickly,' whispered Livvy. 'Teachers usually give me extra exercises.'

'That's good to know.' Mallory had over-prepared for the lesson and knew there was some material she'd never get to in the fifty-minute slot. She went to her desk and found some exercises she'd photocopied from a book in the library and handed Livvy a sheet full of algebra problems. 'Would you like to work through these? You'll have to work on paper though.'

With a sinking heart Mallory watched the girl bend over the problems and begin to write. She'd have them finished in no time and then Mallory would have to think on her feet. She noticed that Livvy's classmates, still wrestling with their own problems, paid no attention to a fellow student whose aptitude was well above their own. It suggested intelligence and diligence were prized talents, which was no surprise given Lowri's personality.

Mallory walked back to her desk thinking of the noisy state school she'd attended where she'd often dumbed down her own abilities in order to fit in with her friendship group. Penbryn Hall in contrast had an air of benign solicitude and Mallory had still to find a crack in its façade.

She glanced out of the window and saw Lowri walk through the inner courtyard speaking to a woman with flame-red hair. Mallory hadn't seen Lowri's companion in the dining room the previous evening but from her manner, she guessed it was Lowri's secretary, Eirin. It was she who'd emailed Mallory instructions for her arrival and, from their tone and content, Mallory guessed Eirin hadn't been let in on the secret of her real identity. She wondered if anyone would spot their subterfuge.

She looked across the classroom and caught the gaze of Livvy who had finished the work. If the teaching staff were as bright as their students, keeping the real reason for Mallory's presence secret was going to be a challenge.

7

After the morning lesson, Mallory had a free period. Lowri had promised a light timetable for her with plenty of breaks and her next class wasn't until after lunch. Mallory wondered what the other teachers thought of her meagre duties but perhaps Lowri had some excuse ready if asked. Mallory couldn't really imagine anyone questioning the head's authority but in a place like this there would be plenty of natural curiosity. The only member of staff who had been informed about Mallory's real identity was Jonathan Mellor, the deputy head. Mallory hadn't yet been introduced to him but had received a message on her police email account that Jonathan wanted to meet at seven p.m. after dinner, in his office. The tone of the missive was terse and unfriendly and had left Mallory worried that a complaint had already been made about the quality of her teaching.

Feeling restless, Mallory wondered if she'd stick with this job until the end of term, the point at which it had been agreed that she would report her conclusions to Lowri. It was only three weeks away but this place was so unfamiliar it got Mallory's back up. She'd never really immersed herself in extreme wealth before. She'd had a decent enough state education in a well-performing school and had gone to Manchester University to study maths. She'd met privately educated students, of course, but her friends had come from similar backgrounds to her. Once in the police, her colleagues had been drawn from across society but if there was anyone from a privileged background, she'd not met them. The gentleman detective was a thing of fiction and nothing to do with real life.

Mallory rubbed her face and suddenly missed her son with a stab of pain. She'd decided not to tell him about her assignment beyond letting him know she'd be out of contact for a while. He'd taken this with equanimity, well used to the demands of her job, but Mallory fretted that Toby's self-reliance masked deeper issues that were only beginning to be revealed. She let out a long sigh, suddenly exhausted. Teaching wasn't for the faint hearted and neither was parenting, come to think of it. Perhaps looking over her lesson plan for the afternoon would take her mind off things, but after running the gauntlet of the lower sixth, she thought year nine maths would be a doddle. Through the window, she saw that the autumnal day was fair with the sun in the cloudless sky making the orange and brown hues of the landscape glow. She'd escape outside.

Mallory stepped out of the building and made her way across the courtyard, heading towards the wooded area in the distance. It was here that Pippa had been found dead, and Mallory, before arriving, had memorised the plans drawn up by the forensic team. She now had the opportunity while she was undercover to look at the spot herself. If Pippa had died by someone else's hand – unlikely but still worth considering, in Mallory's mind – the remote location suggested some kind of rendezvous with her killer, probably after dark. The journey to the woods was too exposed in daylight, and even now Mallory felt as if she was being watched from one of the windows of the school. She wasn't prone to wild flights of fancy but couldn't shrug off the impression that a watcher was tracking her progress across the lawn. The thought made Mallory reassess her plans and she made a point of stopping and inhaling the landscape, her eyes on a pair of figures near a walled garden.

Mallory casually made her way towards them. She had determined that she'd be as unlike Pippa as possible even if that tipped into over-friendliness. The pair drew apart as they saw her approach, both smiling at her.

'Hi, I'm Mallory Dawson, the new maths teacher.'

The woman on the left with rich brown hair held back from her face with tortoiseshell clips held out her hand, which shook a little as Mallory grasped it. She couldn't work out if the woman was a bag of nerves or had a tremor.

'I'm Freya Wells. I saw you arrive last night and have been looking for you to say hello. It's always difficult to join a school well into term.'

'That's kind of you. Dr Rhys explained the circumstances of my predecessor's death at my interview and I'm sorry to hear about it. One of the girls in my first class brought up the incident.'

Freya made a face. 'That's unfortunate but the students like to talk. We're all in this odd state of stasis over Pippa's death. None of us really knew her given she'd only been here a week and yet the school's been knocked on its axis because of the incident. What I'd really like is to try to put it all behind us. Jem and I were just chatting about it now.'

Mallory glanced at Freya's companion. She was as tall as her colleague but with an androgynous appearance.

From her trouser suit over a man's shirt and her short, clipped hair she presented an air of gender fluidity that was intriguing. She also held out her hand. Mallory had noticed this was a quirk of the school. Shaking hands was the norm, far more so than in the outside world.

'I'm Jem Owen. I teach history here.' She had a proprietary manner towards Freya which made Mallory wonder about the relationship between the two.

Jem had the accent of a first-language Welsh speaker and Mallory warmed to her song-like tones. 'I don't know much about Welsh history but it's something I'd love to study. Do you incorporate it into your lessons?'

'It's the basis of our history curriculum.' Jem's voice was proud. 'We don't just teach to pass exams like in the state sector. Is this your first time in a private school?'

Mallory's accent probably gave her away. Guilty as charged. 'I'm afraid so, but this is a temporary position so I need to find my feet quickly. As far as maths is concerned, I'm following a curriculum given to me by Lowri, I mean Dr Rhys.'

'You can refer to her by the name Lowri. Staff don't stand on ceremony here, but we still ask students to address us formally.'

'That's good to know. I'm guessing you have more freedom in subjects such as history and…' Mallory trailed off and Freya came to her aid.

'I teach politics and psychology, and, like Jem, it's good to have the freedom to teach outside the box while making sure the students are exam ready. It's what Lowri prides herself on.'

In the distance a bell rang and the two women's eyes were drawn towards the school building. Lunchtime.

'Will you be joining us in the dining room?' asked Jem.

'Of course. I was just getting some fresh air first. Will I miss out if I don't get there on the dot?'

Freya laughed. 'It's not a scrum if that's what you're asking. People come and go for the two hours that food is served. Come and sit at our table when you get there. We're a welcoming lot.'

There was an emphasis in her voice that suggested hidden emotion. Pippa's refusal to socialise had probably hurt the staff and they were keen to place it as a one-off. They parted, the two women making their way back to the school building while Mallory carried on into the walled garden. Heading to the woods would appear too curious so early in her tenure here so she needed to do it in a roundabout way. She noted that the walled garden was beautifully tended and it was tempting to linger, but she slipped through the gate at the other end and, out of sight of prying eyes, entered the wooded area.

Although the sounds of school – girls' shrieks of laughter, shouts of instructions from the hockey pitch and a strimmer cutting the laurel hedge – had been muted in the walled garden, in the copse the noise was muffled further. Lowri had told her that a bunch of flowers would mark the spot where Pippa had been found. The school would be laying flowers for a month following Pippa's death and then it would stop. Mallory had got the impression Lowri would have preferred not to mark the death at all but students had been laying makeshift posies and the head had been determined to put an end to that. It would be official flowers for a short time only.

Mallory found the bunch of white lilies easily enough. It was a flower she didn't like and it looked incongruous among the elder and oak trees. Artificial against traditional woodland. Mallory thought the flowers were as out of place here as Pippa had been. She stopped for a moment, paid her respects to the dead teacher and went back to work mode. If Pippa had met someone here, the meeting could have taken place in total secrecy. However, if she was looking for somewhere private to take her own life, surely her bedroom was as good a place as any. Why come outside on a cold evening?

Mallory was still regarding the flowers when a snap of twigs made her start. 'Hello?'

Her heart nearly stopped when a figure stepped out of the undergrowth looking momentarily like a monk transported from the fifteenth century.

'Did I startle you?' The figure pulled back the hood of their brown woollen overcoat, revealing a jolly face surrounded by wiry curls. Her smile fell when she regarded the flowers.

'I see you've found our makeshift memorial.'

Mallory decided partial honesty was the best policy. 'I was curious to come to the spot. I hope I don't come across as morbid or anything.'

'It's perfectly natural.' The woman's curly head nodded in agreement. 'I'm Rose, by the way, popularly known to the students as Religious Rose because that's what I teach.' She saw Mallory's confused expression. 'Religious Education, I mean.'

'Oh,' said Mallory, not knowing what else to say.

Rose took no offence. 'You'll find students like to give teachers a nickname to liven things up. They're rarely offensive but it's good to know what they're calling you behind your back.'

'I'll remember that. Did Pippa have a nickname?'

'I don't think they'd got round to it. I mean, she was here for about a week.' Rose gave Mallory an

36

assessing stare. 'Did you know, people are often drawn to places where tragedies took place. It's a well-known phenomenon.'

Mallory inwardly groaned. Rose clearly liked to place people into types and she was going to be known as morbidly curious. This was in fact true but still Mallory resented the assumption.

'It's a miserable place to die,' said Mallory, surprising Rose.

'Is it? I think people are drawn to forests, part of the ancient woodland, the Welsh returning to their past.'

'Did Pippa strike you like this?'

Rose took a step back. 'Pippa didn't strike me full stop. I only spoke to her the once. She was in the library and I tapped her on the shoulder, which made her jump out of her skin. She sprang up, snapped her book shut, making sure I couldn't see the title of what she was reading, and scuttled off. I'm not used to having that effect on people.'

'Sorry, it's just the fact you're visiting the spot where she died, I thought you might have been close.'

'Oh no, it's just that Dr Rhys has asked us all to keep an eye on students. They're a robust lot in my opinion but you never know. I was checking that no one was loitering here.'

'You think Pippa might have made a connection with a student?' If that was the case it was really out of Mallory's remit.

'I don't think so. It's just, well, teenagers can get a bit romantic about death and I'd like to nip it in the bud. I know Lowri feels the same. Shall we have some lunch?'

Mallory smiled and followed Rose out of the wood-land. Another confirmation that Pippa hadn't got close to anyone and yet, she'd died a mere week after her arrival with only commonly prescribed anti-anxiety pills to suggest a mildly disturbed mind.

'Pippa arrived on Sunday I believe. What takes place in the afternoon here?'

'Not much. We have activities for the students and then choral evensong in the chapel. Lowri likes everyone to attend unless there are religious reasons for absenting yourself.'

'Did Pippa go?'

'Apparently not but almost everyone else did.'

It was possible that Pippa saw someone entering or leaving the chapel but Mallory couldn't understand how that could have such a profound effect on the new teacher. She needed to dig deeper below the genteel niceness that permeated the atmosphere. Could she find someone who really wasn't nice at all?

8

Harri drove his daughter to college wondering how Mallory was getting on at Penbryn Hall. It would certainly make a change from the caravan park, and perhaps living in luxury would prompt her to settle somewhere with at least brick foundations. Ellie chatted beside him, oblivious to his distracted manner. She'd recently acquired a new boyfriend after being dumped by his predecessor. It sounded very casual to Harri, who couldn't get used to his daughter dating and had to rely on the reassurances of his sister, Fran, that sixteen was a perfectly fine age to have a boyfriend. As she left the car, Ellie gave the door a slam, reminding him of Ellie's mother, Paula, who had always done the same. She had been dead now for over a decade and Harri still missed her, and the hole in the family had not been filled.

He thought of Mallory again and sighed as he pulled away. He was attracted to her, no doubt about that, but she blew hot and cold and if he was going to be completely honest with himself, so did he. There were others to consider – their kids but also Mallory's ex-husband, the memory of Paula and also Fran, who lived with them. Lives got more complicated as hormones dulled so having a love life was never easy.

Back at the station, there was a message on his desk to go and see Superintendent Morris. Harri immediately knew what it was about. He'd tried to call Mallory's mobile the previous evening looking for an update on her arrival at Penbryn Hall. Given it was early days, he didn't realistically expect her to have uncovered anything but he was interested in how she was settling into what must be a hothouse environment. Mallory would be fine. She had the inner resilience of many ex-coppers. She hadn't even protested when it was suggested she enter the classroom, although Harri suspected it would be this aspect of her new assignment that would cause her the most worry. Teenagers, in Harri's experience, were tough nuts to crack.

Stephanie was drumming her fingers on the large conference-style table which she used to work on. It was apparently part of her new open style of management but in fact the wide expanse of polished teak was as imposing as a chair in front of a standard-issue desk.

'Any news from Penbryn Hall?' she asked without greeting him.

Harri eyed up the coffee pot noting that it only had one cup next to it. He wasn't going to be staying. 'Mallory has only just arrived. I've phoned for an update and she'll call me back when she can.'

Stephanie pouted. 'I want daily briefings on this. If there's a scandal, and I'm inclined to trust Lowri's instincts on this one, then I want to be able to contain it. The reputation of one of the country's top schools is at stake.'

What Harri hadn't told Mallory, and he noticed Lowri Rhys hadn't seen fit to mention either, was that Stephanie herself was an alumnus of Penbryn Hall. The constabulary was probably an unusual choice of one of its former pupils but they must surely be pleased with her rapid rise through the ranks to superintendent before the age of forty.

'If there's trouble, Mallory will find it. She's unerringly drawn to danger.'

Stephanie grunted. 'Well, I'll agree with you on that one. I hope to God it's not one of the pupils who tipped Pippa Evans over the edge. I can cope with rogue staff members but children are a whole different ball game.'

'There's no evidence a student was involved. In fact, I have to say this, ma'am, there's not any concrete evidence that anyone was involved in Pippa's death. She suffered from anxiety and was plunged into a new environment. Mallory's job might be to simply confirm this.'

Steph pulled at her lower lip and Harri saw her pale pink lipstick smudge onto her thumb. The super wasn't someone to worry easily and he wondered what he wasn't being told. In fact, he had quite a lot of questions, not least where they were getting the money from to fund Mallory's wages. A directive had come down from high up that costs needed cutting and a recruitment freeze was imminent. He had dreaded passing the news onto Mallory as it had both a financial implication for her and meant they wouldn't be thrown together as they had in the last two years since their first meeting.

'I have to tell you, I'm getting some pressure from the Chief Constable. She's been contacted by the Foreign Office, who've been leant on, I suspect, by their embassies around the world. We have two princesses from Europe, the daughter of the head of one of the Emirates States plus at Christmas, two children of one of the world's richest men are moving to Penbryn Hall as their school is closing due to the new VAT rules.'

'Christ,' said Harri. 'Can't the civil servants keep out of Welsh education? They pay us scant attention the rest of the time.'

'Now, now,' said Steph, not disagreeing. 'One of the benefits of living in the wild west of Wales is people do leave us alone. Would you rather it any other way?'

'Not really.'

'Exactly, but Penbryn Hall isn't just a Welsh establishment. It has an international profile and people are concerned. It's why the Chief Constable signed off the money for Mallory's role.'

'She didn't go there herself, did she?' Harri asked before he could stop himself.

Steph's brows knitted together in disapproval but she made no denial. Christ, thought Harri, so that's how it is.

'So, as I said, I want daily briefings and once Mallory has confirmed nothing untoward is happening there, we pull her out and close the case. Lowri is a little, well, protective of the establishment at times. She's probably just being over-cautious.'

Harri wasn't so sure. He was an instinct man himself and inclined to respect the suspicions of others. 'Of course. Mallory will have had her first day of teaching so there might not be much to update you with, but I'll make sure I speak to you daily.'

'Come to my office at quarter to nine each morning. I've told my secretary to expect you and I'll have no meetings scheduled before nine.'

Harri resisted the temptation to salute. 'Of course.'

'I need to tell you that Lowri runs a tight ship. I doubt Mallory's colleagues will be inclined to gossip so she's going to have to work hard to find any potential issues.'

'Mallory's an experienced detective and knows what to look for. To begin with, we need to know what Pippa was doing in the library and why she was so desperate not to leave a trail. If I were Mallory, that's where I'd start.'

'And if she gets nowhere with that?'

Harri shrugged. 'Pippa saw someone within hours of arriving at Penbryn Hall. When Sunday comes I suspect Mallory will be watching the routine very closely.'

9

Mallory spent an enjoyable half hour at lunch with Jem and Freya. She kept the conversation away from Pippa as she wanted the two women to feel relaxed in her company before she started digging deeper into the events of the previous week. She could, however, ask some general questions around school life. According to the timeline of Pippa's movements on arriving at Penbryn Hall, she'd been met by Jonathan Mellor, who claimed she'd been perfectly amiable. Pippa had been given time to unpack and told to make her way to the dining hall where staff and students ate together on Sunday evenings. She'd never made it. When Jonathan knocked on Pippa's door that evening, she'd answered, keeping her face in the shadows, to say she was tired and going to bed early. If something had happened to Pippa, or rather if *someone* had happened to Pippa, then the occurrence must have taken place between three and seven thirty p.m.

'What do you do on weekends?' asked Mallory, picking at her hummus salad.

'There are lessons on Saturday morning, of course,' said Freya. 'The rest of the day rather depends on if we've been rostered to help with any extra-curricular stuff, but Lowri is careful to make sure we have time to ourselves. Sundays are free, except we're expected to attend the church service in the morning and evensong at five.' She stopped, casting a glance at Jem. 'This has been explained to you, hasn't it?'

'It has,' said Mallory, 'don't worry. What time is evensong?'

'Five thirty.'

'Right.' Mallory was pretty certain that Pippa hadn't been to the service but supposed she had seen someone going into the chapel from the window of her room. It was just possible in the faint light.

'Everyone attends chapel, do they?' Mallory was repeating the conversation she'd had with Rose but the timing was important and she needed to narrow down attendees.

'Unless you have dispensation,' said Jem. 'We have seven teachers from other faiths and a handful of pupils who don't attend but other than them, you're really expected to.'

Great, thought Mallory, I might have narrowed suspects down by the grand total of seven. As she ate, she noticed again the tremor in Freya's left hand. Her demeanour was calm, which suggested she was suffering from a neurological problem. It probably didn't impact her teaching but it still made Mallory wonder. She glanced down the long table taking in the dynamic of the staff. Lowri had been right when she'd told Mallory that her colleagues were predominantly female. Interestingly, the four men at the table were sitting together at the far end, laughing. She let the chatter wash over her while she finished her meal, determined to make it to the library before her next lesson.

Emiah Jenkins was talking to a student when Mallory entered the huge room that served as the school library. Lowri had been right when she'd said that the library had been allocated the best room in the house. It must have once been a grand drawing room, a ballroom even, and the air of grandeur suited the oak shelves full of books. Mallory waited for Emiah to finish, taking in the tall windows with a clear view to the copse. There were two students at the long tables, both with their backs to the windows, perhaps deciding the view was a distraction. When Emiah was free, Mallory went over to introduce herself. Emiah's smile dropped a fraction when Mallory explained she was the new maths teacher.

'I'm sorry about what happened to my predecessor. It makes things a little awkward when I introduce myself.'

Emiah took a breath, making an effort to calm herself. 'Thank you, although I didn't know her well. I had no idea she was in such torment. She just seemed a bit shy.'

'Can I ask about borrowing books?' said Mallory, her eyes on the computer screen.

'You use your staff ID, which also works as a library card. You can take up to eight books but more are permissible if you talk to me.'

Talk to me, thought Mallory. Here was a way that computers could be bypassed and books borrowed without leaving a trace.

'Do you work every day?' she asked.

'Thursdays and Sundays are my days off, but I have a deputy who works part-time hours to cover my absence. She's not based in the school though.' Emiah's tone was dismissive, suggesting she was queen bee in this space.

'Did Pippa like using the library?'

Emiah frowned. 'What makes you ask that?'

Mallory shrugged. 'I was wondering about the maths section.'

'Oh.' Emiah relaxed a fraction. 'We have a good quality module over to the right. I've no idea if Pippa used it though.'

Nevertheless, Emiah had spotted that Pippa was interested in the spirituality and women's studies section and had included this in her police statement. 'I'll take a look around if that's OK. It's an impressive space.'

Mallory made a show of perusing the shelves slowly, passing without apparent interest the area that had so attracted Pippa. It amounted to two long bookcases filled with books far more specialised than Mallory would have expected in a school. One title was *The Feminine and Divine* a title Mallory wholeheartedly approved of. She had little time for religion and particularly disliked the idea of God as an old man who told you what to do.

She continued her scrutiny, picking up a book from the history section and wondering why Pippa had been so keen to hide the title of her book from Rose unless it was Rose herself she'd wanted to avoid. 'Scuttled away' had been Rose's assessment of Pippa's response. Mallory glanced across at Emiah, who had crossed to the other side of the room to replace books. From this distance, her hostility was palpable and yet Mallory was sure she'd been casual enough when perusing the shelves. She'd need to talk to Lowri about Emiah and find out what was eating away at the woman.

Mallory, about to go to the next lesson, looked down at her cream blouse and saw she'd dropped a piece of lettuce on it, the chlorophyll green spreading into the cotton. Fuck. In the station, she'd have made a joke about it and carried on with her day. Teaching was different and there was no way she was going to run the gaze of fifteen or so critical teenagers with a soiled blouse. Time for a quick change. She'd need to find out the laundry arrangements later.

She opened the door of her room and knew straight away that someone had been inside. Her nose picked up a smell similar to lemongrass, not from artificial cleaner but delicate with the hint of a cottage garden. She looked around and saw her laptop was in the same place and the wastepaper bin unemptied. Not a thief or the cleaner then. She scrutinised the room to find further evidence that her private space had been invaded, and her gaze fell on a note that had been left on the chest of drawers. There was no envelope and the piece of plain paper was unfolded. On it had been typed: 'The Cranogwen room. 2 a.m. tonight.'

Mallory's first thought was that it was one of the students she'd met that morning having a laugh at her expense. There was plenty of opportunity for jokes and pranks in a school and perhaps she was being tested on how she reacted. However, when Lowri had brought Mallory to her room, the same one that Pippa had occupied two weeks earlier, she'd been at pains to emphasise that this wing of the house was for teachers only. No students were allowed in the area, firstly for safeguarding reasons and secondly to allow staff a student-free space to decompress. It wasn't impossible that a student had found a way to sneak in but it was a hell of a gamble. One thing was for sure: Mallory would be outside the Cranogwen room at two a.m.

10

The meeting with the deputy head was abruptly cancelled. One of the lower college students, a girl from Spain, was discovered in the nearby town of Tregaron drinking in a pub with a local boy she'd met on the internet. Jonathan had been dispatched to both retrieve the student and have a quiet word with the boy, who was unaware, or so he said, that his date was fifteen. Christ, rather him than me, thought Mallory. Instead she spent the evening preparing for the following day's lesson and wondering what lay in store for her when she got to the Cranogwen room.

Toby, Mallory's son, rang at half ten that evening just as Mallory was struggling to keep her eyes open. She had no idea teaching was so exhausting and had a new respect for anyone who chose it as a profession. Bloody hell, those students certainly kept you on your toes. The sensible thing to do was to have a nap and set her alarm for half one so she was awake and ready to meet whoever had placed the note in her room. However, Mallory had no idea how soundproof her walls were. They looked thick enough – the whole building had an air of Edwardian solidity – but Mallory was taking no chances. Instead, she'd brewed herself a pot of coffee using the electric kettle she'd brought along with her and added an extra spoonful of grinds to the cafetière.

'Mum, I haven't heard from you for a few days.' Toby sounded put out. "A mother's place is in the wrong" had been her grandmother's axiom and it was certainly true for her relationship with her son, who could never quite make up his mind if he wanted to live with her or his father.

'I told you I had a new job and wouldn't be able to talk much,' said Mallory, trying not to sound defensive.

'Where?' asked Toby. 'Are you still in Wales?'

'Bloody hell, Tobe,' said Mallory. 'I said I've got a new job, not moved country.'

'It doesn't sound like you're in the caravan,' said Toby suspiciously.

'Guilty as charged but I can't tell you where I am as I'm working for the police again and it's a residential post.'

'You're not back on Eldey are you?' This was the island where Mallory had nearly lost her life. A job that had brought her to Wales and to Harri's attention.

'I'm not at Eldey but I'm not answering any more questions. You know the score when I'm working.'

'Is Harri with you?'

Mallory rolled her eyes. More evidence of Toby's protectiveness.

'He's not but he is my boss. OK?'

'OK.'

After a few more minutes of light chat, Toby rang off. Mallory made a mental note to talk to his father, her ex, on Sunday when she had some downtime. Toby struggled with an eating disorder and had finally begun counselling after a long wait for a place. His weight remained stable, which was the best they could hope for so early in the treatment, but the slowness of getting results was making Mallory fret. Not for the first time, she wondered if her own shortcomings as a mother were to blame for Toby's illness.

Mallory was just settling down with her second cup of coffee when her phone rang again.

'How you getting on, Mallory?' Harri's rich baritone voice came down the line. 'I've been trying to call.'

'Well, I've survived my first day of teaching. Those kids are bright, which frightens me more than an unruly classroom.'

Harri laughed softly. 'I don't envy you that. What about Pippa's death?'

So there was to be no chit-chat. 'Lots of disquiet but that's about it. No genuine grieving but you wouldn't expect that after a few days' acquaintance.'

Mallory paused, wondering whether she should tell him about the assignation coming up. On balance, Harri was a good sort and not the kind to moan at her about putting herself in danger. If anything went wrong, she needed to make sure someone knew her plans. He listened in silence as she told him about the note.

'I'm not sure I like the sound of that. If Pippa saw someone who she considered a danger to herself then that person's motives might not be benign.'

'It's a possibility but the note is in effect forewarning me of what's to come. Unless we're talking about a particularly arrogant adversary, they're unlikely to want to inform me about their plans. It's as likely to be someone with information.' Mallory looked at her watch. Only five minutes had passed since she had last checked. It was going to be a long night.

'Where is the Cranogwen room?' asked Harri.

'In this building in the opposite wing. I've looked it up on the school map and it seems to be a supersized classroom which has been made into a lecture theatre. You could probably get three hundred people in there, going by the size.'

'Makes sense. You need somewhere to get everyone together other than the assembly hall. It's probably used for parents' days as well. Will you call me when you're back?'

'It could be three-ish.'

'Still, call me. Good luck Mal.'

Mallory resisted the temptation to look at her watch again and instead pulled across a pile of marking. She'd set her lower-sixth students an exercise in the classroom and taken in their books to mark rather than ask them to complete the task online. It was interesting that you could tell personalities from their approaches to the exercises. Isabella's work, the thin student who had reminded her of Toby, was painful in its neatness suggesting a personality under iron control. Lucy, who Mallory had caught looking her up on her laptop, was creative and methodical. The star of the group, however, was Livvy Mason who had finished the algebra in record quick time. Livvy had not only solved the equations Mallory had set but had moved on to the next chapter in the module.

To help Mallory settle in, Lowri had given her a potted history of each student and Mallory reached for it now. Livvy's father was a diplomat from Cardiff currently stationed with his second wife in Cairo. Livvy had no contact with her mother but this was by mutual consent, and she was close to her stepmother. Mallory grunted. Not much there and yet it hinted at upset and trauma. Livvy in this intensely academic environment was possibly an outlier with her quick brain and she wondered how the girl was coping.

By the time Mallory had finished her marking it was gone one and time slowed down once more. She considered leaving early and arriving at the Cranogwen room to catch whoever was there by surprise but she assumed that whoever had written this note had anticipated this possibility. At ten to the hour, she slipped on her trainers and softly locked the door to her room. The school was silent with just the faint glow of the corridor safety lighting to lead the way. Clutching the school map, she descended into the huge hallway and took a corridor to the right towards the classrooms. The girls' sleeping accommodations were in three separate buildings known as houses and were monitored twenty-four seven by staff.

Passing a window, Mallory saw the light of a guard in the distance. Mallory had asked that the security team be informed of her presence but this idea had been overruled by Lowri. She employed an external team without any particular loyalty to the institution beyond adopting a professional approach. Lowri couldn't be assured of their discretion, so it was a no. Mallory, who wanted an unimpeded run of the school with the exception of student rooms, wasn't particularly looking forward to coming face to face with a professional security guard, who would usually be ex-army or police, but she would just have to take her chances.

After taking a right turn, Mallory saw the Cranogwen room at the far end of the corridor, a heavy panelled door at its entrance. She turned the handle and it opened easily – there was no need to lock the classrooms. The room was in darkness and Mallory was torn between turning the light on or using her torch. Each would attract attention in the dark night. In the end, if challenged, Mallory would come clean about the note, and she switched on the light, preferring to see whatever awaited her away from shadows.

At first she looked around, her brow furrowed. The room was exactly as she'd imagined, a circular lecture theatre clad in pale wood with olive-green pull-down seats. At the front was a huge interactive whiteboard, its screen blinking. Mallory made a sweep of the room even though her instinct told her it was empty. When she got to the bottom of the auditorium, she went over to the computer and moved the mouse to wake up the screen. On the whiteboard, someone had written a message:

> In the shadow of the sundial underneath the prince of beauty you'll find me.

Mallory looked at it twice and rubbed her face. What the hell was this?

11

Harri received a text in the night from Mallory saying all was well and that she'd call in the morning. She'd promised to ring him, which wasn't the bloody same as a WhatsApp message, and he resisted the temptation to throw his mobile at the wall. The text had woken him up, and because of his diabetes, he had to get out of bed to answer a call of nature. Once out on the freezing landing, he'd known that going back to sleep would be impossible. After slipping back under his warm covers he tried to read but began doomscrolling on his phone, looking up the average life expectancy for diabetics.

To take his mind off his demise, Harri looked up the history of Penbryn Hall, which added little to what he already knew, although he did spot that when Lowri had taken over as head in 2012, she'd not replaced the previous long-standing incumbent as he'd thought. Between 2011 and 2012, a Dr Arabella Prytherch had been in post, either a temporary appointment or someone who'd decided early on that the role wasn't for them.

Harri lifted his head at a knock on the door and his sister Fran entered with a cup of tea.

'I saw you were awake and thought you might like this.'

He took the steaming brew off her with a grimace. 'Did I wake you too?'

Fran smiled. She'd pulled one of Harri's old jumpers on over her pyjamas and she looked like a teenager with her mussed hair. 'I'm getting hot flushes in the night. It must be my age so I was already awake. Are you working? I can leave you be if you want to be alone.'

Harri hesitated. He couldn't discuss Mallory's assignment with his sister but she would have read about the suicide of Pippa in the *Western Mail*, her preferred choice of newspaper. Fran was a solicitor and a useful sounding board, especially at four in the morning.

'I was looking up Penbryn Hall and thinking about its reputation.'

'The school?' Fran sat on the side of the bed, retrieved Harri's cup out of his hand and took a sip. 'I should have made one for myself. Go on.'

'There's not much I can tell you except what's in the public domain. A new teacher at the place took their own life recently and I was mulling it over.'

'Right. I remember reading the article.' She shot him a glance but didn't dig any deeper. 'In my profession, I do come across former students of the place. They're all of a similar ilk. Poised, very bright, excellent in an adversarial context.'

'Good God,' said Harri, taking back his tea. 'You're a corporate lawyer, surely that's the default for you lot.'

'You'd be surprised. I come across a lot of very nice chaps and wonder how the hell they got into their Oxbridge college. That's not true of women educated at Penbryn Hall.'

'Do they ever talk about their schooling?'

Fran shrugged. 'A little. I'm not a natural confidante as I clearly don't come from a financially privileged background. But generally I'd say they were a good lot. What's the matter – trying to understand why the teacher did what she did?'

'In essence, yes.'

'Perhaps she had existing mental health problems. You can carry your burdens from one place to another.'

'True.' Harri thought back to Lowri's comment about Pippa having changed schools often. 'It's possible an early encounter at the school affected her state of mind, which is why I'm doing some digging.'

'How's Mallory?' asked Fran, adopting a nonchalant tone. She'd resolutely kept out of any budding romance between the pair and had refused to come on the holiday to Spain, preferring instead to visit a spa for the week.

Harri looked away. 'All right.'

Fran frowned. 'Oh my God, she's not actually in Penbryn Hall is she?'

'What makes you say that?'

'I don't know. Your face went all secretive like it does when you're discussing a case but you've told me enough.'

Harri caught Fran's eye and they both sniggered.

'Mallory in Penbryn Hall,' said Fran. 'God knows what they'll make of her there.'

'Do you think,' said Harri, mulling over the wisdom of his request, 'that you could do some digging for me? Obviously it's been quite a time since your acquaintances were at the school but I got the impression that former students often sent their own children to the place. Could you ask around?'

'I guess so. I work remotely so it's harder to drop things into conversation but perhaps I could say a friend is thinking of sending her daughter there. Is there anything in particular you want to know?'

Harri grimaced and set the cooling tea on the bedside table. 'I'm scrabbling around in the dark. Anything that feels out of the ordinary.'

'Harri – what's going on?'

Harri pulled the pillow behind his head higher and settled back. 'I've no idea.'

12

Mallory decided it must be a feature of private schools that they had lessons on a Saturday morning. She wasn't sure what she'd have thought of it as a teenager as weekends had been a time for lie-ins, a habit that Toby embraced with fervour too. Perhaps Lowri had decided to allow Mallory free Saturdays to do her investigations because she had no lessons allocated on her timetable. When she woke just after seven, she looked at the note on which she'd scribbled the words from the whiteboard.

> In the shadow of the sundial underneath the
> prince of beauty you'll find me.

A riddle, and Mallory hated puzzles of any kind, ignoring the crazes for Wordle, Sudoku and all TV quiz shows. In the evenings, all her tired brain wanted to do was watch a Netflix drama, the grittier the better. Even during her periods of unemployment, the thought of crosswords made her shudder. The message, however, was a challenge – solve me if you're clever enough. Mallory wondered if her cover was blown given she'd been the target of the message. Perhaps it was just because she was new and a maths teacher. The writer might think she was an expert problem solver, which was a laugh given her level of expertise in the subject.

After showering, Mallory went in search of Lowri but was told by her secretary, Eirin, that she had been called away to Cardiff for a meeting. Up close, Mallory saw that Eirin was slightly older than she'd appeared in the courtyard talking to Lowri. Her pale skin was covered with matte powder, possibly to hide her freckles, which were just visible under her make-up. The severe bun her fiery red hair was pulled back into accentuated Eirin's leanness and gave the woman a forbidding air. Mallory didn't envy Eirin's job as Lowri seemed difficult to please.

'Don't you get Saturdays off?' asked Mallory.

Eirin smiled. 'From lunchtime. If there's a crisis, it usually happens on a Saturday.'

The day Pippa had been found. She glanced at Eirin, wondering if she'd been referring to Pippa but the secretary was back to looking at her screen. 'Dr Mellor is available if it's urgent. He's in his office. Lowri will be back on Sunday evening.'

'Thanks.' Mallory walked to the room that had the name of Dr Jonathan Mellor, three to the right of Lowri's office, and rapped on the door.

Jonathan's office was small but beautifully furnished – with better fittings than Lowri's, to Mallory's eye. She'd not had the chance to properly meet the deputy properly and felt slightly daunted after the cold tone of his emails. Jonathan was a tall man in his early forties dressed in an expensive-looking suit that certainly hadn't come from M&S or wherever Harri bought his suits. Mallory silently cursed. What the hell was the matter with her? Every time she met a man, good looking or not, she mentally compared him to Harri. Jonathan, however, was certainly attractive with a toned physique you only get from working out in the gym.

'Sorry to disturb you. Could I have a word?'

He looked up from the laptop he was typing on and shut its lid. 'Of course, take a seat. I've been meaning to check how you were getting on, both in terms of the teaching and also Lowri's concerns around the death of Pippa Evans. How *are* you getting on?'

Mallory sat down, conscious of the stifling heat of the room but relieved to find his tone helpful. 'Teaching-wise, fine. Well, maybe that's a little optimistic but it's not as terrible as I thought it might be, and you have lovely students. In terms of looking into Pippa's death, I'd have said slowly until something occurred in the early hours of this morning.'

Mallory related the discovery of her note which had led to the message on the whiteboard. Jonathan frowned and picked up a pencil, jabbing the blunt end on his desk.

'There are a couple of things that are giving me cause for concern. First of all, entry to your room. The only person with keys other than yourself is the administrator, who keeps a set for every room in a locked cabinet. Mrs Jones the cleaner takes the keys for whichever room she's cleaning that day and they're returned at the end of the shift. We are very security conscious here and no one else is allowed access to the keys. If a teacher locks herself out of the room, she is accompanied by the administrator who unlocks it for her.'

'What if keys get lost or the administrator is away?'

'Another set of keys is kept in the safe and only Lowri, the bursar and I are able to open that. I can check with the others but I'm not aware of anyone accessing the safe specifically for a key.'

'Was Mrs Jones working yesterday?'

'She works every weekday, but I'll need to look at the rota to see if you were down for a Friday clean.'

'My room wasn't cleaned so I doubt it was Mrs Jones but I'll need to talk to her when she's in on Monday. The whiteboard might be a better way to discover who left the message. Is there someone who can look at who accessed the computer in the room?'

'I can check. Give me a moment.'

Mallory watched as he opened a program on his laptop and began to search. 'Well, the room wasn't used for teaching at all yesterday – I've checked the timetable. However, at ten past six, the computer login was activated, which meant someone was using it.'

'Can you tell who?'

Jonathan made a face. 'You can log in as "staff" on the classroom computers. We have given all permanent staff their own login but sometimes we have visiting lecturers, casual staff and so on. Our IT technicians can't create a password each time they arrive. Whoever accessed the computer used the generic login.'

Mallory wondered how that fitted with safeguarding rules but if those given access to the staff password were vetted, she supposed it didn't matter.

Jonathan frowned and looked at the message Mallory had laid before her. 'I also don't like the fact that someone's playing games with us,' he said. 'Does the message mean anything to you?'

'Nothing, but they're clearly sending me on a treasure hunt. Does this building have a sundial?'

Jonathan nodded. 'Come with me.'

He ushered Mallory out of the room, taking care to lock the door behind him. Mallory followed him out the front door and to the left of the main building. As lessons were taking place there were no curious gazes to follow their progress, allowing Mallory to scout the area for the stone sundial. She was surprised when Jonathan came to an abrupt halt on the gravel path and pointed towards the horizon. In the distance was a building that had probably once been a coach house. Next to a building with two huge doors was a small cottage, its render white-washed, with a single window on the third floor. Above the wooded frame something glinted gold in the sunshine.

'That's the sundial?'

'It's the only one I know of. What are we looking for in its shadow?'

'The prince of beauty?' Their eyes met. In other circumstances, Mallory would be inclined to laugh but she was sleep deprived and anxious. She tried to imagine how she'd feel if something weird like this was going on at Toby's school and had concluded she wouldn't like it one bit. No wonder Lowri was uneasy about the circum-stances of Pippa's death. 'Mean anything to you?' she asked Jonathan.

'Nothing.'

Mallory had already done an internet search on the term and it had thrown up references to *Beauty and the Beast*, which didn't sound particularly helpful but you never knew. She looked around the space and saw only grass, flowerbeds and a small sculpture of a young woman. 'Who's that?' asked Mallory, noticing the statue was modern in style.

'A student who died in the 1980s, Karen Moore. She loved it here apparently, and her father commissioned the statue in her memory.'

'What did she die of?' asked Mallory. Perhaps this was the origin of the puzzle around Pippa's death.

'She was an epileptic and had a seizure. If you're interested, you ought to ask Lowri about it as she was a student here at the time. I can't see how it could be a reference to the prince of beauty, though.'

Neither could Mallory but it was an interesting line of investigation.

'You're happy for me to continue looking into this? Lowri's not here but I think it could be important.'

Jonathan shrugged. 'I don't think we really have a choice, do we?'

13

Mallory managed to discover more of the story of Karen Moore in the library. She'd clocked during her previous visit a section dedicated to alumnae and although Karen had never graduated from the college, there was an 'In Memoriam' section dedicated to those who were now deceased, their names also inscribed into a book with thick cream pages. Mallory found the date of Karen's death easily enough – 14 August 1984 – and discovered she'd died in Florence during the school holidays. While her grieving parents might have decided to commemorate Karen with a statue at the school, her death appeared unconnected with the institution. Mallory flicked through the book and saw nothing out of the ordinary. Undeterred, she looked at the glass cases that detailed the achievements of former students and came face to face with Superintendent Stephanie Morris. Great. Well, that explained why this investigation had been given priority status.

She wondered if it was significant that Lowri had been a student when Karen Moore was here. All roads, it seemed, led back to Lowri but then the head had made no secret of her long affiliation with the school. Wondering what to do next, Mallory glanced around the room and saw in the distance Livvy, bent over a book. She appeared engrossed in her reading and Mallory almost went past, but on impulse she bent down next to her.

'Studying hard?'

The girl jumped and caught her breath. 'Sorry, just catching up on some stuff.'

Mallory was an experienced mother of a teenager and recognised the catch in the girl's throat. She was shocked to see Livvy's eyes were rimmed with red.

'What's the matter?' asked Mallory, pulling out a chair. 'Why are you upset?'

Livvy shook her head and swept the book she was reading into her bag. She got up to leave but Mallory held her back. She was on dangerous ground here. She'd read the school's code of conduct before starting and it had made clear that physical contact was prohibited unless the student was in danger. However, if Livvy made a fuss, Mallory could probably argue that the student was distraught and she was trying to calm the situation. No one else was in the library except Emiah's deputy, who was bent over the computer.

'Let's get out of here,' said Mallory. 'Do you fancy a walk? I've actually got a problem that you might be able to solve. Let's get that brain of yours working on it.'

Mute, Livvy nodded and followed Mallory out of the library and into the bracing air.

'Follow me,' said Mallory and retraced the steps she had taken that morning with the deputy head. She felt Livvy next to her relax as the cold wind swept across them. Neither was dressed for outdoors but they ploughed on. Mallory knew from experience that demanding her student open up to her would lead to more resistance. Far better that she distract Livvy with something to take her mind off things. She looked about, checking to see if their progress was being followed. They passed a line of girls heading out towards the sports field with hockey sticks in their hands but no one paid them any attention.

Mallory stopped in the courtyard and nodded towards the coach house.

'Do you know what that is?'

Livvy frowned. 'It's where the school buses are kept. There's also a car for us to practise our driving skills but you can only use it after twenty hours of lessons.'

'Surely someone sits in there with you.'

'Of course. Any teacher as long as they have a licence.'

Mallory made a mental note to turn down any student's request to have her accompany them. The thought of Toby learning to drive was bad enough.

'Do you know much about the sundial?' asked Mallory casually.

Livvy knew immediately what she was talking about. 'Under the roof. I've always wondered why they put it on this building. I mean clock towers are often over stables but I'm not sure why they put a sundial.'

'It's probably from when the house was built. Do you know what a prince of beauty is?'

Livvy frowned. 'Prince of beauty? It sounds familiar but I can't think why. Is it some kind of puzzle?'

'Yes, but I can't tell you what. Dr Rhys might know the reference but I believe she's away from the school for the weekend so I'm trying to solve the riddle myself. The internet is no help at all.'

'Riddle?' Mallory could see Livvy was intrigued, her upset forgotten.

Mallory made a decision. 'If I show you something, would you promise not to breathe a word to anyone else?'

'There's no one to tell. You might have noticed that I'm a bit of an outlier here.' There was no bitterness in the girl's voice. Whatever the issue was, it wasn't a problem with the other students.

'To be honest, I think you're the best person to help me but before I lay the problem before you, would you tell me what's made you upset?'

Livvy kicked the gravel and made a face. 'I had an email from my father last night. My mother, I mean my natural mother, is having a baby. We're not in touch but her new partner occasionally makes it into the papers and Papa was worried I might read it there so he emailed me the news.'

'Couldn't he have rung?' asked Mallory, conscious of her own fragile relationship with her son.

'Calls are hard for me as I don't really like talking over the phone. I prefer emails so he's really only communicating in the way I asked him to.'

'And that's why you're upset. Do you feel like reaching out to your mother? I'm sure your father, whatever their history, would be happy with that if it makes you feel better.'

'I don't… I don't know. I don't think so. She had me when she was twenty and left my father soon after. I see my stepmother as my real mama so I don't know why I'm so upset.'

'Emotions are rarely rational,' said Mallory. 'My advice would be to send an email to your… um… papa… and tell him how you feel. Opening up usually helps, you know.'

'Is that something you'd do?'

Mallory laughed. 'No.' She was relieved to see Livvy was also grinning. 'Are you spending Christmas with them in Cairo?'

Livvy nodded. 'That's the plan.'

'Then maybe talk to him then if you find phone calls difficult. In the meantime, make an appointment to see the student counsellor. Talking, even if it resolves nothing, often helps.'

Livvy shrugged, looking up at the sundial. 'A complex problem would help.'

Mallory smiled. 'OK, but I'm going to need to tell Dr Rhys that I've spoken to you about this, all right. Secrets can in some instances breed violence.'

There was a glint in Livvy's eye. 'OK.'

There was no way Mallory was going to break her cover but she thought she could tell Livvy about the note in her room and the message on the whiteboard. She gave the girl a quick résumé of what had happened, watching in satisfaction as colour returned to her cheeks.

> In the shadow of the sundial underneath the
> prince of beauty you'll find me.

'So we have the sundial but in its shadow is the prince of beauty.' Livvy glanced around the landscape, her gaze falling on the statue of Karen Moore, as Mallory's had done. 'It should be easy to discover what a prince of beauty is.'

'I was wondering about the statue,' said Mallory but Livvy shook her head.

'It says "underneath", and look at the grass – it's pristine. There's nothing buried under there unless it was left when the statue was erected.'

It was a good point. Livvy was pulling at her lip. 'You're going about the problem in the wrong way. What you need to do is look for inconsistencies in the way the puzzle is set up – the workings, if you like, and I can see one immediately.'

'Go on.'

'Whoever left you the puzzle had access to your room, a place where no one else really goes. So why leave a note telling you to go to another place? Why not write the message on the note they left in your room?'

The thought had already occurred to Mallory, and she'd dismissed it, assuming the mystery person wanted to either frighten her or increase the sense of drama. She couldn't shake off the feeling she was being led on a wild goose chase.

'Someone just teasing out the puzzle,' suggested Mallory.

'I don't think so. I think the room is part of the puzzle. Do you know who Cranogwen was?'

Mallory shook her head. 'The name means nothing to me.'

'She was a mariner, feminist, poet, nationalist, lesbian. She plays a part in the puzzle. The question is, what?'

14

Mallory made an arrangement with Livvy to meet after chapel on the following day. Livvy might be on to something about Cranogwen but Mallory would need to do some serious mugging up to find any reference, which meant a trip to the library that was now closed for the day. She warned Livvy not to do any investigating on her own beyond looking at Cranogwen's writings, and when they met they'd compare notes. Mallory, who'd been thinking about Toby all day, tried his mobile but it was his dad, Joe, who picked up the phone.

'How are you doing Mallory?' he asked. 'Toby's in the shower.'

'Not bad. I'm working undercover would you believe it. Don't tell Toby, though, as he'll only worry.'

'Undercover? You?'

Mallory bit back a retort. She and Joe had been getting on much better since he'd acquired a new girlfriend, and she didn't want to break the fragile truce between them. To be fair, she and Joe had joined the Met at the same time and she'd always moaned about doing undercover work. The endless waiting around hadn't suited her personality – well, there was precious little downtime when she was living in a school. 'Is Toby all right?' she asked him.

'I suppose. He doesn't say much as usual, but he seems a bit happier. He's certainly not exercising as much as he used to, which is good news.'

'He told me he was still running.'

'Yes, but it's no longer three times a day. This is what progress looks like, Mallory.' Joe's exasperation with her was a reminder that he was on the coalface of parenting, not her.

'Tell him I'll call him again when I can, OK?' Mallory said and cut the call.

The highlight of Saturday evening was dinner, with all teachers and students eating together, the staff on a separate table. Mallory had the impression everyone had a fixed seat – Jem was next to Freya, Rose sitting next to Jonathan – so she hovered by the table waiting for everyone to be seated. It was Jem who came to Mallory's rescue, pointing at a chair next to her.

'You're right, of course,' she said as Mallory sat down. 'Technically you can sit anywhere but like in church, we all have our favourite places.'

As they were served their starters, Mallory became aware of an undercurrent of tension between Jem and Freya. It wasn't menacing but had the air of a lovers' tiff. She wondered what the school rules were in relation to staff fraternising and was soon put right by Jem.

'My wife says that you're a hit with the students.'

It took Mallory a second to catch on. 'Oh, I hadn't realised you and Freya were a couple.'

Jem looked across at her wife. 'We got married in the summer holidays. Up to then, we tried to keep our relationship secret but you know what students are like. They could wheedle a secret out of Greta Garbo.'

'Are there any other married members of staff?'

'Not teachers but there are houses for families. Jonathan's wife is a primary school teacher in Tregaron but they live here on site. We're the first same-sex marriage among teachers.'

Mallory remembered Livvy's reference to the woman after whom the lecture room was named.

'Are you a fan of Cranogwen?'

Jem raised her eyebrows as she poured a glass of water. 'Cranogwen? Well she's a Welsh icon and I've been to see her statue at Llangrannog. Did you know that before its unveiling there were no statues of named women at all in Wales?'

'I didn't. Is that why the lecture theatre is named after her?'

'Of course. Lowri is a big fan.'

Is she, thought Mallory. Interesting. She glanced across at Freya, who appeared disconcerted at the conversation, and turned the discussion to the coming Christmas holidays. Freya and Jem were planning a trip to Iceland and soon the chatter turned to Scandinavian cuisine, although Mallory could still feel Freya's anxious gaze on her. Could Freya have left the note for Mallory? She certainly had access to the staff wing and an indirect approach might have felt more comfortable than approaching Mallory direct. Freya was definitely on Mallory's list as one to watch.

–

Later in her room, her prep done, Mallory took a call from a furious Harri.

'Well,' he demanded. 'I've been sitting here waiting for you to call me all day.'

Mallory exhaled, trying to keep calm. 'Look, I'm sorry but this place is full on. I'm serious, it sucks you in and before you know it, you're in your room with another day gone.'

'You've not gone there to bloody teach, have you? How am I supposed to update Steph on a daily basis when I get silence from you? I nearly drove up there to see what the hell was going on.'

Christ, that would have been a disaster. Harri wasn't a man to fade into any background, especially not at a girls' school.

'I'm sorry. Look, this is what happened today.' For the third time, she related the events of the previous evening. Unlike speaking to Jonathan and Livvy, she was aware of a weight being lifted from her shoulders. She definitely should have spoken to Harri before now.

'Someone's pissing about with you,' he said.

'You know who Cranogwen is?' she asked.

'I do but I'm not sure I agree with what your student told you. It might be the writer has a sense of drama and simply guided you to the largest room in the building.'

Mallory exhaled, feeling a wave of exhaustion wash over her. 'I just don't know what's going on Harri. Can you leave it with me? I'll call you Monday morning, OK?'

Mallory closed her eyes and crashed out with her bedside lamp still on. She was fully clothed but happy to sleep the rest of the night in this state gathering her resources for the day ahead. She was faintly aware of footsteps walking past her door – other teachers had stayed up late – but she slept on fitfully. It was still dark when she was awoken by a steady rap on her door. She'd wedged a chair against the handle which was the best she could do in the circumstances. It would give her a head start against the person with the key, nothing more. But the knocking suggested someone who was prepared to wait. Mallory went to the door and said softly, 'Who is it?'

'It's me, Livvy.'

Livvy, shit – what the hell was she doing in the staff wing? Mallory unlocked her door and opened it. 'What's the matter?' She saw the girl was shivering and her hands caked with mud. 'Livvy, what the hell have you been doing?'

'It's the puzzle, I've solved it.'

Christ, thought Mallory. Lowri will kill me when she realises I've involved a student. She pulled Livvy into the room, and then wondered if she should wake Jonathan so the girl was chaperoned. Livvy, nobody's fool, shook her head.

'We're allowed in staff rooms if there's an emergency.'

'It's three o'clock in the bloody morning. I'd say it was an emergency. What have you found?'

Livvy had an olive green army bag slung across her body, which she removed and put on Mallory's bed. She kept her eyes on it as she spoke.

'It was straightforward in the end. Cranogwen wrote poetry but not much is available online. She's yet to be discovered beyond Wales.'

'I was going to the library tomorrow before classes to look up her writings.'

'The lit department has reference poetry in the classroom so I just went in there. Her most famous poem is called "Fy Ffrynd" which means "My Friend" and it talks about a rose which she calls a "prince *in* beauty".'

Livvy frowned. The grammatical mistake by the author of the riddle was a jarring note to her precise brain.

Mallory, however, was still trying to catch up with Livvy's actions.

'Are there rose beds underneath the sundial? I just saw autumn bedding plants.'

'There's one,' said Livvy. 'So I didn't have to dig much at all.'

'Dig? Jesus, Livvy. Why the hell didn't you come to me to help you and where did you find a spade?'

Livvy laughed. She looked a different girl to the one Mallory had happened across in the library.

'I'm part of the gardening team so I have access to the tool shed. It used to be kept unlocked until some expensive stuff was stolen last year.'

'And the fact you started digging in the middle of the night?'

Livvy coloured. 'I just wanted to be sure before I came to you with my theory.'

'So you go to the flowerbed and start digging around the rose.'

'Underneath the rose. I had to pull it up and… I found it straight away, only I've not looked inside.'

Livvy opened the flap of her bag and pulled out a metal object. She had made some attempt to clean it as smears of soil arced across the lid. Mallory took the metal tin from the schoolgirl's trembling hands. The puzzle had been a straightforward one and Mallory twenty years ago might have got to the treasure before Livvy. While Livvy might have outsmarted her, what she didn't have was Mallory's wiles. The girl assured her that she hadn't opened the tin and Mallory believed her.

It was an old sweet tin, at least thirty years old judging from the rusted lid and dated look. Mallory wanted to tell the girl to go while she opened the contents but

Livvy surely deserved a share of the spoils. Mallory prised open the lid and was initially disappointed to see a small notebook with a pale blue cover. She took it out, and stamped on the front in gothic lettering was 'The Solstice Sisterhood'. Mallory could feel Livvy's hot breath on her cheek.

'Who are they?' asked Livvy.

'I've no idea. Some kind of religious order maybe.' It didn't sound very orthodox to Mallory. The solstice was about the earth's orbit around the sun so nothing to do with the Bible as far as she could make out. She opened the book and saw a list of what looked like dates, but they were impossible to read because of their smudges. Against these dates were various markings. Sometimes a tick, other times a crescent or full moon with occasionally a hash sign and teardrop.

'What the hell is this?' muttered Mallory to herself. Someone had set an elaborate series of puzzles to lead them to – what? A book of code.

'Look at this.' Livvy pointed to the writing on the inside cover. It said: 'Punishment is a vital need of the human soul.'

'What crap,' said Mallory loudly, making Livvy jump. 'Who makes up this shit?'

Livvy pulled out her phone and typed in the quotation. 'It's from Simone Weil. She was a French philosopher and mystic. We'd need to check if she actually said this. The internet's full of misattributed and made-up quotations.'

'Was she a member of the Solstice Sisterhood?' asked Mallory.

'I'm not sure. There's nothing on her Wiki page. Only... hold on...'

Livvy was frowning into her phone.

'What is it?' Mallory struggled with the temptation to snatch the phone out of the girl's hand.

'Look.' Livvy turned her phone to show a newspaper article that screamed 'Punishment cult disbanded after reign of terror'. The first picture showed a woman in her early thirties hiding her face in the shoulder of a man who was leading her away from an imposing town house. Mallory knew she should be focusing on the woman but her eyes were drawn to the man who was pushing his way past a throng of reporters. Harri.

The school clock chimed loudly making both of them jump. Mallory looked at her watch in the faint moonlight. 'You need to get back to bed, Livvy. I'll walk you over.'

'No need.'

'There's every need.' Mallory's voice was harsh. There was someone at Penbryn Hall who'd instilled terror into Pippa, although Mallory wasn't necessarily sure if they had been the one to leave the series of clues leading them to this tin. It was possible they had worked out who Mallory was and were playing with her. An alternative was that someone else knew what was going on and was guiding her. Either way, it suggested her cover was blown.

'I'm going to accompany you back to your room. When you get in, bolt the door and push something up against it. Even if it's your desk chair. If someone tries to get in, shout loudly asking what they want. Do you have someone on each side of you?'

Livvy nodded. 'What shall I do when the bell goes for breakfast?'

'Act normal. The message was meant for me, and I'm sorry I brought you into the trouble but I am going to sort it out.'

'OK. Look, if there's some kind of code that needs breaking—'

'Please Livvy. I need to talk to my boss about this first.'

They left Mallory's room in silence and Livvy fell into step beside Mallory. 'I can keep a secret,' she said.

Mallory smiled faintly. 'I know but I am going to Dr Rhys tomorrow morning to tell her all I know.'

'You know,' said Livvy. 'You're the coolest maths teacher I've ever met.'

15

11 March 2014

Angharad retrieved the book from behind the Port-meirion vase and opened the pages. There was a symbol for each form of punishment, a means of keeping track on whether one of their community was improving or remaining slack with respect to their duties. The symbols were a form of code, which appealed to Angharad's sense of intrigue. A triangle for canes on the hand, a square for birching on the back of the thighs or buttocks and a circle for a slap across the face. The ultimate punishment, denoted by a teardrop, had yet to be placed inside this girl's pages but the time would come.

She put in the day's date and a triangle symbol and handed the book back to Pippa. The girl took it mutely but there were no tears in her eyes. She was a defiant one but much worse, she was also very bright with a watchful manner. She was the type of girl who tried to hide her intelligence but that stupid Branwen had left her punishment book on the table in the hallway and Pippa had picked it up and deciphered the symbols immediately. Oh well, she didn't suppose it mattered. The brightest people didn't always have the best self-awareness so perhaps all would be well. They were paying the girl enough to keep quiet.

After Pippa had gone back to the kitchen, Angharad climbed the stairs to the room at the back of the house. She cast an eye over the counterpane and noticed a slight wrinkle. That would be Sister Ceridwen's mistake and she'd be punished for it accordingly when Angharad next encountered her. Really they needed more staff but plans were afoot to remove themselves from the city into the countryside, something Angharad wholeheartedly agreed with. It wasn't true that cities were more anonymous. In Angharad's opinion, it was the countryside where people minded their own business.

Sitting in the hard-backed rocking chair, Angharad mentally marked the whereabouts of the five other resident members. Branwen had made herself scarce by disappearing into the garden during the punishment, a regular occurrence in Angharad's experience. Rhiannon should have been supervising Pippa in the kitchen, but had disappeared with Branwen when the plate smashed. Another member who wasn't fully embracing the discipline at the heart of the group. Luned and Kigva were much better in this respect and would soon be back from the hospital, where words would need to be had to ensure the status quo remained. That left Ceridwen, whose hammer could still be heard in the distance, fashioning the new clogs for Branwen.

Angharad rocked slightly in her chair. Had she made the right choice? Penbryn Hall had felt such an ideal opportunity, but their plans had quickly turned to dust. This was a chance of a new start, if everything went well. If she could receive as well as give.

16

Harri made the long drive from Carmarthen to Penbryn Hall at the crack of dawn on Monday morning. Mallory had rung him about the discovery of the punishment book early the previous day, but they'd agreed there was nothing to be done on a Sunday, not least because Lowri was away. She would have plenty to say on the Solstice Sisterhood he was sure, and it would be from a different perspective to his. The discovery of the slim blue book was very bad news indeed and he'd already phoned Steph to put off their morning meeting until he could give her a full update. He had a feeling she'd also share his disquiet.

In the distance, the sun was just beginning to rise over the horizon as he sped through Lampeter taking the road past the recycling yard towards Tregaron. Some idiot was powering towards him in the opposite direction with their lights on full beam and, irritated, Harri flashed his own headlights. God he hated these early morning call outs and, if anything, driving behaviour on the roads was getting worse. Ellie would soon be seventeen and wanted driving lessons. He'd try and put that off as long as he could, he'd decided. God knows he didn't need more stress in his life.

As the school came into view, Harri pulled over and took in the vista. The Welsh countryside was dotted with these huge homes now, often crumbling or with long-term 'For Sale' signs mouldering at their entrances. The lucky few found rich owners who turned them into luxury hotels or private family homes. Penbryn Hall had been chosen in the early Fifties as the location of a new upmarket school and Harri could see why. It was a handsome Edwardian house so it was probably well built, but not so large that upkeep would be prohibitively expensive. Its grey stone also lent itself to the inclusion of modern construction. The new-looking building to one side, probably the sports hall, should have looked incongruous but again gave off an air of solidity and privilege.

Harri switched the engine back on and motored down to the house, where he was gratified to see Mallory stamping her feet in the frosty car park.

'Couldn't wait to see my smiling face again?' Harri asked as he got out of the car.

Mallory rolled her eyes and folded her arms tight across her chest. 'I wanted to talk to you before we see Lowri. I can tell she's seriously wound up and I was wondering if there was anything you wanted to tell me in private first about the Solstice Sisterhood.'

'How much do you know about them?'

'Just what I've read on the internet, which isn't much. The scandal seemed to flare and die – do you remember the case?'

Harri felt his mood darken as she told him about the punishment book. He remembered them perfectly well and had hoped to God to never hear the name again.

'I'm very much hoping it's an old case that in some way impacted on Pippa in a negative way and led to her death. What have you told Lowri?'

'For the moment, very little. I told her I needed an urgent meeting and it was in relation to the Solstice Sisterhood. Do you know what her reaction was?'

'What?'

'She said "fuck".'

In other circumstances, Harri would have laughed. There was something incongruous about the ice-cool Lowri Rhys swearing. However, he felt like uttering a curse or two himself.

'Let's go and see her, shall we?' he said.

He followed Mallory into the main building, noticing that she was wearing different clothes from her usual get-up. A skirt, for instance. She looked more like a school mistress, and the outfit suited her.

The interior of the house had none of the institutional feel he associated with schools. If anything, it was like a plush country club replete with thick carpet and discreet lighting. Only the muted chatter and occasional laughter reminded him that this was a place where a hundred and fifty girls were educated.

They went up the central staircase and along a corridor. It was clearly an administrative wing of the house – a closed door was marked 'Bursar' and another 'Administrator'. Mallory knocked on a door which opened on to a small office where a red-headed woman tapped into a computer.

'I've got DI Evans here. Dr Rhys is expecting us.'

The woman glanced up and pointed at two chairs. 'Will you take a seat for a moment? Dr Rhys is with a student.'

At that moment, the door opened and a girl of about fourteen with hair the colour of pale straw came out. She glanced with curiosity at Mallory and Harri but left

84

without a word. In the doorway stood Lowri, imposing in a long black skirt and high-necked jumper.

'Come in. Eirin, can you make sure there are no interruptions while I talk to Mallory and DI Evans? I don't even want anyone waiting in your office. Can you also message Phoebe's form tutor and tell her I've excused her from lessons for the rest of the day.'

'Of course.' Harri glanced back at Eirin. The name suited her. In old Welsh it referred to berries and she definitely had the autumn look about her. She had turned her attention back to a spreadsheet on the screen, a pair of large tortoiseshell glasses perched on her nose.

There were no formalities when they sat down. Lowri gestured towards a pot of coffee and let them serve themselves.

'Mallory has updated me about what went on in the middle of the night. It's my fault, of course, for going away. If I'd been here, I'd have told her not only about the sundial but I'd have got the Cranogwen reference. "Fy Ffrynd" is her most famous poem.'

Her professional pride was dented, Harri could see, which was a shame because they all needed to keep a rational head on them, especially if they were coming up against the work of the Solstice Sisterhood.

Mallory glanced over at Harri, wanting to explain her actions. 'I don't think it was a particularly difficult puzzle but Livvy was upset in the library and I wanted to give her something to take her mind off her problems.'

Lowri sniffed and reached for her coffee. 'I'd have preferred if a student wasn't involved as I've now the added headache to ensure she's kept safe.'

'Livvy has done all she can to help. Now I've found the tin with the correction book in, there won't be any further need for Livvy's excellent brain. I'm sure this is the end of the matter as far as Livvy's concerned.'

'Then you don't understand teenagers.'

Harri watched Mallory flush. The fact her son Toby preferred to remain with his father, in addition to his barely controlled eating disorder, was a source of shame and worry for her. She nodded slightly, as if accepting Lowri's words and turned her attention to him.

'I think in order for me to carry on doing my job, I need to know about the Solstice Sisterhood and the correction book I found. I've done a brief search of the internet so I know what's in the public domain but I'd like to hear the rest. It appears both of you have some kind of involvement with the organisation.'

Mallory's dark eyes were on him. Things had been a little strained since their Spanish holiday. Their respective kids had got on great but their presence had inhibited him from even taking hold of Mallory's hand, even though he'd wanted to on plenty of occasions. About halfway through the week, without any discussion, they'd both realised that the holiday would be more relaxing if they just let the kids take the lead. Harri had resolved, once they were home, to take Mallory out on a date but there had never been a right time to broach the subject, especially as he was pretty sure what Mallory really wanted from him was employment above anything else.

'I'd like to know what this bunch of nuns was up to,' said Mallory. 'I don't like religion, especially when they're dishing out punishment.' Harri remembered she had lived in a former convent on Eldey Island, her first job in Wales, and had nearly lost her life in unmasking a poisoner.

'They weren't nuns,' said Lowri, unable to hide her irritation. 'The Solstice Sisterhood was a loose group of women with no affiliation to a recognised church. Their principles were authenticity, wisdom and worship of earth spirits. They were particularly devoted to the Welsh book of myths, the Mabinogion.'

'Like a cult?' asked Mallory.

'More or less,' said Harri, 'although they wouldn't have seen themselves that way. It's probably best if I start the story as I had dealings with one of the members a few years ago. The sisterhood began in a house in Cardiff in one of those tall, roomy terraced houses that now go for a fortune near Roath Park. They were pretty settled there and blended into the usual hubbub of a city but after a series of set-tos with neighbours – there were rumours of screams and sobbing late at night – the group moved to a more isolated house in the Ceredigion countryside.'

'Near here?' asked Mallory.

'It depends what you call near. About ten miles from this school on the road to Aberystwyth. The house was more isolated than the group's previous residence and I guess they hoped there would be no nosy neighbours to stir things up. However, one day about eight years ago, a girl fled to a neighbouring house claiming she'd been forced to accept a whipping as part of her role, receiving six strikes of a birch over her hands. The family at the house called in the police and inquiries were made.'

'And you visited the sisterhood?' asked Mallory. 'I saw your photo in the paper.'

'The family had already tipped off the *Western Mail*, who arrived as quickly as I did. Given the nature of the allegations, we arrested all members of the sisterhood, six in total. It wasn't a large group and I got the impression that they'd had trouble recruiting members. It was all about austerity and self-deprivation, which isn't for most people.'

'Six is enough to cause trouble,' said Mallory.

'Well, exactly. During the interview process the group was split. Three admitted that chastisement was a feature of the house while the other three denied any knowledge of the practice whatsoever.'

'Which group did you believe?' asked Mallory.

'The former, of course, especially given what the accuser claimed. However, all six said the girl was troubled and prone to fancies. Plus, she'd been in the house for three months before anything happened and had been happy up to that point.'

'The girl wasn't Philippa Evans, was she?'

Harri shook his head. 'Definitely not, although they were about the same age. The complainant was a girl named Bethan Rossi. Her family owns a well-known café called Rossi's in Carmarthen where she now works.'

'So were there any prosecutions made?' asked Mallory.

'The CPS decided there wasn't enough evidence for a charge to stick so that was that. However, for about a year, I kept an informal eye on the group with the occasional drive by. One time, I even stopped and rang the doorbell.'

'Did anyone answer?' asked Mallory.

'An Irish woman who went by the name of Kigva. She was pleasant enough. If anything, I'd say she was the most sociable of the group. She said they were fine but I wasn't invited inside and then the next time I passed, the place was empty. I subsequently discovered that the lease had lapsed.'

'You think they set up somewhere else?'

Harri considered. It was a good question and one he'd asked himself a few times over the years. 'As far as I'm aware the group disbanded but I thought I saw one of the sisters – Branwen – in Aberystwyth when I was there with the kids.'

'Six members you say?' said Mallory. 'Think one of them might be here in Penbryn Hall?'

Harri glanced across at Lowri who looked furious. 'I'd like to think that highly unlikely,' she said, 'but I'd better tell you of my knowledge of the sisterhood.'

17

Mallory could feel her headache returning, a pulsating behind her forehead that was refusing to subside. These constant pains inside her skull were a new phenomenon since she'd started teaching. She guessed it was a mixture of stress from being in the classroom and two broken nights' sleep. Her headache was exacerbated by the palpable tension in the room. It was the first time she'd seen Lowri properly discomforted. Even when she'd come to seek help around the circumstances of Pippa's death, she'd been clearly in charge. Now, she looked towards Harri for reassurance but lowered her eyes when she found none.

'I like to say that if you cut my heart in two, you'd find Penbryn Hall stamped there. I went here to school, went away to Oxford for my undergraduate and doctoral studies and then came back here to teach. Most of the staff and students assume I never left but I did briefly go to another boarding school in the north of England for a year in 2011.'

'Did you want to experience life in another school?' asked Mallory.

Lowri flushed. 'I suppose that's one of the reasons. I was deputy head by then, the youngest the school had ever had, given I was only thirty-seven, but I'd studied for an MBA alongside my teaching duties and thought I had the leadership skills for the post. However, when the headship came up unexpectedly, I was unsuccessful.'

That must have stung this proud woman, thought Mallory. Harri, she saw, knew some of the story.

He said, 'I was looking at the history of the school and I saw a Dr Prytherch was here for only a year. It stood out, as your heads are usually in post for ten years plus.'

'Dr Prytherch, Arabella, did not suit Penbryn Hall. She was an outsider and the trustees had developed a new vision for the school which involved recruitment of more students from North America. Arabella was from California, one of the best schools there, and wanted experience of a British education. Her family were originally Welsh, as you can probably tell from her last name.'

'So you moved schools when you didn't get the post?' asked Mallory.

'Yes, but I'd already met Arabella Prytherch and I knew we'd never get on. The head and deputy in a school exist in a delicate balance. You've met Jonathan and we rub along very well together. Arabella was abrasive and inflexible. So I applied for a new school and moved.'

'So what went wrong?' asked Harri.

'She was abrasive and inflexible as I just said. Three teachers left during the first term and one put in a claim for constructive dismissal. Then she began to fall out with the trustees so, at the end of the year, she was sacked and I was asked to return.' Lowri examined her fingernails. 'It's not an episode in the school's history we're particularly proud of.'

'Is this important to the case? Don't tell me she was one of the sisters arrested in 2015,' said Mallory.

'I'm afraid so. She called herself Sister Angharad and was, it seems, in charge of the five other women. While she was here, some of the teachers spotted that she liked to be known as Angharad but they put it down to her rediscovering her Welsh roots. In fact, she was already adopting a name from the Mabinogion as part of her assimilation into the group of women.'

'The Mabinogion being a collection of Welsh myths?' asked Mallory, looking at Harri for confirmation.

He nodded. 'From what I can see, Angharad, as I knew her, was one of the ringleaders of the group.'

'But how do you go from a major public school to a small farmhouse living out a mediaeval fantasy?'

Lowri shrugged. 'I've no idea. Aren't these groups usually dominated by a forceful personality? She certainly had one of those. The interesting thing was that the development of the group took place outside her role at Penbryn Hall, or so we presumed. Given the predomin-antly female teaching staff, it was always possible that Dr Prytherch had been recruiting for her vision from among her colleagues but it appears the Solstice Sisterhood came into being after her stint in Penbryn Hall. She probably gathered together a loose group of women who shared a similar outlook in terms of embracing Welshness and, well, correcting supposedly deviant behaviour, and set up home in Cardiff.'

Mallory stared at the pair in astonishment. 'But it's completely bizarre, given the accusations of this Bethan Rossi, that a scandal didn't emerge about her former role as head teacher. It would have been perfect headline fodder. Didn't the papers make the connection with the school in 2015?' asked Mallory.

'I can answer that,' said Harri. 'They didn't and neither did we. When we interviewed the sisters, we noted that Angharad Prytherch had US citizenship. We didn't run background checks on any of the women because it was hard to prove criminal activity.'

'She changed her name officially to Angharad?' asked Mallory.

'She must have done. The thing is, the case was a flash in the pan. Bethan Rossi made her claims, the women were interviewed, then the girl went cold on us and said she didn't want to pursue the matter further. We had other crimes to investigate and the matter was allowed to drop.'

'So where's Dr Prytherch now?' asked Mallory.

'Not here,' said Lowri grimly. 'When I read about the sisterhood in the paper in 2015, I recognised my predecessor immediately. It gave me a sleepless night and I called the chair of the trustees immediately the following morning. I wanted Dr Prytherch's name taken off the list of former heads but I was overruled about that. We did have a reactive press strategy in place but it was never needed. No one connected her to Penbryn Hall.'

'And you're sure the sisterhood came into being after Angharad left the school?'

'There was no evidence that anything untoward was happening during her brief tenure here. The three members of staff that we lost were extremely upset at being forced to leave and none of them were among those arrested.'

'Then what is a punishment book from the sisterhood doing under a rose bush in the school grounds?'

Lowri looked suddenly exhausted. 'I don't know but it's got to be connected to my concerns around Pippa's death, hasn't it? We could try to look at things methodically, starting with who left the message for you to find the book. Do you have any idea?'

Mallory made a face. 'At the moment, it's difficult to say. Most staff have been friendly enough and I don't think my cover has been blown. The main resistance I've had to my presence here has been from your deputy, Jonathan Mellor, who knows my true identity, and Emiah Jenkins, the librarian, who doesn't. Or at least I think she doesn't.'

'What has Jonathan said to you?'

'Nothing specific and he was polite enough when I told him about the note, but I get the impression he doesn't like the fact I'm here.'

Lowri's fair skin reddened. 'It's not his call to make. I'll speak to him when I get a chance. It's now clear something is going on and my decision to involve the police has been justified. What's Emiah said to you?'

'Nothing specific. I went to the library to check out what you told me about her interest in women's spirituality. Obviously that now makes sense – Pippa must have recognised someone from the Solstice Sisterhood – but I got a strong sense of animosity from her.'

'Interesting.' Lowri was more relaxed about the librarian's attitude. 'Emiah's nobody's fool so she's probably wondering why you're asking questions. I'm not prepared to take her into my confidence but if she mentions anything, I'll say you're just curious.'

'So you're happy for me to remain incognito, with the exception of Jonathan?'

Lowri hesitated. 'I think we'd better leave it at that for the moment. There's still plenty we need to discover. Do we think the punishment book belonged to Pippa?'

'The dates are impossible to read but it's surely something Harri can look into. Pippa was from Cardiff so it might well be that she was connected with them in some way from their time there.'

'But why would she have such a visceral reaction to seeing one of the former sisterhood here?' asked Harri. 'I interviewed them all, and other than being off the wall I didn't find any of them overtly threatening.' Mallory saw him pause, start to speak and check himself.

'I don't know,' said Mallory. 'It's one of the conundrums but it's possible Pippa was a victim herself. Seeing a former member working here might have brought back a raft of memories.'

'So what you're saying,' said Lowri, 'is that a member of my staff might be one of the former sisters. I have to say that's highly unlikely. I conduct extensive background checks on all my staff, including five years of references.'

'We're talking ten years since they were in Cardiff. It's not enough.'

Lowri shook her head. 'I think you're on the wrong track but if you can provide me with pictures of who you interviewed, I can tell you for sure.'

'I don't have them,' said Harri. 'They were interviewed under caution, nothing more. I need you to look at who has joined here since 2015 and double-check their background. I can't do much more as there's still no evidence that a crime has been committed.'

'Will you be updating Steph about what happened last night?'

Here we go, thought Mallory. The old girls' network.

Harri kept his expression neutral. 'Of course.'

18

Mallory and Harri left Lowri's office to discuss the next steps. There were three distinct lines of investigation and they had been prioritised.

First was the identity of the person Pippa might have recognised on her first night at Penbryn Hall. Given that Angharad Prytherch was no longer at the school, the most likely culprit was either a long-standing member of staff who had interacted with Angharad while she was in post, or someone connected to the sisterhood who had since joined the school. The former would be more difficult to weed out but Lowri said she'd provide a list of all long-standing staff and would also scour through the sixty or so résumés of all her teaching and auxiliary staff, which would take time. Gaps in their CVs were investigated at the time of recruitment but she'd be looking with an eye to euphemisms which might have been used to cover up a spell in the sisterhood. Contractors would be harder to pin down. An enhanced DBS check was all that was required to come in and teach judo for an hour each week, for example, but she would try.

The other two mysteries were who had buried the punishment book and the identity of the person who had led Mallory to it, if it wasn't the same person. If the book belonged to Pippa then they were two different people, as Pippa couldn't have left the note for Mallory.

Back in the corridor, Mallory whispered, 'Do you think the sisterhood might be still active in the school?'

Harri put his fingers to his lips. 'Let's go to your room where we can talk freely.'

Mallory led him across the building and up the staff staircase. He looked ill at ease in the environment, his shabby raincoat incongruous in the plush surroundings. She noticed him relax as he took in her room while he shrugged off his coat, revealing a suit older than any Mallory remembered seeing on him.

'You can have the comfy chair,' she told him with a wink. 'I'll take the desk one. It saves us having to use the bed.' She wheeled it out and rolled it towards him. 'I daren't even look at it. I'm so tired I'm worried I'll fall asleep standing up.'

'Have you got any teaching today?'

'Yes, but not until after lunch. It's been agreed that I'll take the class – an absence might cause more comment given the changes in teachers recently – but after that I'm going straight to bed.'

'How secure is this room?' he asked.

'There's a lock on the door but someone has a key because the note with the clue was left on my chest of drawers.'

'Then get it changed today. A place like this will have a raft of maintenance staff but I'd prefer an outside company to come in. Call in a locksmith from Aber.'

'I will, although I'll have to get the OK from Lowri. There's a complex system for looking after keys to the rooms.' Mallory warmed at his concern for her. Harri was a decent sort, so different from her ex, who'd always assumed she could look after herself. She rubbed her leg, which always began to ache when she was tired or stressed, the result of an injury that had invalided her out of the force. 'So, what next? Someone has led us to this correction book and therefore to the Solstice Sisterhood. I'm now guessing it's not the person Pippa saw – why deliberately put themselves in our line of fire? That means there's possibly someone here who Pippa recognised from the group of women and someone else who knows what's going on. Do we have enough evidence to bring a team in to investigate?'

Harri groaned, running his hands through his hair. 'I doubt it, and anyway, Lowri wants things kept discreet so she's hardly likely to press for a full investigation. OK let's split it into two parts. Let's say that Pippa was somehow involved with the sisterhood and she comes to Penbryn and recognises a former member of the group – most likely coming out of the chapel given she didn't make it into dinner. How about I give you a description of three of the six women I interviewed back in 2015? But I have to tell you I'm relying on memory only.'

Mallory pulled across a notepad as she was so tired, she might easily forget something important. 'Three of the six? What, not all of them?'

'Because we know about Angharad even if we're not sure of her present whereabouts. There's no way she's at the school. I know for a fact that one of the former members is dead and the other living in Australia. She'll be easy enough to check up on.'

'You have been keeping tabs on them,' said Mallory, wagging her finger. She saw Harri colour slightly. 'Tell me about those two anyway so I've got a feel for the group of women.'

'I'll do my best.' Harri folded his arms, lost in thought. 'There was an older woman in her sixties called

Lizzie Styles who looked ill when we interviewed her. I subsequently discovered she was being treated for leuk-aemia and she died in 2017. Her name in the group was Sister Luned and I considered her a victim of the sister-hood rather than persecutor. She seemed frightened of the other members and admitted to having borne the brunt of punishment herself.'

'Any evidence of this?'

'We didn't conduct a physical examination but she'd been admitted to hospital in Cardiff the previous year with infected lacerations on the back of her thighs. The A and E doctor remembered the case distinctly but Luned said she'd inflicted the wounds on herself as part of a cleansing process.'

'You think that's likely?'

'It's possible but when I interviewed the doctor he said Luned had been accompanied by someone calling herself Kigva. She had a proprietorial air with Luned that struck him as odd.'

'So we suspect she was being punished when she was in the early stages of leukaemia. That's nice when you're feeling sick.' Mallory put down her pen and pulled some aspirin out of her bag, dry swallowing a couple. 'Go on.'

'The other sister I know who is definitely in Australia is a woman named Jane Finch, who went by the name of Sister Ceridwen. She was one of the first members of the group. A degree at Oxford followed by dropping out and helping Angharad set up the sisterhood. She was very practical and I believe she made shoes for the group to wear. Some kind of clog, I think. When I interviewed the group in 2014, I wondered if she was the brains behind the group's ethos, except...'

'Except what?' asked Mallory, pouncing on his hesitation.

'I'll come to that later. Let me tell you what I do know and also what I think. Angharad, who we now know to be Arabella Prytherch, was the most verbose of the group and freely admitted that punishment was at the core of their ethos. It apparently freed the spirit and there was joy in physical pain.'

Mallory glanced at Harri, whose face showed disgust.

'The thing is Ellie did an essay on cults for her A-level RE, and she was researching modern-day groups. I happened to glance over her shoulder and saw Ceridwen's face just staring out at me on the screen. My heart sank as I thought she'd unearthed some info on the Solstice Sisterhood but in fact it was a new group of women in the Australian desert near Alice Springs who'd set up an alternative community.'

'A town like Alice,' murmured Mallory. 'So how do you know Ceridwen is still there?'

'Because I looked her up when we were talking to Lowri. Here's a photo from yesterday on the group's Facebook page.'

Harri passed his phone to Mallory, who looked at the woman staring out at her. She was dressed in pale blue giving her the air of a Madonna, her face, unadorned with make-up, lined with exposure to the sun. The caption underneath said, 'Blessed Jane checks on the Golden Wattle' and was dated the previous day.

'Blessed Jane?' asked Mallory. 'So she's elevated herself from sister to blessed.'

Harri shrugged, taking back his phone. 'She wasn't short of ego. Even if the photo is old – which I think unlikely as there's a traceable timeline of Jane in Australia – there's no way she's teaching in this school.'

'So we rule out Ceridwen and obviously Luned who died,' said Mallory keen to get on. 'Plus Angharad whose whereabouts are unknown. What do we know of the other three?'

'They were named Sister Branwen, Sister Kigva and Sister Rhiannon. I can give you a rundown of all three but I can't see any of them getting into the school incognito.'

'Why no—' She stopped abruptly as, in the distance through the window, they heard a scream, followed by another.

Mallory and Harri were on their feet immediately, flinging open the door and running towards the sound. Mallory was used to girls' shrieks but this was something fearful and she dreaded what she was going to find. Her leg, for the first time since the accident, was strong under pressure despite the ache as they came down the stairs.

'Around the back,' said Mallory. 'Near the sundial where the book was found.'

Once outside, they could see a huddle of girls in the distance, a couple of whom had turned away sobbing.

'Shit,' said Mallory. 'There's someone down.'

The group parted at their arrival and Mallory saw with a jolt it was Livvy on the floor, her dark hair matted with blood.

Christ. 'Livvy, what's happened to you?' She knelt down and felt for the girl's pulse while Harri pulled out his mobile to call for an ambulance.

Livvy was trying to speak. 'I… I… thought I saw someone looking at the rose bush.'

'Who?'

Livvy's mouth worked but no words came out.

Mallory looked across at the rose bush, which had been replanted with much care the previous day by Livvy. Even the soil around it had been carefully hoed to remove all trace of Livvy's presence. So why had someone returned once more to the spot?

19

4 August 2015

Angharad had been watching Bethan Rossi for a while. The girl wasn't like Pippa, the previous maid whose departure had helped seal the decision to move to West Wales. She was less nervy for a start and more competent at her job. The other members of the group liked her, and once Angharad had caught her throwing a tea towel at Rhiannon as they'd washed up together after dinner. The group dynamic was beginning to change. She could sense a restlessness that she couldn't put her finger on and felt something needed to be done to bring everyone to heel. The August heat didn't help, making everyone sticky and irritable.

The garden was lush with produce. Branwen had grown more than they could eat and had suggested selling some to villagers on a cart outside the farmhouse to raise funds for the sisterhood. Angharad still hadn't decided if this was a good idea or not. Prying eyes were what she feared and a produce stall would encourage the curious to loiter and stare.

Bethan came into the room with a tray of tea things. She set the teapot and cup carefully down but a slop of milk from the jug fell onto the table.

'I'll get a cloth.' She hurried out and returned a moment later with a piece of kitchen roll, dabbing it at the spill. 'Oh, I think it's going to stain the table.'

Angharad forced a smile and followed her out to the kitchen. Rhiannon was drying a large saucepan by the sink and avoided eye contact with Angharad, probably still sulking after the previous night's punishment. 'You like it here, don't you?' she asked Bethan.

Bethan raised her eyebrows in surprise. 'Of course. I mean, it's a long way to travel but the pay is good. It's more relaxing than working in the restaurant.'

'You know we're a community here, don't you?'

'You're the Solstice Sisterhood.' Bethan stopped. 'That's all I know except that you also have names from the Mabinogion.'

'We do. We also live by certain rules that you've probably noticed. We prefer to keep mod cons to the minimum, for example, and live a simple life.'

'Like the clogs.' Bethan looked down at the shoes she slipped on every morning on arrival at the farmhouse.

'Yes, like the clogs. We also have a system of light chastisement for when one of us does something wrong. It helps remind us that we're all here for the benefit of the others. I'm not sure if you've noticed.'

'Chastisement?' asked Bethan shooting a glance at Rhiannon. 'Are you going to give me the sack?'

'No, of course not. The thing is, in the group, we administer a little light corrective punishment but only with the receiver's consent. That is very important. Obviously as you're not a member we've not involved you, but it might make you feel more at one with us if you began to participate in this. Would you like me to show you?'

Angharad noticed that Rhiannon had stopped pretending to wipe the pan and was staring at the pair in trepidation.

'Well all right,' said Bethan. 'It's nothing weird is it?'

'Of course not. Would you just hold out your hands.' Angharad was secretly amused to see Bethan hold out her arms with her palms down. It would hurt her more that way. 'Turn over your hands, Bethan.'

The girl showed Angharad her palms. Angharad grabbed the nearest thing to hand, the riding whip that had seen much use since their move to the farmhouse. She brought it down three times onto Bethan's hands and watched the girl's face turn puce.

'You fucking bitch,' said Bethan and Angharad felt a blow to her eye. As she doubled over, she heard the door to the kitchen open forcefully and Rhiannon's head knock against the wood.

'You bunch of weirdos,' wailed Bethan, fleeing into the sunshine.

20

The beat underneath Livvy's skin was faint but steady, which gave Mallory hope. It was all her fault, of course. She should never have dragged Livvy into the mystery surrounding the note and, not for the first time, Mallory cursed her impulsiveness when under pressure. The school nurse sprinted across the courtyard to join them and tended to the girl's injuries while Mallory whispered words of encouragement. Lowri, who had arrived ashen-faced, shepherded the group of girls back to their classes and made arrangements to put the school into lockdown. There seemed to be a system in place for emergencies involving messages sent to teachers' whiteboards. It was a relief to be left alone with Livvy, Harri and the nurse, as the sound of a siren wailed in the distance.

Mallory stood back as the paramedics attended to Livvy, the sight bringing back her own memories of the stab wound to her neck and thigh when she had been a full-time member of the force. Triggering, her son Toby would have called it, but for Mallory there was something cathartic about watching how competent the medics were.

'I think she's going to be OK,' said Mallory. 'Her breathing is normal, which is a good sign.'

'You never know with head injuries.' Harri's tone was downbeat and as she glanced across at him, Mallory saw that he was pale. Livvy, she remembered, was about the same age as his daughter Ellie.

'You OK? I meant what I said. Livvy was semi-conscious, and the cut looked superficial.'

'It's what's going on inside her skull that I'm more concerned about. It was no accident. Look.'

Harri pointed to a stone lying on the ground, about ten centimetres in diameter.

'That's odd,' said Mallory. 'She was hit on the back of the head but said she saw someone at the rose bush. Either she was attacked by someone other than the person looking at the rose or she turned when she saw she was about to be assaulted.'

The stone was large and heavy enough to be held in one hand and Mallory could only imagine the damage if Livvy had received the full force of the blow.

'The attack on Livvy puts a whole new perspective on things. I'm going to ring Steph now with an update. I hope to God the girl's OK. According to Lowri, her parents are in Cairo. That's a long way without family when she's injured.'

Mallory sighed. 'It's her father and stepmother. She's not in touch with her natural mother but her father might have relatives here. Lowri's secretary will ring the family.'

It was the girl's head of house, Freya Wells, who travelled with Livvy to the hospital. Mallory had already learnt that this relationship was the closest to a substitute parent, and Livvy had looked glad enough to be accompanied by Freya. Mallory surreptitiously watched Freya as she tended to Livvy. She was competent, of course, given that Lowri was hardly likely to employ anyone who wasn't, but if Mallory had been laying bets, she'd have said the expression on Freya's face was one of confusion.

'Where are our colleagues?' grumbled Harri looking at his watch.

'At least the ambulance was quick.' In the distance, she could see two cars approaching, their sirens silent but with lights flashing.

'It's going to be hard to keep this discreet now,' said Mallory. 'Staff and students will need to be questioned, which means parents will be informed.'

'Agreed, although Lowri does wield some influence. She might just be able to keep the lid on things. Only the three of us suspect it's connected to what you and Livvy found last night.'

'Livvy must have been attacked because she could reveal the identity of who was looking at the rose. It tells us one thing – the person who hid the book and left the message isn't the same person Pippa saw.'

'I'd already thought of that. I'm going to ask Siân to get hold of Pippa's post-mortem results. If she was assaulted by the sisterhood at some point in her past, there might be scars on her body that were overlooked in the autopsy.'

Mallory made a face. 'I don't think that's very likely. Abusers are excellent at not leaving scars. I'm just worried this might not be the end of it. We've potentially opened a can of worms.'

'Then we need to make it known that we're aware that someone here is possibly a former member of the Solstice Sisterhood so at least that stops any more attacks on Livvy.'

Mallory took a breath. 'What I can't understand is, even if one of the staff is unmasked as a member of the sisterhood, so what?'

Harri rubbed his face with his hands. 'We need to go back to what I was telling you. There are three women, one of which may be employed here, and… well… there's something else.'

Mallory stared at him, annoyed by his prevarication. 'What something else?' she demanded. 'Would you stop talking in riddles?'

This infuriated him. 'All right but don't blame me if you think I've gone round the bend. Just let me speak and then tell me what you think afterwards. It'll have to wait until later. Right?'

'Right,' hissed Mallory taking a step back as the cars, ignoring the parking round the building, drew up beside them.

It was around three hours before they finally had time to themselves. Harri had rung home, and his sister Fran was tending to his kids, although as older teenagers they were probably happy to look after themselves. Harri had taken a long call from the super and had ended it grim-faced. One of the sixth form students was the daughter of European royalty whose representative had already been in touch with the Chief Constable.

'What the fuck am I supposed to do about it?' he said to Mallory. He had apparently said something similar to the super and had been told to 'solve the case', which had made him even more furious. Mallory, who had decided long ago that telling men to calm down was a complete waste of time, let him stew before dragging him to one of the work pods set up in the library. Emiah glanced over as they entered but quickly returned to her book pile.

The pod with its stark white interior and teak desk felt more intimate than Mallory's room.

'You were telling me about the sisterhood and the three members including Angharad Prytherch. Give me quick bios of the others, as much as you remember, and we can look up the women's real names on the computer afterwards.'

'No need. I've spoken to Siân and got their details. As soon as she said the names it all came back to me.'

'Go on,' said Mallory impatiently, wondering who was taking her class. Perhaps they'd doubled up for the afternoon.

'OK. Well we'll start with Sister Rhiannon, who was a thirty-five-year-old Welsh first-language speaker. She was the group's cook and claimed she spent most of her time in the kitchen, where she never saw any trouble. Given that Bethan Rossi said that she was punished every time she broke a glass, burnt the porridge and so on, I find that very hard to believe.'

'The cook? It's possible Pippa might have seen one of the catering staff the first night she arrived but that wouldn't account for her shunning the staff room.'

'True.' Harri shifted on the hard seat. 'And I can't see Rhiannon having the brains to become a teacher. We'll be looking into the backgrounds of all staff but I'd be very surprised to see her here. Next up was Sister Branwen, real name Joanna Christie. She was in her sixties when I interviewed her. Physically very robust, she was responsible for the gardens and general maintenance. I have absolutely no problem imagining her picking up a rock and hitting a young student over the head. The problem is that she'd be nearly seventy now and again reasonably easy to identify.'

'And there's no resident gardener. I've seen a firm from Tregaron come in with their vans.'

'Well Branwen could more or less turn her hand to anything but I'll recognise her if she's on site.'

'And of course, they should both be easy to discover if they're living elsewhere.'

Harri grunted. 'I wouldn't be so sure about that. It was a very closed group, which nicely moves me on to Kigva. She was from Ireland, Laois I think, and in her late twenties, real name Carmel Byrne. She was the outward face of the group – received passing visitors, shopped in town for provisions. She even went on radio talking about the sisterhood just after the arrests, claiming they had been victims of an injustice.'

'So media savvy.'

'Very, but she had the air of the zealot about her, which was off-putting. She might be harder to recognise as she had a kind of nondescript look about her. Pale blue eyes, I remember, but light-brown hair with a slight curl to it. She might be harder for me to identify but I've asked Siân to send over photos on file for all three – all six in fact – to see if anyone here can recognise them.'

Mallory picked up on his tone immediately. 'You don't think any of them are here?'

'It's probably just me.' Harri was inspecting his finger-nails, a slight colour visible on his cheeks.

On impulse, Mallory reached over to him and grasped his hand. 'What is it Harri?'

He didn't respond to her touch but screwed up his face. 'Do you think I'm a straightforward kind of bloke?'

Mallory smiled. 'Harri, you're the most normal person I've ever met. Why are you asking?'

'Because what I'm about to tell you is going to sound preposterous.'

'Try me. I'm the one that usually deals with off the wall stuff.'

'Well, OK. I think there was a seventh member of the group that no one ever saw.'

Mallory sat back in the seat and stared at him. She needed to tread carefully as it had cost him a lot to make this confession but she was also his colleague and needed to stress test every assumption. 'But surely with a group so small you'd know if there were six or seven members. You can't just hide that number.'

'I know and when I brought it up in 2015 no one took me seriously and I began to wonder if the job was getting to me. Paula had recently died and I thought grief was sending me doolally.'

'And now?'

Harri stared at her, his eyes troubled. 'I think there was a hidden member. Someone who masterminded it all.'

21

3 August 2015

Harri pushed open the door to the first bedroom in the farmhouse feeling a little like Goldilocks. The six members of the sisterhood were still in custody, but they'd need to be released by that evening, which gave him a short window of time to take another look at the house.

He had little doubt that Bethan's allegations were truthful. An initial search had found two bunches of birch twigs and a horse's whip. Angharad had been most forthcoming about the items, explaining they were for light punishment only. A horsewhip? Harri would have liked to use it on Angharad but he had a horrible feeling she would enjoy it.

Harri shook the thought away and looked inside the bedroom. It was the largest room on the first floor and in the centre was a large double bed. He lifted one of the plump pillows and noted the folded, pink-striped pyjamas underneath. A quick rifle through the handbag on the nearby table revealed this to be the room of Angharad. While she had the most generous room in the house, she didn't appear to share it with anyone. He looked around for books that might give an insight into the origins of the sisterhood's ethos but the space only contained a romantic novel by an American author.

The room next door had two single beds which had been made up with a precision he usually only saw in hotels. The one next to the window had a chair nearby with a pair of corduroy trousers thrown over that were caked with mud. He presumed this was the bed of Branwen, named after the daughter of Llyr in the Mabinogion, an association which ill-suited the no-nonsense red-faced woman he'd spoken to that morning. She shared the room with a woman whose bedside table was awash with prescription medication, from asthma inhalers to beta blockers. It was Luned who had insisted on collecting her tablets before the trip to the station and the label confirmed that the medication had been dispensed to an Elizabeth Styles. Harri had arranged a social worker to speak to Luned before her release. Given that Bethan was back with her family, Harri didn't much care what the group got up to in their spare time, although he was concerned for the vulnerable. There was something about Luned's pallor that set off alarms in his head.

The three bedrooms at the back of the house were much smaller, with barely enough space to house the single beds and a peg rack for clothes. The smallest had the smell of pastry and apples and he guessed it belonged to Rhiannon. The second's occupant was harder to identify but Harri guessed at Ceridwen because of the two books on clog making by the bed. The final room at the back of the house, although also tiny, had the air of a studied portrait of simple living. The Welsh blanket, for example, cost a couple of hundred quid and the white sheet underneath looked like linen. He remembered his interview with Kigva and her air of arrogance when she'd admitted the use of punishment. She was the thinnest of the women, possibly a size eight like his wife had been, and this was confirmed by a quick glance at the jumper on one of the pegs. Size extra small.

Her room was next to the bathroom, decent sized with a claw-footed bath in the centre. Harri was about to leave when he opened the door which he assumed led to the airing cupboard and saw with surprise that it led to another room. He walked in and saw another double bed, immaculately made up with no other signs of occupation. This couldn't have been Bethan's room as she had told them in her statement that she either travelled in by bus or slept downstairs in a bedroom at the side of the kitchen. Harri opened the drawers of the mahogany dresser and the door of the matching wardrobe. Both were empty of clothes and clean although a bird's feather rested on a shelf at the back of one of them. Harri picked it up and inspected it. It was long, brown and white in colouring and came from a large bird. He placed it back on the shelf and shut the door. Perhaps it was a guest room where prospective new recruits were housed, or they were saving it for a new member. And yet...

Harri sniffed the air that smelled of polish and something grassy and fresh. He and his colleagues had arrived at eight a.m. that morning just as the sisters were cleaning up breakfast. As per procedure, there was someone stationed at the back door as well as the front, where the two detectives and uniformed officers waited for admittance. No one had left the house and after all six women had been put in the back of two police vans, the house had been checked for other occupants. There was nothing to tease Harri's suspicions that there was anyone else there.

It had been the testimonies of the six women that had planted the first seed of doubt. Their responses had been pat but that was to be expected. Cults thrived on order and regularity. The answers of the three who'd been happy to admit the rules of the order – punishment was always consensual and mild, yes people were free to come and go – were as synchronised as expected. Yet underneath, Harri could sense something else, a shared anxiety that there was something much larger than the complaints of a former kitchen maid. And once, and only once, Sister Kigva had said that she would 'need to check with Sister—' before she had stopped abruptly, and he had been sure she was about to say something other than Angharad.

He would have to interview Bethan again despite her reluctance to push matters any further. She had willingly made a complaint to the police so there was no reason for her to hide the presence of another member. Perhaps they hadn't asked the right questions.

22

Mallory was sure her mouth was open. There was something hypnotic in Harri's storytelling, whether it was his baritone Welsh voice or the way he left the tale on a cliffhanger.

'Well?' she asked. 'What *did* Bethan say?'

'I never got the chance to interview her again. All the charges were dropped after the girl withdrew her allegations. I always thought that some pressure had been applied to her, but I was a sergeant at the time and the instructions from my guv'nor had been clear. Drop it.'

'Who was your guv'nor?'

'Steph Morris.'

'The super? I never knew she had a spell as a detective.'

'For a short while but it never suited her. I think she thought it would be high-profile stuff but as you know, serious crime is thankfully rare around here. It's how we get to employ civilian investigators like yourself.'

'I can't see the super as a detective, I have to say.'

'No, well she soon left to join the corporate governance team and got her first chief inspector role soon after.'

'It figures. You know she's a former student here?'

'Ah.' Harri slid his gaze away from her.

'You did know! So, have you told her about the sister-hood?'

'Yes, but to be fair, she doesn't really recall the case. She remembers the arrests and most definitely knew that Bethan dropped the allegations. So as far as she's concerned, the fact the case stalled wasn't anything to do with her. Her main concern is the attack on Livvy today, but my guess is she'll be poring over the old files like the rest of the team.'

'Hmm. So, what next? My cover has been clearly blown. Not many maths teachers, especially in their early weeks, go haring across a courtyard towards an injured girl.'

'You know, I wouldn't be so sure about that. You might still be OK. I'm asking the team to probe gently when they're conducting the interviews about how people are viewing you. Your cover might hold yet.'

'Think the attacker might come after me?'

'It's possible but I suspect Livvy, with the innocence of the young, gave some kind of clue about her nocturnal activities. That rose has been lovingly replanted and someone saw her do it at a time she shouldn't have been gardening. This place is probably a hotbed of gossip and I wouldn't be surprised if Livvy's activities have come to the attention of our attacker.'

'OK, if I stay here what do you want me to do next? I can't do much in relation to the sisterhood from here without blowing my cover.'

Harri sighed. 'Leave that to me. I'm going to pay a visit to Pippa's mother and also speak to Bethan, a conversation I should have had years ago. What we really need to do is start thinking of motive. Pippa saw someone she recognised. So what? Why would that person want to kill? Whatever was going on within the farmhouse is still happening here. I guarantee it. I need you to find out what it is.'

'You think it's to do with corporal punishment? I could ask around about discipline, although I'm pretty sure anything untoward would have already come out. It's hard to keep deviancy going in today's safeguarding environment.'

'Hard but not impossible. Think wider than just punishment. Control, zealotry, I don't know Mallory, I'm in the dark myself.'

Mallory thought of Livvy's bloodied head on the path. 'I'm kicking myself I got Livvy involved in the case and yet, what we need is Livvy's mental thinking.'

'No!' Harri's voice grew loud in the pod. 'No access to Livvy. You're the adult and a professional. Keep the students out of this from now on.'

'Sure,' said Mallory.

—

The Solstice Sisterhood punishment book had been taken away for evidence but not before Mallory had photographed each page. She sent the images to the shared printer in the staff room and stood by the machine waiting for the images to come out. Phones were frowned upon at Penbryn Hall and Lowri promoted a digital-free attitude outside lessons. It would look less suspicious if Mallory carried papers around with her while she tried to decipher the code. Rose was the only teacher in the room, sitting in an armchair with one leg slung over the arm. Mallory could see she was reading *Cosmopolitan* and smiling slightly at the subject matter.

'God, it's been a long time since I read that. Who's the agony aunt now?'

'No longer Saint Irma Kurtz I'm afraid, and they don't use that title any longer either. I don't really know why I'm reading it as it's definitely not written for millennials. Perhaps I just like to see what my students are thinking.'

Mallory had the sheaf of paper in her hand. She folded it into a square and placed it in her back pocket. She switched on the kettle and took a seat opposite Rose who, putting the magazine to one side, appeared to welcome the company.

'I'll have one too if you're brewing up. Milk, no sugar. How's Livvy?' asked Rose. 'It sounded like she had a nasty gash to the head. Was she attacked?'

'I assume so. I mean, there was nowhere for a rock to fall from so we have to assume someone deliberately hit her over the head with a stone.'

'Christ. Some student feud?'

'I don't know. I get the impression Livvy's a bit of an outlier. I'm not even sure if she's got a friendship group.'

'It's not surprising with a brain like that. I had her for GCSE RE and the only advantage I had over her was experience not intellect. That sort of thing can cause resentment, especially in an achievement-orientated place like this.'

'How long have you been at Penbryn Hall?' asked Mallory. 'I get the impression staff stay exactly because of the high motivation of the students.'

'That's one of the reasons I suppose. I've been here for about six years. Lowri headhunted me from my previous school. She's done that with quite a few of us. She's got no qualms about swooping in when she hears of a good teacher and offering them a higher salary here.'

Mallory made the tea and returned to her chair. 'She wouldn't like it if it was the other way round.'

'Of course not. It's why she's often away from the school. She goes to conferences and networking events not only to schmooze prospective parents but to listen out for information about outstanding teachers. I've heard other heads are inclined to play down their teaching staff attributes in front of her because the next thing you know, they're teaching here.'

'Is that what happened with my predecessor?' asked Mallory knowing full well it wasn't.

A sharp expression came into Rose's eyes. 'You seem to ask a lot of questions about Pippa. Did you know her?'

'Never met her. She was younger than me and our paths never crossed teaching-wise. It's just that I'm not one of those high-flying teachers Lowri recruited – I came through an agency and I believe Pippa did too.'

Rose shrugged. 'We have emergencies like everyone else, and you're popular with the students, as was Pippa.'

Mallory tried to hide the rush of pleasure she felt at being called popular. Perhaps she wasn't making as much of a hash of things as she thought.

'I heard she was reserved.'

Rose took her time over taking a sip of her tea. 'If you ask me, she was afraid.'

'Why do you say that?' Mallory kept her tone casual.

'She gave the impression she was always looking over her shoulder for someone. If she was relaxed in the classroom then it clearly wasn't a student who was bothering her.'

'A member of staff?'

Rose carefully placed her mug on the table and looked Mallory square in the face. 'Looks like it, doesn't it?'

Their eyes locked. 'Do you know who?'

'I've no idea. Something's going on isn't it? I can see you're not going to tell me but I'd appreciate a heads-up if there's a scandal brewing. I'm in the process of applying for other jobs and I'll take the first one offered if I have to.'

'Isn't it unusual to be looking for a job in the academic year? I got the impression people waited until summer.'

'Let's just say the atmosphere doesn't suit me any longer. Lots of people are jumpy, and before you ask, I don't know why.'

'When you say people, who do you mean?'

Rose considered. 'You're not actually a teacher are you? My sister-in-law's a copper and you've got that lean and hungry look I recognise.'

'I am a teacher,' said Mallory. 'I don't think Lowri would let unqualified staff teach here.'

'If you say so.' Rose picked up her magazine and began to fan herself.

'So who's jumpy?'

'Jem Owen for one. For a newly married woman she's clearly not happy. Emiah too has something on her mind. Some of my students are positively avoiding the library because of her attitude.'

'Any idea why they might be behaving strangely?' asked Mallory.

Their eyes locked again. 'You tell me.'

23

Harri was torn between reinterviewing Bethan Rossi and speaking to Pippa's mother. He felt both conversations were important but because he needed to establish a definitive link between Pippa and the Solstice Sisterhood, he finally decided to make the trip to Cardiff first accompanied by his colleague Siân. There was no evidence that Pippa had been in the area before she arrived in Penbryn Hall, which meant if she knew of the sisterhood, it was from her time in Cardiff. Siân was unusually talkative in the car, probably because Mallory was safely tucked away in an all-girls school and not interfering, as Siân thought, in the process of modern policing. Harri could never fathom the rivalry between the two, although it was Siân who was the most antagonistic, Mallory usually preoccupied with the needs of her son and personal circumstance. Whatever the issue, Siân was enjoying her time alone with him.

'I've been reading up on the sisterhood. Did you notice they were all named after characters in the Mabinogion?'

'It was the first thing I spotted back in 2014. That at least I have no problem with.' Harri had been brought up on the collection of Middle Welsh stories and loved in particular the story of Pwyll, Prince of Dyfed. He didn't mind a group of Welsh women taking the names, but it was the association with deprivation and punishment that turned his stomach. The stories were ones of survival and beauty, not subjugation of those weaker than yourself.

'I never got into the tales myself,' said Siân. 'I think it was being made to read them at school that put me off. Was Pippa given a name, I wonder?'

'If she was in the same position as Bethan then I doubt it. Mabinogion names were reserved for full members, not servants.'

'Right but not punishment. That was available to all, lucky them, but difficult to prove. Didn't you say Luned showed signs of beatings?'

'She did but we never got to the bottom of it.' Harri winced at his choice of words. Bethan, when interviewed, had said she was sure a switch was used on the other members, and she'd spotted one of the sisters, Ceridwen, hitching up her trousers after a beating.

They were nearing Cardiff and he kept his attention on the road. Every time he came to the city, he was surprised by how much it had changed and how little was familiar. He navigated the one-way system and finally arrived in Roath. It was one of the oldest suburbs of the city, full of terraced houses which had once been affordable to the ordinary person. Now they were being bought by busy professionals and individualised so there was no longer a homogenous feel to the roads. Number ten was one of the few that looked unchanged although Harri noticed the windows were freshly painted.

They were shown in by a woman in her early fifties who took them into a room at the back. A TV was on, which Lucy Evans turned down but didn't switch off.

'You've come to update me on Pippa,' she said flatly.

Siân had called ahead to arrange the meeting but had told Lucy nothing of the reason behind it.

'Can we sit down?' Harri asked, taking the sofa along with Siân. Lucy looked like she wanted to continue standing but in the end pulled out a stiff-backed chair from behind a small table. It reminded Harri of the sitting room of his childhood, a square table tucked away in the corner used for tea and chat. He wished he'd waited to be invited to sit there but he was now stuck with the sofa.

'DC Lewis and I are continuing to investigate the death of your daughter, which we're treating as unexplained.'

'Not suicide?' asked Lucy. 'That's what I was told.'

'Unexplained, which is how we treat all suicides before the coroner's inquest. What we're trying to do is get an insight into Pippa's state of mind before she died. I can see from your statement that she came to see you just before she left for Penbryn Hall, is that right?'

'The day before. She was like the cat who got the cream going to that school. Said the headmistress had asked for the cleverest maths teacher they had and that was her.'

Harri frowned. 'You mean Lowri specifically asked for Pippa or that she asked for their most able teacher?'

'I... I don't know. I thought she'd asked for Pippa but maybe I misunderstood that.'

'Did you hear from Pippa while she was at the school?' asked Siân, making notes on her tablet.

'No, but she'd only been gone a week. We talked once a month or so.'

Harri tried not to wince at the thought of his own children talking to him so irregularly but experience told him every family was different. He already knew that Pippa was in touch only now and then with her father, who Lucy divorced when Pippa was a child, and it appeared to be a family where parental responsibility ended at eighteen.

'Can I ask about Pippa's employment before she went into teaching?' asked Harri.

'Before? She only ever taught, when she wasn't travelling, that is.'

'I heard Pippa liked to travel. Is that why she was supply teaching rather than employed in a permanent position?' Harri kept his eyes on Lucy Evans. She appeared to have a similarly restless personality to her daughter, her concentration shifting from the TV to the movement of a cat just outside the window.

Lucy shrugged. 'Pippa was still only young. This new generation doesn't stick at anything for long.'

Out of the corner of his eye, Harri saw Siân make a face. 'Back to before Pippa started teaching. Did she have holiday jobs while at university, for example?'

'Only in KFC, but what's that got to do with anything? It was a long time ago.'

'Just KFC?' Siân glanced up from the screen. 'No other kitchen jobs, for example.'

'No… Oh, there were those women who had a house in the next street but that only lasted a few weeks. Pippa couldn't abide the place but she stuck it for a while. Then one day she walked out and never came back.'

'Can you remember anything about the women?' asked Harri. 'Did they have a name, for example.'

'Well…' Lucy frowned. 'I think they *did* have a name but I'm not sure what it was.'

Harri could feel Siân's glance on him.

'What about the address?'

'That's easy. The women had a house on Radnor Road although I can't remember the number.'

Harri glanced at Siân. That was good enough confirmation for him. 'Were they called the Solstice Sisterhood?'

'That's it!' Lucy stopped. 'What have they got to do with Pippa's death?'

'Were you aware,' said Siân, 'that the group relocated to West Wales shortly after Pippa left them?'

'No, but there's no way she would have anything to do with them – she used to recoil whenever I mentioned them. I'd occasionally see one of them walking down the street wearing clogs even in winter. It caused quite a stir around here I have to say. Pippa thought they were a bunch of weirdos and I couldn't get her to talk about her time there at all.'

'We're trying to check all of Pippa's past. You might not have heard but there was a criminal investigation into the lifestyle of the women in the group.'

'Criminal? You must be mistaken. Pippa would never get involved in something illegal. She only went in to help with the housework. A bit of extra money in the summer holiday to stop her getting under my feet here.'

Harri was beginning to get annoyed by the woman's attitude. Her lack of curiosity about the reasons for his questions and her dismissal of Pippa's time there suggested a shortage of maternal concern. 'But did Pippa mention how she'd been treated in the house on Radnor Road?' asked Harri. 'The group were accused of causing harm to a female similar in age to Pippa. Did she mention anything about being physically assaulted?'

'Of course not. Pippa would have stood up for herself.'

'Did you notice any assault marks?' asked Siân. 'The palms of her hand might have had scars, or there might have been weals on her legs.'

'You've had her body, why didn't you check?' asked Lucy, her voice tart.

Harri was once more appalled but he already knew the answer. The post-mortem hadn't identified any recent scars on Pippa's body, nor evidence of old healed ones. That wasn't to say she hadn't been a victim of the assaults by the Solstice Sisterhood but the physical scars at least had not been permanent.

'I'm asking you,' he said evenly.

'I saw nothing.' Lucy folded her arms.

'So you say,' said Siân 'that Pippa worked for the sisters for about a month and then she left. Did she give you a reason for leaving?'

'Nope, but she came home in tears one day and said there was no way she was ever going back. It was late at night, after midnight, and I couldn't get it out of her why she'd stayed so late. She'd usually be back gone nine once she'd cleared up after dinner but this evening it was much later.'

'Did she give you any clue about what might have made her so upset?' said Harri. If it had been Ellie, his daughter, he'd have bloody well made sure he got it out of her.

Lucy shrugged. 'You know what teenagers are like – secretive. I just let it go but I told her she'd need to earn her keep, which was when she got the job in KFC.'

'You never asked her further about her time there?' asked Siân.

'Of course not. Why would I?'

'Were you aware she was taking anti-anxiety medication?' asked Harri.

'Been on it for years,' said Lucy. 'Have you finished? I need to go out.'

'I just want to be sure that Pippa never said anything about the Solstice Sisterhood after she left. Anything at all. It might help explain her death.'

Lucy shook her head. 'It's that school you should be looking into. She should have stayed at the comp here. It's what happens when you stray away from your class.'

—

After the interview, Harri and Siân walked to the adjacent road and found the house once occupied by the sister-hood. Harri was fuming after the interview.

'Jesus Christ. Pippa was clearly traumatised by what happened there and the mother doesn't even sit the girl down and ask her what happened.'

'Take it easy, boss. You know what families are like.'

'It starts a cycle of keeping secrets though, doesn't it? Pippa's death can probably be tracked to the fact she was unable to talk about her experience with the sisterhood.'

'I think that's a bit harsh.' Siân stopped outside a dingy-looking terrace with a broken wheelie bin stationed next to the front door. 'I think this is it.'

To Harri's eyes, the farmhouse in Ceredigion had been a significant step up from this terrace and he wondered who had financed the move. There wasn't any place to hide in this tall terrace and Pippa must have had a good insight into the life of the sisterhood. But what had she seen? He really needed to speak to Bethan Rossi and start tracking down the remainder of the group. The answer, he was sure, lay with them.

24

Mallory was glad to get back to the classroom. Initially the lower sixth had been subdued – Livvy was liked even if no one was especially close to her – but with the robustness of the young, they'd soon started pumping Mallory with questions. Given Harri was now going to have to do all the legwork surrounding Pippa's past and the previous history of the Solstice Sisterhood, Mallory was determined that her time here wouldn't be characterised by her merely picking up tidbits and school gossip.

'Any Cranogwen fans here?' asked Mallory and a few girls put up their hands. 'What about among your teachers?'

Isabella pulled the sleeves of her jumper over her hands which she jammed under her armpits, a gesture of comfort that Mallory had seen Toby do many times. 'The teachers *love* her. There was even an exhibition in the library last year where we all illustrated quotes from Cranogwen's poetry.'

'Can you remember which teacher organised that?' asked Mallory.

'It wasn't a teacher,' said Isabella. 'It was the librarian.'

Emiah, thought Mallory. She really did need to get beyond the woman's antagonism towards her and see how much she knew about either the message or the buried punishment book. She noticed Molly wanted to speak.

She had seen Mallory run to Livvy the previous day, easily outsprinting Harri, who needed to lose a few pounds anyway.

'Were you an athlete when you were young, miss?' she asked.

Mallory bit back the rejoinder that she was hardly over the hill. 'I used to run every morning but I got an injury and my leg's never been the same. I've clearly got muscle memory, if you think I was fast.'

'My dad's got stress on his plantar fascia,' said Molly, commiserating. 'He's had to give up running.'

Mallory recalled the knife that had sliced into her thigh after she'd tried to arrest a suspect in London while at the Met. Even now, the thought of her blood spilling on the pavement made her wince. Instead, she smiled.

'Who's up for some trigonometry?'

–

There was an Amazon parcel waiting for her at reception, which Mallory unwrapped back in her room. It was a portable door lock, the type bought by female travellers who wanted to secure their rooms from unwanted attention. She'd had no time to speak to Lowri about changing the locks and this would be a temporary solution. Mallory fixed the device to her door and tested it. It held firm and would give her plenty of warning if someone tried to get into her room while she was asleep. When she was teaching or otherwise occupied around the school, there was not much she could do. However, in terms of her personal safety, it would help.

Harri's theory of a seventh member of the Solstice Sisterhood was a little left field but Mallory wasn't inclined to shrug off a colleague's instincts. From what he'd told her, it did sound like Angharad Prytherch was the type to lead a group of women. She was a teacher, for starters, who'd risen to become head of this notable school. She'd have had her leadership qualities closely scrutinised at interview and had clearly impressed the trustees. She was presumably also used to being with women.

Mallory retrieved the photocopied pages of the punishment book and looked again at the symbols. There was something about the assignment of shapes to actions that suggested a mathematical brain and she wondered if this was important. Harri had said a member of his team would be going through the statements of the sisters again, but the punishments that Mallory knew of were switching across the palms and slaps across the face, which Bethan had endured, and, based on the injuries of Luned and Harri's discovery of the horsewhip, some form of chastisement across the back of the legs and buttocks. All of these punishments would have been given a symbol but Mallory doubted her ability to decipher each one. She tried to get into Livvy's way of thinking, as her student would have had some ideas on deciphering the symbols although Mallory wasn't convinced that separating birching from another form of chastisement would actually bring her nearer to solving what had happened to Pippa and Livvy.

Punishments, like those meted out by most abusers, were painful and humiliating but didn't leave long-lasting scars like broken bones if Pippa's post-mortem results were anything to go by. What Mallory needed to do was get to the reason why Pippa had brought the book to Penbryn Hall, if it had in fact belonged to her. The smudged dates were an issue and to Mallory's mind looked like they were from tears shed over the ledger. Of course the book would hold terrible memories for Pippa, and Mallory personally would have put it on the fire if she'd been in the girl's position. But Pippa – maybe to prove to herself that she had been beaten during her time with the sisters, or perhaps to one day give to the police as evidence of her assaults – had kept hold of it. But why take it to a new post unless she knew she would have use for it?

Mallory was still musing on Pippa's motivations when there was a knock on the door.

'Hold on.' Mallory slid off her bed and walked to the door. 'Who is it?'

'It's Jonathan.'

Mallory unlatched the door and let in Lowri's deputy. She was once more struck by how attractive he was. Mallory had overheard him telling a colleague at dinner that his father had come to Wales from Namibia to work at Morriston hospital near Swansea. He'd met a Welsh nurse there and they'd married. It was all she knew about him but it suggested an interesting backstory that she'd not been allowed to engage with. He was the only teacher, apart from Lowri, who knew Mallory's real identity but he'd not attempted to speak to her about her investigations in a meaningful way beyond deputising for his boss. Mallory was left with the impression he disapproved of the plan so it was a surprise to see him in her room.

'I came to check on you,' said Jonathan. 'You had a busy day yesterday, followed by a class today. Teaching isn't for the fainthearted, although neither I suspect is policing. How are you feeling?'

Surprised, Mallory shrugged. 'I'm fine but worried after what happened to Livvy. Do you have any news?'

'She'll be back with us later this week. She was observed overnight in Bronglais hospital and they're happy with her progress. Her scans show a slight hematoma but outside the skull, which is what we want to see. Her brain's not showing any swelling but they're keeping her in just in case.'

'Thank God. I've been beating myself up for involving her in my plans. I thought it was just someone playing games with me when I first got the message. Now we know it's a lot more serious.'

'I'm blaming myself too. I've not been able to stop thinking about it all day. I get the impression Lowri is annoyed that I didn't ring straight away to tell her about your discovery.'

'Impression? I think with Lowri you'd know straight away she wasn't happy. What did she say?'

'That it counted as an emergency, which wasn't the view I took when you brought the book to me. Like you, I wasn't quite sure what was going on and I thought it could wait until Lowri returned.'

Mallory realised Jonathan was on the verge of tears. She went to her wardrobe and pulled out a silver flask. Not much of a drinker, Mallory had anticipated she might need the odd nip of something strong after a day's teaching, and now was the occasion. 'Drink this – it's some Fino sherry I bought in Spain. Not exactly the hard stuff but it'll help. Go on.'

Jonathan took a sip of the amber liquid and Mallory watched as the alcohol revived him. She took the flask off him and had a nip herself. 'You know, it's really easy to be wise after an event. We get it all the time in investig- ations, people telling us we should have done this or we missed something important. Finding the book wasn't an emergency and that's exactly what I'll be telling Lowri.'

'She hasn't come to see you after Livvy's attack?'

'No, but I believe Harri has spoken to her.' The head teacher, Mallory was discovering, had a strict view of hierarchy in the school and in the outside world. She preferred to deal with Harri while most communication with Mallory went through her deputy. Well, that was fine but she couldn't have it both ways. She was told about the book on her return and if she'd thought it an emergency, could have put the school into lockdown straight away. 'Don't worry about it, OK? The whole point of being a deputy is that you sometimes make decisions on your boss's behalf. Lowri is probably panicking about her reputation and that of the school, which is fair enough.'

'OK. Thanks, Mallory.'

'Look, you could help me, though. I'm trying to discover which teachers have been here for fifteen years or more. From about 2010. Have you been here that long?'

'Only just. I came to teaching a bit later than usual. I'm a qualified psychologist but decided to retrain and I came to Penbryn Hall from my previous employment as deputy head at a state school in Bristol. If I'm honest, I was glad to leave. I was shocked at the racism I received.'

'I always thought Bristol was a multicultural city.' Mallory had been struck by the lack of diversity in Dyfed Powys constabulary, which really needed addressing, but knew from experience the Met had worked hard on its recruitment from minority groups. At a conference in Bristol, she'd also been impressed by the diversity of the speakers and attendees.

'It is and has historically always been so. But I was teaching in a white working-class area and the students were merciless. In the end, when I saw the advert for the deputy post here, I decided to apply on a whim.

Sometimes these spur-of-the-moment things work out and Dr Prytherch and I hit it off.'

'You were recruited by Dr Prytherch?' Mallory narrowed her eyes. 'So this was presumably the year Lowri was teaching elsewhere.'

'Oh, you know about that.' Jonathan smiled. 'I was a little anxious about meeting Lowri given I'd taken over her job but we've got on well. She's quite a demanding boss but I've learnt a lot from her and she encouraged me to do an MBA to improve my management training.'

He'd clearly forgotten about the incipient tears a moment earlier. 'What did you think of Dr Prytherch?'

'Arabella? Keen, a little over-keen, and she never really seemed to settle here. She had these high plans but they were disjointed. She wanted to attract more students from the US and Asia, for example, but these ideas never really got off the ground. Instead, she got sucked into the minutiae of running a school, which really is what you need a deputy for.'

Mallory frowned. 'Can you give me an example of this?'

'Well, sure. Eisteddfods, which are Welsh celebrations of culture – singing, music recitals, poetry and so on – have always played a role here, but Arabella embraced the whole ethos with fervour. These things aren't difficult to organise and can really be left to the teachers to put together, but Arabella seemed to want to be in the heart of things.'

'Rediscovering her Welsh roots maybe?' said Mallory.

Jonathan shrugged. 'Maybe, but it wasn't the best way to run a school like this. It didn't go down that well among staff, who saw it as interfering.'

'So which other teachers are here from that time?'

'Not that many. There's Jem Owen, who you know, and me. To be honest that's probably about it but I'll have a think. Most of the staff have retired from that time. Lowri sort of had a clean sweep when she arrived back but I have to say the teachers she recruited have largely stayed as she's a good boss.'

'Jem Owen? Is she an old girl too?'

'No she's not, but she might as well be. She fits in perfectly in Penbryn despite her eccentric dress. The funny thing is fifteen years ago it might have been seen as an affectation. Now it's bang on trend.'

He doesn't like Jem, thought Mallory. I wonder why that is. 'What about other members of staff? Cooks, gardeners, cleaners.'

'God I don't know. Mrs Jones has been here for years and Emiah the librarian is a fixture of the place. She was certainly here when I arrived. Is there any reason you're asking about long-serving staff?' asked Jonathan, his gaze on Mallory. 'I have a horrible feeling I'm not being told something. Care to share it with me?'

Mallory grimaced. 'I can't. Not yet.'

25

Over the following days, Mallory taught maths by keeping one step ahead of her students, and fretted as she quietly observed the comings and goings of the school. The atmosphere was subdued – although the students outwardly behaved as normal there was a false brightness to their manner, and another counsellor was drafted in to speak to those who were anxious about the attack. Among the staff, there was a new watchfulness. There wasn't much speculation about Livvy's attacker, which suggested to Mallory that her colleagues were looking among themselves for the culprit. No one, however, mentioned the Solstice Sisterhood, and it seemed in this respect the lid was being kept on things.

Mallory borrowed a book on the Mabinogion from the library using her ID card. She was relieved she could take it out without attracting the attention of Emiah, although the librarian could search for information on her loan if she wanted. Mallory didn't suppose it mattered. Rose had guessed who she was and others must be wondering why she'd been speaking to the police team for a few hours in the aftermath of Livvy's attack. Mallory took the book into one of the sitting rooms tucked away at the back of the house and immersed herself in tales of heroic acts and tragic sacrifices. She couldn't for the life of her think why the character names had become the focus of a religious group. It was Angharad Prytherch who would be able to give some answers and Mallory found herself desperate to meet the former head.

A click of heels in the corridor outside the door warned her someone was approaching and Mallory shut the book using the cover flap as a place marker. The door opened and Lowri stood on the threshold.

'I was wondering where you are. You have a class in half an hour.'

'I know,' said Mallory. 'I'm fully prepped and I wanted a bit of downtime before I started teaching. If you wanted to speak to me, you could have sent me a message.' I've lost my psychic abilities, thought Mallory, wondering why the head suddenly wanted to speak to her.

The comment annoyed Lowri. 'I've been busy ensuring the security of the school. I'm beginning to wonder if this plan of ours was a big mistake.'

Mallory went cold. She might not think she was a good fit for the school but she was damned if she was going to be sent away because of the incident with Livvy. 'What did you think might happen by inviting me in to look into Pippa's death? Of course I've shaken up things and if it wasn't me who'd received the note it might have been one of the students. It's to your benefit that you have a professional inside Penbryn Hall.'

Lowri took a deep breath. 'I'm not so sure about that, although I will say that I've been hearing good things about you from the students. I'll let you get on with your reading.' She turned to go.

'It's fine. Come and join me. I wanted to speak to you anyway about some of the things we discussed in your office.'

'In relation to the sisterhood? I'm really not the best person to ask.' She nevertheless shut the door and took a chair opposite Mallory. She had on a brown suit with a long narrow skirt, which on anyone else would have looked dowdy. On her, she reminded Mallory of a Fifties movie star. Tippi Hedren in the countryside.

'How is Livvy? Isn't she expected back soon?'

'She'll be home later today. She gave a statement to the police that she was attacked by a woman she saw looking at the rose bush but she didn't get a look at her face.'

'Definitely a woman?'

'It would seem so, wearing a long coat with a hood covering her face, which I have to say isn't that unusual. I've got one myself to protect me from the worst of the winter.' Interesting that she was both putting herself in the frame as a suspect and then eliminating herself. I can do the detecting on my own, thanks, thought Mallory.

'The coat is a useful detail but limited. Well, we can rule out the male staff then, but that's about it.'

'You know, I wouldn't rule anyone out based on their gender.' Lowri frowned at the book in Mallory's hand. 'What are you reading?'

'I took this from the library. I've been mugging up on the Mabinogion but I can't say it's given me any great insights.'

Lowri smiled. 'I'm glad you're discovering our literary history even if it's under such dire circumstances.'

'Do you think the fact that the members of the sisterhood named themselves after Mabinogion characters is significant?'

Lowri pursed her lips. 'I doubt it. The tales are well known and are often repurposed by new-age figures for their own ends.'

'Tell me about Angharad Prytherch, or Arabella as you knew her. I feel she's the key to linking the sisterhood to the school even if she's not physically here.'

'I only met her the once on the day of her interview. I'd had my own meeting with the trustees in the morning and it had gone fairly well. I knew I was in with a good chance of getting the role and prepared to be friendly with the other candidates.'

'What were your impressions when you did meet?'

'I've already told you. I found her arrogant and dismissive. I also, I suppose, thought she was fairly charismatic, so she'd make a good impression on the trustees.'

'There was no hint of her being, I don't know, interested in alternative religions? I mean you have a strong Anglican ethos here, don't you? Perhaps something struck you as odd.'

'I'm afraid our conversation was purely superficial. As the existing deputy head, I was tasked with showing prospective candidates around the school. I was happy to do so, it was a competitive process after all, but I was also checking how well I'd be able to work with a successful candidate if I didn't get the job.'

'I'm struggling to grasp Angharad's motivations, especially given she ended up running the sisterhood, which she presumably brought into existence. If when she was appointed she didn't find the post to her liking, why didn't she go to another school? It's what most people would have done.'

'I can't answer that for you. Perhaps when you find her you can ask her yourself. Harri tells me he's trying to track down her whereabouts and those of former members of the sisterhood.'

'I've not had an update on that. How have you got on looking at your existing teachers?'

'All of the staff I've recruited appear to be exactly who they say they are. Where I can, I've even telephoned their previous employers for the period 2014–15 when we know the sisterhood was active. I've not discovered anyone with a gap in their employment for that period.' Lowri stopped.

It was a longshot, and Mallory was beginning to think that someone they hadn't yet identified was also at the school with a relationship to the Solstice Sisterhood.

'There *is* something I need to tell you,' continued Lowri. 'I've discovered that Pippa had applied for a position in a school in Ledbury while she was here. I was speaking to a head about a teacher I was checking out, and he mentioned that he'd received an application from Pippa. They were planning to invite her for an interview when they read of her death. It would have meant leaving her post at Christmas, which would have left me looking for another teacher. During her interview with me, Pippa was adamant she would work a full school year.'

'So we know she was definitely planning to leave. Why do you think she took her own life if there was the potential for an escape route?'

'I don't know.' Lowri raised her hands. 'I thought I should pass that on.'

'In my opinion, there are two possibilities. If the sisterhood has a presence at the school, it's either someone who was here at the school when Angharad was here or someone who joined more recently but has links to the order. You're checking out the latter possibility and I need to focus on the former. Both are important lines of inquiry. Perhaps a new incarnation of the sisterhood exists somewhere and you've inadvertently recruited a teacher from their midst, or there's someone who never left.'

'And Pippa? She's the reason I brought you to the school. What's her connection to the Sisterhood?'

Mallory resisted the temptation to glance at her phone. 'That's what I'm waiting to discover from Harri.'

26

Harri eventually called at three that afternoon and Mallory listened to his update, trying to make sense of where the information left her. While Harri's interview with Pippa's mother was important in linking the dead woman to the Solstice Sisterhood, it didn't prove the punishment book belonged to Pippa nor did it provide any clue to the identity of the person Pippa might have spotted.

'Any luck in locating any of the sisterhood?' asked Mallory.

'Give us a chance, Mallory,' said Harri, his voice cross. 'I've an interview with Bethan Rossi this afternoon, which will help clarify what went on in the house in 2015. Siân is on the case tracking down the missing sisters. The priority is Angharad, and I can tell you now she's not appearing on any database under any of her names.'

'Is it just you and Siân working on the case?' said Mallory. 'Christ, I thought this was a priority.'

'Well Steph wields a lot of power but if you ask me, now she's realised that there is something wrong at Penbryn Hall, she's looking to cover her back so the emphasis is on proportion. Don't forget, the idea of putting you in the school incognito was cooked up by Steph and Lowri together.'

'And there I was thinking you just wanted to work with me again,' said Mallory.

She heard him laugh softly down the line. 'You know, you should pretend to be the school mistress thing more often. It suits you.'

'Yeah right.'

Mallory was smiling as she cut the call. She looked out of the window and saw it was getting dark despite being only three in the afternoon. There was an end-of-term feel about the school, probably due to the Christmas productions and concerts being rehearsed wherever Mallory ventured. Students were discussing their holiday plans in the classroom, many of which involved exotic holidays in places Mallory could only dream of going to. In a week she'd be out of here and the momentum would be lost. Mallory had already decided that there was no point in returning to the school come the new year. It was one thing putting her into a classroom for the sluggish December weeks, quite another as students looked towards exams to achieve their required grades. From Lowri's attitude this afternoon, it appeared she'd happily see the back of Mallory too.

They were nearing the winter solstice, when daylight would last just a few hours. She counted on her fingers – it was five days away, and if there were the remnants of the cult in the school then surely the date must have a significance. It was also a potential crisis point for the school. She needed to find out what the group used to do on the two solstices, the winter one in particular.

She tried to ring Harri back but the phone rang out unanswered. He was planning to interview Bethan Rossi, who might know the nature of solstice celebrations, but one of the original members would be the better bet. She typed in a quick message telling him what she wanted.

Mallory was still by the window when a car drew up and she watched as Livvy was helped out of the rear door by Freya. Livvy looked pale but otherwise OK. The rear door on the other side of the car opened and a woman got out who Mallory had seen recently at Carmarthen HQ. It looked like Harri was taking no chances with Livvy and she'd be getting officer protection. On impulse, Mallory hurried to the door that led onto the courtyard.

'Are you all right Livvy?' she asked and saw all three heads turn towards her.

'Livvy's fine,' said Freya, 'but she needs to get into the warmth and rest as soon as possible. No visitors.' Freya had dark rings under her eyes which hinted at sleepless nights.

The two adults busied themselves around the girl, who held Mallory's gaze and – she was sure of it – winked as she was led away. Mallory looked at her phone again. 'Come on Harri,' she said.

'First sign of madness,' said a voice and Mallory saw that Jem was smiling at her. 'Talking to yourself, I mean. Who's Harri?'

Mallory groaned. 'Someone I'm trying to contact.'

Jem was following the progress of Livvy and the adults with an expression of concern. 'You know,' she said with a distracted air, 'Lowri doesn't really like staff using their phones during school hours. She thinks it sets a bad example to students.'

'Of course. I'm sorry.' Mallory put her phone in her pocket. 'I'm still getting to know the rules and I rushed out to see Livvy when I saw the car arrive.'

'How is she?'

'She seems OK but I didn't get a chance to speak to her. What has Freya said about her? It must have been a shock for her.'

The question got Jem's attention and she turned her gaze to Mallory. 'She's not said much. Why do you ask?'

Mallory noticed the change in Jem's attitude. She was clearly protective over her wife but her question was tinged with suspicion.

'I thought that as head of Livvy's house, she might have some ideas about what had happened.'

'If she has, she hasn't shared them with me. In fact we're not sharing much at the moment. Freya has moved out of our shared accommodation and is staying onsite with her students.'

'She must be concerned about her students' welfare.'

'I think it's much more than that but I'm not being let into what it is.' Jem rubbed her face, looking shattered.

'Look, I know I'm new here but it's a strange time for the school, first with Pippa dying and then the attack on Livvy. I'm sure Freya is feeling it as much as anyone.'

'OK maybe.' Jem was grabbing at any comfort she could get but it got Mallory thinking. Perhaps Freya knew more about the attack on Livvy than she was letting on. She needed to tread carefully as Jem's first instinct would be to protect her wife.

Mallory moved closer to Jem. 'Can I ask you something in confidence? You said you taught Welsh history. Do the Welsh have any celebrations for the turn of the seasons – I'm thinking winter, in particular beyond Christmas?'

Jem frowned. The question had taken her by surprise but she answered willingly enough. 'The Welsh have lots of celebrations you might not find elsewhere. In New Quay and Aberaeron they commemorate the end of the fishing season with a mackerel festival which ends with them burning an effigy of the fish on the beach. Is that what you were thinking of?'

Fish? Christ. 'Not exactly. I was wondering what might happen in a Welsh solstice. We're coming up to the period now.'

Jem adjusted the bag on her shoulder, her eyes straying to the door of the student house that Livvy, Freya and the officer had disappeared into. 'Well, if you're into that kind of thing, people try to recreate the druidic celebrations at various points of the year – the equinoxes and solstices, for example. The problem is that no one actually knows how the winter solstice was celebrated as it wasn't written down anywhere. It doesn't stop people speculating, though.'

'So it's common for people just to make up their own thing.'

Jem frowned, a little offended. 'I think "make up" is a little strong. When you talk about Welsh culture, it means different things to different people. I like to redefine what it means to be Welsh – our national poet, for example, is of Iraqi–Welsh heritage – but others see Welshness as having ancestors who've farmed the same hill for six generations.'

Mallory didn't really want to be getting into a conversation about Welsh identity. She had quite enough of that with Harri. What she wanted to know was what she might expect if she was still here on 21 December.

She tried again. 'So what are modern-day solstice celebrations?'

'The Welsh figure Iolo Morganwg came up with the idea of four annual festivals on the equinox and solstice. The winter one is called Gwyl Alban Arthan.'

'And what happens on that day?'

'It depends. It could be poetry readings, some might incorporate holly or mistletoe into some kind of ritual. There's also likely to be fire in some way. The burning of the yule log, for example, they think is inherited from pagan times.'

Mallory swallowed. 'There could be a bonfire?'

'I was thinking more lanterns and candles but if you're planning to do something like that with your students, I have to tell you that Lowri won't give you permission for anything like that.'

'Sorry, I'm staying in my lane as far as teaching is concerned. I was just wondering what might happen here,' said Mallory, moving away.

'Term finishes at the end of the week so there'll be no students here except those whose travel plans have been delayed. The school shuts for Christmas.'

'Any idea where I could look up information about solstice celebrations?'

Jem shrugged. 'There are plenty of books in the library. I think your predecessor was also interested. I caught her reading a title called *Druidic Rites* and that must have had something about the solstice in it.'

'Caught her?' asked Mallory.

Jem flushed. 'I only use the term because she flipped it over when I approached. She clearly didn't want me to see what she was looking at but I recognised the title anyway. The book has a distinctive cover and is well known.'

Jem had lost interest again. There was a lack of curiosity in her response to Mallory's questioning. Either she had decided that life was easier at Penbryn Hall if you didn't ask too many questions or she had other concerns that were taking precedence over Mallory's questions.

'Thanks. I might take a look at the book myself.'

'It's not there. When Pippa died, I went to see what was in the book myself. I thought, well, that there might have been a ritualistic element to the suicide given she was found in woodland. I wanted to make sure the students weren't getting any ideas.'

'But the book has gone?'

'Exactly. It should be in stock, according to the system, but it's not there.'

A bell rang and Jem looked at her watch. 'I need to get going. Look after yourself, Mallory.'

It was an odd comment to end their conversation. 'I'll try,' she muttered to herself.

27

Bethan Rossi had hardly changed in the years since Harri had last interviewed her. Her brown hair was still streaked with golden highlights and she had the same wing-eyed eye make-up, her lips outlined with dark pink lip pencil. Harri's daughter Ellie had gone through a phase of lining her lips in this manner and he'd never taken to it. He preferred the more natural look but perhaps that was what all fathers said about their daughters. He'd spotted Bethan occasionally over the intervening years working in the family diner and she'd maintained an angry expression that never seemed to waver. Of course, she had plenty to be angry about after her spell with the Solstice Sisterhood and Harri very much hoped she'd had some kind of therapy to talk through the punishment dished out to her.

Rossi's was full when he walked in, a testament to its reasonable prices in a world where the high cost of living was affecting everyone. Bethan was waiting for him, hovering next to the counter and ignoring a customer who was trying to pay his bill. She recognised Harri and pointed to a table for two near the till with a reserved sign on it.

'I'm sorry I caught you on one of your working days. Given what we're about to discuss we can go elsewhere if that makes things easier for you.'

Bethan pulled out a chair and made a face. 'Go to another café? It'll be home from home. I spend all my time in this bloody place.'

'You're only in your late twenties,' said Harri. 'The hospitality industry is always looking for staff. You could just leave.'

This didn't go down well. Bethan picked up a menu and glanced over it. She must have known its contents off by heart. 'I'll have the puttanesca. You?'

'Same.'

The spicy tomato dish would be perfect for this weather although his diabetic nurse had warned him off eating too many carbs.

'You want to talk about the sisterhood,' she said after giving their orders. Her voice was flat but her gaze direct.

Harri nodded. 'I'm afraid so. I know it's a difficult subject but it's important. I need to revisit some of the content of your statement to us back in 2015 as I'm trying to track down everyone who lived in the house while you were there.'

'What for? I've been trying to put all this in the past. Why drag it up now?'

Harri had thought long and hard about the question. He decided partial honesty would be the best approach. 'Someone died who we think might have had a similar job to you in the sisterhood. We're investigating her death to check if her employment history might have had a bearing on her death.'

'Died how?'

Harri saw the girl had paled and tried to reassure her without resorting to outright lies. 'We don't know. It's possible she took her own life, which is incredibly sad, but we don't just stop with a presumption of suicide – we try to work out why.'

'You think she was a maid in the sisterhood like me?'

'Yes we do. Is that how the other members referred to you? As a maid?'

'God yes. I should have realised how utterly bonkers they were when they told me I had to wear a uniform. I mean, I didn't think anything of it at first as I have to wear a black shirt and trousers in this place. But they gave me something out of Dickens. A long skirt and blouse.'

'Did they say why you needed to wear a uniform?'

'It was all part of their ethos apparently. They all dressed in a similar manner, wearing long skirts and high-necked blouses. It was only me as the maid that had to wear black. As I said, I didn't think anything of it.'

'You travelled there every day by bus, I know, but occasionally you slept overnight. Why was that?'

'Twice there were late-night celebrations. Don't ask me what but I had to prepare a wild garlic dish and mushroom risotto using ingredients Branwen had foraged from the nearby forest. I didn't like cooking these ingredients as I was worried they'd picked poisonous stuff by mistake. Now I think it would have served them right if they died, the mad bitches.'

So Bethan had changed. In the intervening years she'd hardened her memories of her time there. 'The name of your predecessor was Philippa Evans but she was known as Pippa. Did you ever meet her or hear her name?'

'No. I don't know any Pippa. They wouldn't have mentioned her to me because no one ever spoke to me except to tell me what I was doing wrong. Was she young like me?'

'We think that when she worked for the sisterhood she was seventeen.'

'Jesus, that's the same age as me.' Bethan folded her arms. 'Do you think they chose us because we were so young?'

'I don't know. Possibly. Every group like the sisterhood, no matter how self-sufficient they are, needs people to help out.'

Bethan looked towards the counter and lowered her voice. 'Was she beaten like me?'

'I think it's almost certain that she was.'

Bethan turned her palms to his and Harri saw with shock that the welts were as vivid as the first day he'd seen them.

'Jesus.' For a moment he thought the girl was harming herself, reopening ancient wounds.

'Keloid scars.' Bethan had adopted the flat tone once more. 'I rub cream into them when I remember but they're impossible to get rid of. Did she have them too?'

'I don't think so. There was nothing in the post-mortem report to suggest beatings of any kind and yet she left suddenly, a little like yourself.'

Bethan made a face. 'You'd think with my Italian olive skin I'd be better blessed but no.'

'Maybe you were…' Harri faltered.

'Hit harder than your girl. Maybe. Angharad certainly raised that switch high.'

'I'm sorry. This must be bringing back bad memories for you.'

'Yes.' She sat back into her seat as the pasta arrived. 'But the weird thing is that hearing someone else was a victim makes me feel a bit better. Does that make me a bad person?'

Harri picked up his fork. 'No. I guess we all feel when we're being preyed upon that there's some weakness in our character that has made us a target for bullies. Often it's as simple as being in the wrong place.'

He stopped and saw two fat tears sitting on Bethan's cheeks. He looked around but no one was paying them any attention.

'Are you OK to carry on?'

'Of course.' Bethan picked up her fork. 'Why did you want to talk to me?'

'The thing is, we're trying to track down the whereabouts of the other members of the group. Pippa was working in a school and we believe she recognised someone.'

Bethan had stopped. 'Was it that teacher who died in Penbryn Hall?'

'You read about it?'

'Of course. Sometimes a group of students from the school comes in here when they go to the theatre. They try out their Italian on my dad, which is funny because he's from Sicily and claims they're impossible to understand. But I heard them talking and they sound great.'

'Was it your dad who suggested you drop the accusations against the sisters? I remember him being furious about the incident.'

'Maybe. I just wanted to forget about the whole thing too. I started working there as Kigva, one of the group, came in for a meal and saw me dishing up. Dad's never forgiven himself for suggesting I take the decent money they were offering.'

'Bethan.' Harri chose his words carefully. 'I'm going to put something to you and I want you to hear me out. In your statement, you talked about six members of the group. Angharad, Branwen, Ceridwen, Rhiannon, Luned and Kigva.'

'They were awful. I wish they were all dead.'

'Luned is dead. She died a few years ago from leukaemia.'

'Good.' Bethan picked up a forkful of pasta. 'What about the others?'

'We're trying to track them down. Ceridwen went to Australia but she's the only one I can definitely place. Have you seen any of the other four?'

'Rhiannon is here in Carmarthenshire. I've seen her from a distance. She's probably spotted me but we give each other a wide berth.'

'The cook? Interestingly she was one who claimed she never saw any evidence of punishment.'

Bethan shrugged. 'Turned a blind eye. The farmhouse was a decent size but you can't keep something like that secret. One thing I will say is when I showed her my hands she was totally shocked.'

'Were you whipped the once?'

'Once was enough, wasn't it?'

'Of course, and you did the right thing to run for help. I worry that Pippa, your predecessor, wasn't so brave.'

'You know,' said Bethan pushing her plate away, 'it eats away at you. I can understand why she might have been horrified if she saw someone from that time, especially Angharad.'

'She was the person in charge?'

Bethan hesitated. 'She claimed to be. She was certainly the person who hit me. I *thought* I saw her about a year ago on the beach of all places and my heart was in my mouth. I can imagine how Pippa felt.'

Harri's food was untouched as he was sure he was on the cusp of learning something important. 'The thing is, are you absolutely sure there wasn't another member of the sisterhood? Another member that you omitted to mention in your statement.'

Bethan's fork had frozen in the air and she stared at him in shock. Harri thought she was going to faint and he picked up a glass of water and walked around the table to her. 'Drink this.'

She took the beaker gratefully and downed it. 'Sorry.'

Harri went back to his seat. 'You've nothing to be sorry about. Tell me, was there someone who you didn't mention?'

'I told you about everyone. Angharad who loved hitting me with the cane, Branwen who spent all the time in the garden but slapped me with the back of her hand when I trod on her tomato plants. I thought it was just ill temper, not part of the group's regime.'

'So why did you react just now when I mentioned another possible member?'

'She comes to me in my dreams,' Bethan whispered. 'Someone who isn't one of the six. She stands at the bottom of my bed holding a cane which swishes up and down.'

'What does she look like?' asked Harri, leaning forward. 'Is she tall? Young or old?'

'I don't know. Tall maybe. Taller than me, I'd say. I don't see her face as she's wearing a hood. That's the worst of it. I can't see who scares me.'

'Do you have many nightmares?' Harri put a forkful of the rich pasta into his mouth to give the girl time to compose herself. It tasted heavenly. A pungent tomato sauce sliced through with anchovies and capers.

'A few,' said Bethan, her face bent over her food.

'So why do you think you dream about this figure? Do you think you've made it up?'

'No.' Bethan's head shot up. 'There was someone else, I'm sure of it. She didn't always live with the group but I only stayed overnight twice. She could have been there on other nights and I'd never have known.'

'I know this is hard but can you think why she might be in your mind? It's possible that other people did come and go in the sisterhood. Why is this person who you've never met creeping into your dreams?'

Bethan took a gulp of water. 'Because I think she told Angharad to whip me. Whatever was going on in the group, I wasn't included until the second time I stayed the night. There was something going on. A feast that I helped prepare but was sent to the room off the kitchen once it was ready.'

'You were punished the following morning. Did Angharad say what for?'

'The cake I made was burnt around the edges.'

'And was it?'

'Possibly. The thing was, when Angharad lifted the cane, I'm sure I saw a person behind her in a long cloak with a hood.'

'The figure in your nightmare.'

'Yes.'

'It could have been one of the other women.'

Bethan opened her palms again and regarded the scars. 'No. This was someone new.'

28

4 August 2015

Angharad knew the moment that Bethan had made the complaint that it was all over for the sisterhood. The family that Bethan had run to had never liked the presence of the group in the farmhouse. The village had one place of worship, a huge chapel that only a handful of elderly attendees frequented on a Sunday morning. But the chapel mentality lingered on in the village – tea and sandwiches at funerals, early closing at the pub on Sundays and the tending of the bleak graves on anniversaries. Angharad wasn't sure how the news had leaked out about their presence. Admittedly six women living together invited gossip but they'd deliberately recruited their maid from Carmarthen, a fair distance away, who came up each weekday morning on the bus.

They'd told her not to speak to anyone from the village, but it was clear now that she'd been stopping to talk to the young family in the end stone terrace at the curve in the road. When Angharad had administered the first punishment on Bethan, the blank book ready for its first entry, the girl had attacked first her and then Rhiannon. She had been left with a black eye and Rhiannon a ringing head. The girl had fled and Angharad knew it was useless going after her. It had been a question of sitting and waiting.

'What do we do now?' asked Kigva as she joined Angharad in the sitting room.

'We need to make plans. Some of our pictures will be in the paper and the news will already be around the village.'

Kigva folded her arms, her expression difficult to read. 'Someone has already thrown a brick through the greenhouse window. Probably one of the Jones boys.'

'It'll be the start. We can't stay here.'

'I was thinking,' said Kigva, 'that my time with the sisterhood is coming to an end.'

Angharad had expected this. Of all the sisters, it was Kigva who promoted the ethos with the most fervour but had remained essentially aloof from the others. Leaving would cause her no great hardship. As a trained PR professional, she'd find a job easily enough and the sisterhood would become a distant memory.

'Where will you go?'

Kigva shrugged. 'I have a friend in Newcastle. It's far enough away from here for me to start afresh. What about you?'

Angharad rose from her seat. 'I think I'll go and help Branwen pick up the broken glass. It's a thankless task.'

'What about you?' repeated Kigva. 'Will the sisterhood carry on despite this?'

'I doubt it,' said Angharad. 'But it's not really up to me.'

29

Mallory spent the weekend immersed in reading about solstice celebrations. As she descended deeper into the rabbit hole of alternative lifestyles, she began to wonder if she was on the wrong track. Surely if someone was baking acorn bread or fashioning themselves a real-life yule log, she'd find evidence of it somewhere? All around her in Penbryn Hall, staff and students were focused on what she considered traditional celebrations – a school concert, the sending of Christmas cards and a production of *The Snow Queen*. In the entrance hall, a huge pine tree from a nearby forest had been dressed with decorations made by every pupil. Mallory was touched by the homespun nature of the tree and her heart ached for Toby. On impulse, she retreated to her room and called him.

'How's it going, Tobe?'

Her son sighed theatrically down the line. 'Dad's being a complete pain. He wants advice on what to buy Josie for Christmas.'

Mallory made a sour face, grateful that she wasn't being observed. Josie was his father's new girlfriend and she'd tried to keep discussion of her to a minimum. 'What did you suggest?'

'Perfume.'

'Well, that's not a bad idea but it could be expensive. What about gloves?'

Toby considered this for a moment. 'What's Harri going to buy you for Christmas?'

Here we go again, thought Mallory. 'I've no idea. You'll be there, won't you, so you can see for yourself.'

'You going to tell me where you are?'

'Nope, but I'll pick you up on Christmas Eve in Carmarthen as promised. Don't, whatever you do, miss the train or you'll be spending Christmas with your dad and Josie.'

Toby made sick sounding noises down the phone. 'I'll be there an hour early.'

After the call finished, Mallory looked at her watch. Sunday afternoons were a dead time in the school and she was feeling restless. There was a carol concert in the chapel at five, which gave her a few hours of daylight before darkness fell. Despite the excitement of the impending holidays, she was stuck with the sense that something was about to happen. People were behaving oddly – Jonathan had gone from unfriendly to confidant, Lowri was having second thoughts about Mallory's presence in the school and Freya had something on her mind that even her wife didn't appear able to identify.

To get some fresh air, Mallory pulled on her coat and made her way outside, scouring the landscape for anything untoward. It was now only three days to midwinter.

'There's a storm coming.' Mallory started and wheeled round to see Emiah with an armful of dried twigs in her arms. 'I thought I'd collect these before they're scattered around the grounds.'

Odd, thought Mallory, that she was bringing attention to her actions. 'Making some decorations?' she asked.

'What?' Emiah looked down at the dead wood in her arms. 'No, I'm going to light the fire in the library. The temperature has dropped and some of the students are feeling the cold.'

'People are still studying on a Sunday afternoon?'

Emiah shrugged. 'This is Penbryn Hall. You've got to keep on top of things.' She eyed Mallory's coat. 'You going for a walk?'

'Just clearing my head. Tell me, those twigs look dry. Is there a log store somewhere?'

'The wood for the fires is kept in the shed behind the coach house but I've gathered this lot from the pile of dead leaves at the edge of woodland. It's underneath tarpaulin but it won't last in high winds. Why do you ask?'

'I might light a fire in my room.'

'Head over and get yourself some kindling then.' Emiah sounded almost cheerful and Mallory wondered if she'd misread the woman's attitude before or if this was another example of an about-change in attitude towards her.

'Can I ask you,' she said. 'Are you in touch with the old head, Dr Prytherch?'

Emiah froze and stared at Mallory. 'Dr Prytherch? Do you know her?'

'Not at all. I saw her name on the list of former heads on the library wall and I saw she'd only been here a year. I know you're one of the longest-serving members of staff so I wondered if you're in touch.'

'What do you want to know about her?' Emiah stepped forward and Mallory experienced the thrill of fear. They were out in the open, alone but visible to anyone passing by. In the distance there was a group of girls chatting and laughing. Emiah had her eyes on the girls too before returning her hostile gaze to Mallory.

'I believe she was American. I wondered if she returned there when she left.'

'How would I know?' snapped Emiah. 'I barely got to know her.'

She stalked off but not before retrieving her phone from her coat pocket and switching it on.

Mallory first checked the wood store near the coach house and found it open. Split chunks of wood were piled against three sides and there were instructions to take logs from the far left. There must have been a grounds person, and Mallory thought she ought to speak to them – when she discovered who they were – to see if more wood had been used than usual. The tarpaulin with the kindling was harder to find but gave Mallory the opportunity to continue scouring the grounds for any solstice activity. Strings of lights had been put up around the school grounds, one set running across the courtyard garden to the woodland where Pippa had been found. Mallory hadn't returned to the spot since her first day at the school and she wondered if flowers were still being left now that term was reaching its conclusion.

The grass was soggy due to the recent temperature rise although Mallory had seen a storm was forecast for the following week, which might be good news. There was nothing like a downpour of rain to dampen fire. The school noise got quieter as Mallory neared the edge of the trees and she was glad of the silence, missing the solitude of the caravan. In the distance, however, she could hear a gasping and it was in front, not behind her. Mallory slowed, her senses on high alert.

'Is anyone there?'

There was no reply. Mallory moved forward, picking up a large stick from the ground to use as a weapon if necessary. She remembered the attack on Livvy and the girl's lucky escape. Pippa too had been frightened of someone, and Mallory was under no illusions that she faced danger. However, for both their sakes, she had to keep going. She stepped forward, the gasping noise getting louder, and she wondered if it was a fox or badger trapped in undergrowth. Here goes, she thought and charged forward, the stick in the air. In front of her she saw Jem Owen kneeling over a figure on the ground.

Fuck. She rushed forward and pushed Jem out of the way. She'd expected it to be a student, given they were fascinated by the spot where Pippa had died, but she saw it was Freya lying on her back, her unseeing eyes open. Beyond help, Mallory thought, although she noticed the body was still warm. Glancing down at Freya's pale neck, she could see red weals where fingers had choked the life out of her. The fact it had been done with bare hands and not a rope or wire suggested a lack of planning on the killer's part. It also meant that the forensic team would have much more to work with. Bare hands on skin left DNA traces, although results could be painstakingly slow.

Mallory put her arms round the shoulders of the weeping Jem. The woman was shaking hard while hyper-ventilating, both signs of shock. She needed to be in the warmth but there was no one to take her and Mallory didn't want to leave Freya unattended even for a moment. If it had been dark, Mallory would have used her torch or other means of light to attract attention. As it was, the day was the worst kind, a grey murk surrounding the trees.

'Is anyone there?' Mallory shouted into the gloom. 'Can someone help me?'

Mallory cursed the fact she had left her phone in her room. It was a rookie mistake. There was a rustling sound and Mallory felt the finger of fear on her heart. She wasn't out of danger yet. There was a killer in Penbryn Hall, no doubt about it now, and there was only so much she would be able to do without the means to defend herself.

'Hello!' The rustling got louder and Mallory saw the security guard burst through the undergrowth.

'What's going on?' He stopped as he saw Freya's body lying on the ground. 'Oh my God, is she dead?' He looked as if he was about to faint.

'She is, I'm afraid. I need you to take Jem to Dr Rhys's office. If Eirin tries to stop you seeing her, tell her it's urgent. There, Lowri needs to ring the police, an ambulance and DI Harri Evans in that order. Do you have all that?'

The man nodded. 'I can get to my hut quicker.'

'I know but Jem is suffering from shock and needs medical attention and warmth. You need to take her out of the cold now as a matter of urgency. The school also needs to activate lockdown procedures. Dr Rhys and Eirin will know what to do.'

The man finally understood Mallory's instructions and led Jem away, her body still wracked with convulsions. Mallory was in a dilemma. She knew she should not go back to Freya's body while she awaited the forensic team and yet her eyes were drawn to the figure lying prone on the ground. She'd been at pains to pull Jem away without disturbing the scene but the soil was claggy and their footprints would be clear where their feet had sunk into the loam.

Mallory sat on the stump of a recently felled tree, the exposed wood like a wound, and contemplated Freya. She tried to think why it had been so important to kill the politics and psychology teacher. Although she'd been nervy and shown signs of sleep deprivation, Mallory had put it down to her concern over Livvy's attack. She'd

166

shown a lack of interest in Pippa's death and, if anything, it had been Jem who was the more curious, but no one could mistake Freya for her wife. The killer had been intending to kill Freya, who might have had knowledge of the Solstice Sisterhood.

Mallory could hear voices in the distance and there was no mistaking their urgency. It was her last chance before help arrived and she seized the moment. She retraced her steps as best she could, placing the soles of her feet in the imprints she'd already left, and bent over Freya, turning over one palm and then another. Her skin was unblemished. Shit, she'd got it terribly wrong and needed to get the hell away from the scene before forensics gave her hell. Then, on impulse, she parted the two lapels of Freya's coat and pulled down the collar of the lightweight jumper. A series of burn scars criss-crossed her pale chest, teardrop in shape. Mallory sat back on her heels and swallowed the flash of fury that had swept over her. It wouldn't help Freya, who she was now sure was another victim of the sisterhood.

–

Help arrived as Mallory made her way back to the branch she'd been sitting on. Lowri came first, took one look at Freya and said the school was in lockdown and all students would remain in their respective houses. Her face was haggard and grey with exhaustion and for the first time Mallory felt the tug of compassion for the woman.

'I'll stay here so please don't worry about me. I'll step away from the scene when the forensic team arrives.'

Lowri's expression was cold as she regarded Mallory. 'I'm trying to convince myself that this would still have happened if I hadn't brought you into the school.'

Unlikely, thought Mallory, but perhaps it was time for some hard truths. 'Maybe not now, but another time. There's something rotten going on here.'

Lowri turned her back on Mallory and left through the woodland, leaving Mallory once again in the silence. The police team were there in twenty minutes, followed by Harri half an hour later.

'I've been trying to call you to find out what the bloody hell was going on. When I heard about a death I thought it was you.' His voice cracked, leaving Mallory aghast.

'My phone's in my room and I needed to stay here to look after the body. You know the procedure Harri.'

He nodded, turning his face away but not before she saw the glint of tears in his eyes. Bloody hell, that was a first, a man crying over her. Her ex had departed from their marriage without a backward glance, and it was she who had done all the weeping. Not for the first time, Mallory wondered if her professional life had hardened her or whether it was just her character. Harri must have had his fair share of knocks, especially when his wife died, but he was emotionally open. She sighed and resisted the temptation to give him a hug.

'I need to tell you something,' she said. 'It's important.'

Harri listened as she told him about the burns on Freya's chest, only giving her a look of despair when she described returning to the body while she was waiting for help to arrive.

'Have you told forensics this?'

'I did and no one is happy with me.'

Harri sighed. 'You know what you were meant to do but I can understand protocol goes out of the window in a case like this. So now we know what the teardrops stand for in the diary. Burn marks.'

'Exactly but there's no mention of them in Pippa's autopsy report. So now I'm wondering if the book we found actually—'

'Belonged to Freya.'

'Yes exactly. And that might give us a motive for why she was killed. If she was happy to lead us to the record of her punishments, perhaps there was a possibility she'd eventually tell us who is administering them. She was showing signs of strain, which I stupidly attributed to upset over Livvy's attack.'

'Did the marks on Freya's chest look fresh?'

'They didn't look like they were ten years old.'

'Fuck,' said Harri. 'Which means we have to face the possibility that there's not only a member of the Solstice Sisterhood in the school but that it's active again too. I hope to God it's only staff involved and not pupils.'

Mallory nodded. 'This is too big for me to remain incognito and for our knowledge of the sisterhood to be kept hidden. Every student needs a welfare check, and once we've talked to them, we then question the staff.'

Harri reached out his arm and pulled Mallory to him. 'I'm so relieved you're safe. When this mess is over, we're going away on holiday and this time the kids can bugger off.'

30

Harri wanted Mallory to join the team interviewing students. She'd have personally preferred to be speaking to staff as she was sure the death of Freya Wells had nothing to do with the girls studying at the school. The thought of these well-educated, polished girls strangling one of their teachers was preposterous. Mallory was also reluctant to interview the students because she wasn't brilliant at speaking to teenagers about their problems, probably because of her fractious relationship with her son. Lowri came to Mallory's rescue by suggesting to Harri that, rather than traumatise or possibly excite each student, there should be a general assembly where anyone with information would be invited to speak to female members of the police team. Harri, to his credit, agreed.

The assembly took place not in the usual hall, but the Cranogwen room, where Mallory had received the cryptic message that had led her to the punishment book. While waiting for the meeting, she'd been doing some thinking. There were teardrops in the blue book she'd found under the rose. It suggested that it belonged to Freya, who had buried it in order to lead Mallory to its hiding place. But why not just leave the book in her room? She must have thought it too dangerous, which suggested that Mallory was up against someone who had access to every part of the school. The strangling was an act of desperation, which meant they were getting closer to revealing the woman's identity.

Mallory stood to one side next to Emiah, watching as the girls filed in. She saw that some of the students were crying but most were composed under Lowri's steady gaze. Their head teacher was a woman who encouraged resilience and control. She lifted her hand and the noise dampened.

'I'm sure you've all heard the news that one of our teachers, Ms Wells, died this afternoon. I'm sorry we've had to cancel the carol concert but, under the circumstances, we're now in the hands of the investigation team. I'd like you all to refrain from indulging in idle speculation. Any death that is unexpected involves the police and all I can tell you for the moment is Ms Wells died suddenly.'

Would the students buy that, wondered Mallory. She very much doubted it.

'The police naturally want to speak to anyone who might have information about Ms Wells's state of mind. If anyone has any information or is worried about anything, please let your house mentor or tutor know and we will arrange an interview.'

Mallory looked at the students' reactions. Most looked relieved that they wouldn't be interviewed as a matter of course but Mallory also noticed that a few eyes strayed towards her. It was clear the news was out about her real identity but, given the circumstances, there had been no real way of disguising it. She caught the gaze of Molly Jessop, whose lips lifted in a conspiratorial smile. Mallory had the feeling she had suddenly become significantly more interesting. Mallory turned her attention to the staff that had accompanied the students. Jem, naturally, was absent and under the supervision of the local GP who served the school. The ten or so staff who were with the students Mallory only knew by sight, although she was intrigued to see Emiah standing at the back of the hall with her arms folded. Emiah, as far as Mallory knew, didn't have pastoral responsibility for any of the students so her presence at the briefing was a mystery. Mallory wondered if it was more than natural curiosity. Lowri certainly appeared unperturbed by her presence as she continued her address to her pupils.

'I've also decided,' she said, 'to shut the school a week early. An email has gone to all parents and guardians informing them of my decision.' Mallory hadn't expected this but it was a clever move. The removal of vulnerable teenagers would help focus on the hunt for the killer among the staff. The students reacted to the early closure with undisguised glee and Mallory wondered if their parents would be as cheerful. While the girls were at an age where they could look after themselves, Mallory suspected some Christmas plans were about to be severely disrupted.

As she pushed her way through the students streaming out of the Cranogwen room, Mallory bumped into Eirin, Lowri's secretary. Eirin reached out to steady Mallory, her expression concerned.

'Are you all right?'

Mallory frowned and made to move away. 'I'm fine.' It was an odd question. Eirin surely also now knew Mallory's identity and that she was used to unnatural death.

'You're looking very thin, you know.'

Mallory stopped. She was used to questioning her son's eating habits but knew she'd been neglecting her own need for sustenance.

'I'm fine. It's just that dramas seem to unfold around mealtimes and I've been skipping food.'

'Come with me.' She took Mallory away from the throng towards the back staircase and they went up to the first floor. Out of the staircase window, Mallory could see Siân talking to the security guard who had answered Mallory's call for help. Siân was probably taking his statement, routine policing which needed to be undertaken even if the answer to this killing lay within this building. Eirin's room was about Mallory's size but expressed the secretary's individuality with original artwork and a Turkish rug on the floor.

'Sit yourself down while I prepare tea.'

The cake was from a tin, not something Mallory would have associated with fine food, but one look at the label assured her it was out of her budget. She let Eirin fuss over her, feeling directionless after watching Siân and wondering how she could help the investigation while still within the school. She was in a dilemma because if she asked to leave her post, chances were there wasn't a role available to her within the team so it would be the end of her brush with the Solstice Sisterhood. No, she had to remain in situ until Christmas and focus her attentions on the staff left on site. She let out a sigh. The combination of the sweet currant slice and strong tea was reviving and Mallory felt her spirits lift.

'Thanks for this. I forget to eat sometimes and fear I've passed my indifference to food to my son Toby.'

She told Eirin briefly about Toby's struggles with bulimia and her guilt that Toby preferred to live with his father.

Eirin listened, slowly sipping her tea. She was about Mallory's height but stronger looking. Staff were allowed to use the gym equipment out of school hours and Eirin gave the impression she took advantage of this. It must be a relief after a day sitting at your desk. Her auburn hair was her crowning glory, its amber tresses enhanced by the fireside light. 'As you can imagine, we have plenty of experience with eating disorders here. There's an excellent onsite counsellor, and we've found therapy does help.'

Mallory took another bite of her cake. As much as she was grateful to Eirin for feeding her, she was clearly naive. Not everyone had access to free counselling; it had taken a lot of effort to get Toby registered with an NHS therapist and this support would stop abruptly when he turned eighteen.

'We do our best.' Mallory put down her plate. 'Eirin, you're close to Lowri. I'm not asking you to betray any confidences but what do you think is going on here?'

Eirin gathered her long hair and secured it with a scrunchie she retrieved from a pocket. 'I don't know, to be honest. I know it's something to do with the Solstice Sisterhood. Lowri updated me about your real identity after the attack on Livvy, although I'd had my suspicions about you. Without wishing to be rude, your qualifications weren't really comparable with the rest of the staff.'

'You didn't mention it to anyone, did you?' asked Mallory. 'Freya, for example. I got the impression she was keeping her distance from me.'

'Of course not. After Livvy's attack, though, I mentioned that I was unsure why you'd been selected and Lowri told me about the decision to install you in the school.'

'You thought I might be responsible for the attack on Livvy?' It was a fair enough assumption, but Mallory couldn't help but feel hard done by.

'You don't fit in here, but given the reason you're actually here, it's probably a good thing.'

Mallory banged her plate down on the table in frustration. 'I can't help feeling I've done more bad than good. A teacher has died on my watch and I have no idea what's going on. I'm not exactly doing a brilliant job. Tell me what you thought when Lowri mentioned the sisterhood. Were you aware of the group?'

'I only know what I read in the paper at the time they were accused of chastising the girl.'

'You saw the story? I got the impression there was a brief flare of publicity which died down quickly.'

Eirin waved her hand at her iPad. 'The internet is full of it and, to be honest, I'm a bit of a news junkie. People are always surprised because I work in a girls' school, but that doesn't mean I'm not interested in what's happening in the world around me.'

'So you were surprised to see Angharad Prytherch's name there?'

'Surprised?' Eirin laughed. 'I was astounded. I worked for Angharad – or Arabella, as she was known then – before Lowri and I never noticed a thing.'

So Eirin had also been here during Angharad's tenure. That was interesting. 'And did you notice anything unusual about her while she was here?'

'Everything was unusual, to be honest. She was American and a breath of fresh air, but I suspected she wouldn't stay long. Things are done here in a particular way, which is both a strength and a weakness.'

'But what about her interest in alternative religions? It almost certainly started here.'

Eirin frowned. 'The papers said that the Solstice Sisterhood started in Cardiff after she left as head. There was no connection to the school at the time.'

'So I believe, but Angharad must have been forming the ethos of the new order in her mind all the time she was employed here. That's quite a scary thought.' Mallory kept her tone casual. 'You don't think she tried to recruit anyone to the sisterhood while she was here, do you?'

Eirin snorted. 'If she tried, she failed. There was no one I recognised from the school in the article I read.'

'They used pseudonyms from the Mabinogion. I don't think there was a photo of everyone in the news articles.'

'Even so, I've not heard of anyone joining the Solstice Sisterhood.'

Mallory noticed Eirin was on the defence, but that was understandable given everything that had happened. Nevertheless, the arrogance of someone saying that a teacher at Penbryn Hall hadn't been recruited into the order was dangerous given they hadn't yet tracked down the members arrested in 2015. Mallory also couldn't tell whether Lowri had told her secretary about the discovery of the punishment book. They'd kept the existence of the book on a need-to-know basis, and on balance, Mallory thought Eirin was in the dark about it.

'Was Dr Prytherch especially close to anyone while she was here? Were you two close, for example?'

'Us? I'm very good at my job, and do you know the secret to being a good personal assistant? Don't get too close to the boss. I'm friendly with Lowri and it was the same with Angharad. I probably know more about the school after the head than anyone else. Even Jonathan, the deputy, doesn't know as much as me. But I'm discreet and loyal, which my bosses have always appreciated.'

'How did you end up here?' Mallory stopped. 'Sorry, maybe "end up" isn't quite the phrase I meant.'

Eirin smiled. 'Lowri recruited me. I was working as PA to Sir Ben Joseph, who sent both of his daughters to Penbryn Hall. He was quite an absent parent, and I spoke to Lowri a few times when she was deputy head. When the previous secretary left, she offered me the job. The money was London wages, but with accommodation and no opportunity to spend my earnings. My plan, once my nest egg is substantial, is to retire and write poetry. Or learn to, at least.' She saw Mallory's expression. 'I have my dreams too.'

'Of course. I wasn't trying to disparage your plans. I just—'

'Think of me as a PA. Well Philip Larkin was a librarian. We all earn a living somehow. Why did you, for example, become a detective?'

'I was sporty as a teenager and the police seemed a good option. I joined CID because I wanted to do something different from my husband at the time, who was also a cop.'

'I see. And now you've *ended up* in a girls' school.'

Mallory laughed. 'I think I'll be out by the end of the week. Now classes are finishing, I'm not needed, and besides, everyone knows who I am.'

'It'll be much appreciated if you could find the killer as soon as possible. It would be good to get some normality back.'

Mallory let out a long sigh. 'So you've heard about the marks on Freya's neck? You don't have any insights into that, do you?'

Eirin hesitated.

'Do you?'

'The thing is, something *was* up with Freya. She tried to make an appointment to speak to Lowri, but I was asked to schedule it for a few days' time.'

'Asked by Lowri?'

'Yes, but only because she was busy. She's really perturbed about this whole Solstice Sisterhood thing and the potential reputation damage it might cause for her school, so she was looking back over personnel records to see if she could spot something.'

So Lowri had shared Harri's concerns about a potential present-day connection to the school. What Lowri hadn't done, however, was share that Freya had wanted to see her. It could be down to guilt, or something more sinister.

—

Mallory left Eirin's room revived and went looking for Harri, who had his coat on, ready to leave. He was briefing Siân, who turned her back on Mallory as she approached. Mallory waited for them to finish before approaching Harri.

'You're not staying?'

'I've been called back to speak to Steph, and I've got a lot of explaining to do. However, there's something you need to know. After interviewing Jem, it's clear that the punishment book you found isn't a historic one.'

'It belonged to Freya.'

Harri gave a grim smile. 'You've got there before me, then. According to Jem, Freya kept it in her bag next to her purse and was very secretive about it. Jem thought it was a diary or something and was happy to let Freya have her secrets, but one day she took a peek and saw the markings.'

'Has she seen the actual book we discovered? I mean there might be more than one circulating in the school if we have a member of the sisterhood operating here.'

'I've shown her photos. Of course, she can't remember exactly the order of circles, triangles and teardrops. All I can say is she recognised the book. It'll have to do as identification for the moment.' Harri looked over at Siân, who was talking to two uniformed officers.

'If it's Freya's punishment book, she'll have corresponding marks all over her body,' said Mallory.

'Can't answer that until we get the results of the PM, but given you saw the teardrop marks yourself I think we proceed on the basis that the punishment book was hers.'

'And she left the clue in the Cranogwen room?'

'I have absolutely no idea. We've got to start piecing things together. My priority is to interview the former members of the sisterhood. One of them must know the identity of the missing member.'

'Could I accompany you?'

Harri shook his head. 'No chance. Your presence here isn't coming out of CID budget, I've discovered, but is being funded by Penbryn Hall.'

'Christ. How does that work?'

'I don't know, and fortunately that's Steph's issue. But if you leave here, that's the end of your involvement in the investigation, I'm afraid.'

It was as Mallory had thought. 'But we proceed on the basis that there's been a resurrection of the sisterhood within Penbryn Hall.'

'We do, which is exactly what I'm about to tell the super.' Harri drew the lapels of his mac tight against his neck. 'Wish me luck.'

'Harri.' Mallory grabbed hold of his arm. 'If you track down the members, any of them, ask them what happens on solstice night. I need to know what's coming.'

31

Harri's head was pounding as he left Superintendent Steph Morris's office. The meetings last night and this morning hadn't gone well, and he had her words ringing in his ears as he scrabbled around in his jacket pocket for the blister pack of paracetamol he kept there. What a complete fucking mess. He blamed himself as much as his boss.

All right, Steph was an ex-pupil of Penbryn Hall, so was bound to have wanted to help out her alma mater, but he could have been the voice of reason. He could have called in the evidence being gathered into Pippa's death and examined it along with a team member or two in the sterile environment of the police station. Instead, he'd dragged Mallory into a God-awful mess and left her to deal with the fallout. Well, there would be plenty of resources poured into the investigation into the murder of Freya Wells and he would personally make it his mission to ensure that he finally rooted out that bloody missing member of the group who he was sure Pippa had recognised.

The attack on Livvy should have told him that he was dealing with someone increasingly unstable. At that point he should have realised that they were concerned with a live case, not one left in the past in 2015. Whoever had attacked Livvy must have been terrified that she'd be recognised when she was looking under the rose for what else it might contain. If it was Freya who'd buried the hateful book, then she too must have feared what Livvy's attacker might say or do to her. The question was, who?

Harri sat heavily behind his desk. The conversation with Bethan had been useful, and she'd confirmed his hunch – the possibility of the presence of a shadow sister who remained in the background but was in charge of the group. The dynamics of this were still unclear. Surely, if you were going to create a quasi-religious sect based on characters of the Mabinogion, you'd want to be in situ, not popping in and out. Groups like this were based on control and compliance, which was difficult to oversee when you were often elsewhere. One possibility was money – the group was being financed by a wealthy or high-prominence figure. That might account for the subterfuge, but there were likely to be other factors. Harri remembered what Bethan had said about Angharad being the main disciplinarian, and perhaps this was the missing sister's clever way with the group. Everything done through someone else.

If he was honest with himself, one of the reasons the group of women had stayed in his mind was their appropriation of names from the Mabinogion. He didn't like them fashioning Welsh myth for their own use, but it was interesting that some of the members were Welsh, and Rhiannon had been fortunate enough to have been christened with a name from the saga. He wondered what the missing woman's name was in the sisterhood. There were other names from the Mabinogion not yet used – Arianrhod or Blodeuwedd, for example – but which one? A thought struck Harri. If the missing sister had already been working at Penbryn Hall, she wouldn't have been able to get away during the daytime but might have been able to go to the farmhouse for overnight stays.

Harri called Siân into his office.

'Any updates?' he asked.

Siân sat down opposite him looking annoyed. She probably wanted to be at the school, at the heart of the investigation, but until the forensics team had finished, there was little they could do there. It probably didn't help that Mallory was in situ, although she'd been warned not to interfere with the evidence gathering.

'As requested, I've been looking at the financials of the group to see if that will give us an insight into how the sisterhood operated. There was no register at Companies House, and all payments, as far as I can see, went through the administrator, Angharad Prytherch, so the evidence I've managed to gather is slight. We're talking over ten years ago, so I've just managed to find invoices with Angharad's signature on them. There's no evidence of how the money came into the group.'

'Did Angharad come from a wealthy background?'

'I'd say so, even by US standards, which suggests there's no reason to think anyone other than her was bankrolling the group.'

Harri saw that Siân wasn't convinced about his missing sister theory. Fair enough. 'OK – so tell me where we've got to in relation to the four sisters we need to track down.'

'I double-checked all six. You're right – Sister Luned died in 2018 and the woman who called herself Sister Ceridwen is definitely in Australia. I called and spoke to her this morning. I thought I'd receive some resistance, but she was proud of her time in the sisterhood and wanted to talk about it.'

'She hasn't left the country recently?'

'Not since a trip to California last year. I checked with immigration and they verified that. She still has a British passport.'

'Did you ask if she was in touch with other members of the group?'

'I did and she said she wasn't in contact with any of them. I read off the names of the members and she confirmed all had been there during her sojourn.'

'And—'

'And I asked her outright if there was anyone else I should know about and she said "no", but she didn't like the question.'

'Did you push it?'

'As much as I could, considering she lives thousands of miles away and hasn't committed any crime. She wouldn't be drawn any further. One thing, though, she was pretty open about how punishment was used by the group. Her argument was that many religious orders use discipline as a means of getting closer to God – deprivation, obedience, manual labour, fasting.'

Harri frowned. 'They didn't do any of that in my local chapel.'

Siân laughed. 'Nor at mine, thank God, or I'd have stopped going sooner than I did. She likened the discipline to those of flagellants who whipped themselves as proof of their devotion to God.'

'Yeah right. Whipping themselves, I don't have a problem with. It's dishing it out to others that's the issue. Anything else from Ceridwen?'

'Nothing. Which brings me onto the other four. Angharad, real name Arabella Prytherch, should be the easiest to track down given she held a position of responsibility, but she's proving the hardest to find. She's completely gone off radar. However, this is probably easier to do with a US passport. I don't have access to tax records, for example. However, I can start making inquiries with the consulate, but it'll take time.'

'And Christmas is coming up.' Harri threw his pen on the desk. 'What about the other three?'

'Carmel Byrne, known as Kigva, is in Newcastle, still working in PR. I've spoken to Tyneside colleagues only to make them aware of our interest, but I haven't asked them to contact her. The two others are closer to home. Branwen is in Caerphilly and Rhiannon in Llandeilo.'

'That's good and bad news, isn't it? If we've got addresses for the women, it suggests that they aren't in Penbryn Hall causing mischief. They'll need to be checked, though, and I think I'll do the interviews. Newcastle is a bloody long way to go but I might manage a trip to the other two. You stay here and continue to look for Angharad. Push the embassy.'

'I've tried that, boss.'

'Then ring Lowri and ask her for the names of students at the school from high profile US families. Let's use the influence of Penbryn Hall for our own ends. If necessary, try to schedule a call between the ambassador and the Chief Constable.'

'Me?' asked Siân.

'All right, I'll send a message to Steph. It might just stir up things lower down the hierarchy. Shit, I wish we'd done this earlier.'

'No one had been killed before yesterday, though, had they? Why this emphasis on Angharad? It won't be her at the school, will it? I think the staff would recognise their old head teacher.'

'I'm looking for the missing solstice member.' Harri swallowed his irritation. Siân was treating his theory as idiotic, but what else did they have? He was following a trail from Pippa's recognition of someone at the school to the attack on Livvy and Freya. He decided to have it out with her.

'You think I'm on the wrong track?'

'It's just…'

'What?'

'I just think Mallory being in the school might be muddying waters. I mean, you should be here leading the team. Let me and another team member interview the women and see what they say. We also should withdraw Mallory from the school now that her cover has been blown.'

Harri felt his blood pressure rise again. He knew Siân and Mallory hadn't hit it off, but it was far above Siân's pay grade to discuss the hiring of civilian investigators.

'Definitely not. She's got more of an insight there than we have, and I want to speak to the women because I was present at the previous interviews. I'm going to put to bed my missing sister theory once and for all. Any other complaints about my management style?'

Siân reddened. 'No, sorry.'

After Siân had left, Harri opened his window to let in a freezing blast of air. It made his headache subside a little. He opened his desk calendar and saw he had two meetings that afternoon, both of which he could probably send a deputy to. He might as well strike while the iron was hot.

—

Caerphilly had gentrified itself since Harri had last been there. He associated the town with its castle and arcs of suburban bungalows that spread from the north side of town. The woman he had known as Branwen was living in a 1970s detached house in Narberth Court. The front garden consisted of a strip of concrete which served as a driveway, a ring of grass that needed a mow and flower-beds where weeds threatened to take over the established plants. Branwen had been the cottage gardener at the farmhouse, yet here it looked like the place was going to seed.

Harri had revisited the woman's statement before the interview and two things had struck him immediately. Of all the women, she was the person he'd least expected to find in the sisterhood. She had been in her early forties with sandy bobbed hair neatly parted in the middle. Perhaps it was the earth under her fingernails or her sunburnt skin, but she'd given off an air of solidity and reassurance. He'd asked her how she'd come to join the group, and she'd replied that she'd answered an advert in the *Western Mail* for a gardener. She'd been surprised when she arrived at the small terrace in Roath because she'd stressed her background in growing edible plants, but had been told by Angharad that the sisters had wanted to learn that type of horticulture as they were planning a move to a farmhouse in Ceredigion. In the event, she'd moved with them, but had been unwilling to elaborate the reasons for this.

Harri's other memory of this woman was her absolute denial that any punishment went on in the group what-soever, despite the fact that Angharad told them in the preceding interview that discipline was at the heart of the ethos. He wondered if her story would change after the passage of time. He rang the doorbell and saw why the garden looked so unkempt. The woman who answered the doorbell was on crutches, one leg encased in plaster.

Harri showed his badge and was let in. His colleagues in South Wales Police had helpfully telephoned ahead of his arrival, and Branwen looked resigned to her fate. She took him into a sunroom at the back of the house where the small garden sloped towards a tall fence. Here it looked less unkempt, but still overgrown, the autumn business of tidying for winter having been neglected.

'Is your accident recent?' Harri asked, settling himself into a wicker chair that he hoped to God would take his weight.

'Two years ago, I broke my leg, but the fall also damaged the cartilage in my knee. That got infected, so it's been one operation after another trying to fix things. I now have a replacement knee, but it's taking time to heal.'

'I'm sorry about that. I'm not sure if you know the reason why I'm here.'

'No idea whatsoever. The officer who called me wouldn't say, but if I was to guess, I would assume it was to do with my time in the Solstice Sisterhood. It's the only remotely interesting thing that has ever happened to me. Would you like some tea?'

Harri shook his head. 'It *is* about the sisterhood. I've been revisiting your statement from 2015, and the reason for my interest is that a woman who once worked as a helper has recently died.'

'A helper? Not one of the sisterhood.'

'No, although I believe Luned has died.'

Branwen sighed. 'Would you like something stronger than tea? I know it's the afternoon so I could offer you brandy.'

Harri raised his eyebrows. 'No thank you, but have one yourself if you want.'

'I don't think I will, but whenever you mention the sisterhood, I feel the need for alcohol.'

'I'm surprised to hear that. When I first interviewed you, I was struck by how capable you were.'

Branwen grimaced. 'Capable yes, but that place was enough to send you insane. I was more than ready to leave when we broke up after Bethan Rossi's complaint. What happened to her?'

'Beth… It's not Bethan Rossi who's died. It's a woman who had a similar role when the sisterhood was in Cardiff. Her name was Pippa Evans.'

'Pippa?' Branwen swallowed. 'But she was as bright as a button, as I remember. What happened to her?'

'She was bright. She went to university and qualified as a maths teacher. She ended up in a school called Penbryn Hall.'

'Penbryn? But that's where Angharad was head teacher for a while.'

'Exactly. Have you visited Penbryn Hall recently?'

'I've never been near the place. The only person with a connection to the school is Angharad. Why don't you ask her?'

'We're trying to track Angharad down. Have you been in contact with her or any of the others?'

'Not for a long time. When I left, I came back to Caerphilly and used some inheritance as a deposit on this place. I resurrected my gardening business, until I broke my leg and since then I've been living off my savings. I've even sold my van, so I doubt I'll ever get back to it.'

'Who did you last speak to?' asked Harri.

'It would have been Angharad as she's the only person to keep in touch with me. It was Christmas cards, which stopped about four years ago, and I assumed she'd probably moved back to the States. Except...'

'Except?'

Branwen shook her head as if escaping a bad memory. 'Except I saw her in Swansea when I was visiting a friend there. It was last summer and she was coming out of Waterstones with a bag full of books. She always loved reading.'

'Did she see you?'

'No. She was looking at her phone and I ducked into a shop as soon as I saw her. There's nothing we have to say to each other, but I couldn't help looking through the window at her. She'd changed. She looked, I dunno, affluent.'

'What gave you that impression? Her clothes?'

'That partly, but also the gold phone she was holding and all the shopping bags she had with her. She was doing well, and I wondered where she was living.'

The sighting was likely to be accurate, especially as Bethan had also spotted Angharad on a nearby beach. 'If I recall,' said Harri, 'the sisterhood was about self-sufficiency and meeting basic needs only. Angharad as your leader preached that.'

There was a pause as Branwen shook her head. 'Angharad was our administrator but never our leader.'

'So who was that? Kigva?'

Branwen gave a bark of laughter. 'Kigva was good at PR, but can you imagine anyone following her rules? She was too much of an individualist. We didn't have a leader.'

'But who came up with your ethos? The idea was that punishment was a cleansing process.'

Branwen shook her head. 'I don't know anything about that.'

'Come on. During the interviews with the six of you, three admitted that there was a system of punishments in place while the rest said you knew nothing of it. I've seen the size of that house and it was impossible to hide anything.'

'I didn't live with the sisterhood until they moved to West Wales. I can't help you in relation to what went on in the Cardiff house.'

'You knew Pippa, though.'

'Only in a casual way. She'd bring me a cup of tea in the garden, which was more than the others did.'

'So why move with them to Ceredigion?'

Branwen fiddled with the button on her cardigan. 'It's a little embarrassing but if you must know, I fell for someone in the sisterhood. Rhiannon was the cook, and once I knew they were moving, I felt I needed to go with them.'

'Did Rhiannon know about your feelings towards her?'

'I never said anything. Kigva missed nothing, so I suspect she knew.'

'Rhiannon also denied knowing anything about the punishment.'

'There you are then.'

'Did you dish it out?'

'I did not.' Branwen stood in outrage, her leg wobbling as she tried to put pressure on the plaster.

'Then you and Rhiannon must have been victims. I don't buy the notion that you were outside the central ethos of the group.' Harri saw that she was shaking. 'I know this must be an embarrassment for you but it's important. Do you still have your punishment book?'

Branwen hobbled towards a tray of bottles and poured herself a glass of spirit. She knocked it back and used the table to guide her to a sideboard where she pulled open a drawer and retrieved a slim blue book, identical to the one found at Penbryn Hall. 'Here, take it. It's a hateful thing.'

Harri opened it. Unlike the one from the school there was just one symbol next to dates. A circle.

'What punishment is a circle?' he asked.

'I was slapped across the face on four occasions by Angharad. I think she enjoyed it. None of this cleansing nonsense. She liked hitting people and the Solstice Sisterhood gave her a legitimate means to enact her desires.'

Harri wiped a hand across his face. 'Why? Why put up with it?'

'The first time was shocking, then I don't know, they seemed to be isolated incidents. It was the book that bothered me more. It was like someone was enjoying codifying my embarrassment.'

'Is that why you lied?' asked Harri. 'Embarrassment.'

'I suppose so.'

'So you always knew that Bethan Rossi's story was likely to be true.'

Branwen nodded mutely and grabbed a walking stick, struggling back towards Harri.

'Who named you Branwen?'

'It's from the Mabinogion. Branwen married the king of Ireland.'

'I know that,' said Harri. 'But who gave you the name?'

'Angharad, when I joined the sisterhood.'

'No one else?'

'What do you mean?' Branwen had begun to fidget and had turned her face away from him.

'The thing is,' said Harri. 'I'm going to visit everyone I can from 2015, but I'm not getting any answers. Pippa died at Penbryn Hall, but there's also been another death. That of a teacher named Freya Wells.'

'I've never heard of her.'

'That's of no consequence. There's a chain of events which has taken place. When Pippa arrived at the school, she saw someone she recognised and I don't think it will be any of you six. So who did she see?'

'I don't know.' Branwen's voice was a whisper.

Harri lowered his voice to match hers. 'She met your leader.'

'No.'

'Yes she did. I need you to tell me who it is.'

'I can't help you. Please don't ask me this.'

'People are dying, for Christ's sake. Who is it?'

'I don't know,' shouted Branwen. 'I never met her. She'd come at night. When I first joined the sisters in Roath, I used to come back to Caerphilly, as I've told you. There wasn't enough room for me in the house.'

'So how do you know there was another person?'

'Because when Angharad hit me, she said it had been ordered by our founder. But I don't know who that was, I promise.'

Harri scrutinised the woman and recognised that she was telling the truth. 'All right, I have one final question. You were with the sisterhood for over a year. How did you celebrate the winter solstice?'

'Rhiannon cooked things from the garden. It was a lovely time of us working together. Then we lit the fire in the farmhouse and put a decorated yule log on it.'

'There wasn't anything else more sinister? No punishment rituals or grand displays?'

'Of course not. Why do you ask?'

'Because I want to know what to expect on the twenty-first.'

32

Mallory couldn't work out whether lessons were cancelled or if she was supposed to wait in the classroom to see who turned up. Lockdown had been lifted, but neither Jonathan nor Lowri had given her any update on her duties until the last of the students had left. Looking for someone to chat to, Mallory entered the staff room and, finding it empty, assumed that her colleagues were either teaching or being interviewed by police. As she was leaving, she bumped into Rose.

'Thank Christ I've found you. What the hell is going on, Mallory? I heard you're part of the police team.'

'I thought you'd already worked it out.'

'I knew you weren't a regular teacher, but I thought you might be private security or something. I didn't realise you were an actual officer.' Rose's eyes glittered with tears. 'It's appalling, everything that happened.'

'I'm a civilian investigator. Lowri called in the old girls' network after Pippa died and I came here to see if I could spot anything wrong. Have you been interviewed yet?'

'Mine's at two this afternoon. I'm glad I found you, though. I called at Jem and Freya's rooms earlier and Jem is distraught, of course – angry about everything that's happened. She wants to talk to you.'

'Me? She's already given a statement to the police, so what does she want with me?'

'I don't know. I heard you found her with the body. You don't think she had anything to do with Freya's death, do you?'

'I don't know. She seemed stunned by the scene.' Mallory took a step away not wanting to discuss it with Rose.

'Please go and see her.' Rose looked at her watch. 'Do you think they'll let us leave school before the official end of term too? I wouldn't mind getting away early if possible.'

'You'll have to speak to Lowri.' Mallory hesitated. 'Rose, you're an RE teacher. Has anyone ever asked you to join in anything like a secret group, or embrace an alternative form of worship?'

Rose frowned. 'I don't know what you mean. Can you be more specific?'

'I can't, I'm afraid. It's just that, while Penbryn Hall caters to all faiths, chapel attendance is clearly important. But there are other religions besides the organised ones.'

'You mean cults? I certainly teach that aspect of religion to my sixth formers. It's a subject that goes down well with them – teenagers are often attracted to the more bizarre aspects of our society – but no one has mentioned anything about one being present at the school.'

'I wasn't thinking so much about the students, more among your colleagues.'

Rose frowned. 'There's nothing that I'm aware of.'

Mallory sighed. 'You might get asked something similar this afternoon in your interview. If there's anything unusual that springs to mind in the meantime, be sure to let the interviewing officer know.'

'All right. Will you go and see Jem?'

Mallory, who had intended to see a different person in the same house, thought she might as well combine the two visits.

—

Mallory showed her ID to the officer stationed outside Livvy's room. It was a different woman to the officer she'd seen the previous day and Mallory suspected that her colleagues would now be protecting Livvy in shifts. Really Livvy would be safer elsewhere, but like other offspring of overseas parents, her choices were limited.

'I'm sorry it's taken me so long to come and see you,' whispered Mallory as she approached Livvy, sitting bolt upright in her bed, reading a book on physics.

'I've heard what happened to Ms Wells. Dr Rhys came to see me to tell me in person, and I could see she was upset too. It could have been me, if I hadn't turned away when my attacker came at me with the stone.' It was to the girl's credit that it was said without a shred of self-pity. Mallory had heard Livvy's father was 'preparing to fly over to see his daughter'. What someone needed to do to prepare to fly, Mallory wasn't sure. Like Livvy's father, Mallory didn't live full time with her own child, but would have been on the first plane out of Cairo if Toby had been injured.

'When's your father arriving?' she asked, keeping the question light.

'He's in the middle of a diplomatic incident,' said Livvy. 'It may be that I'll have to get a taxi to Heathrow and catch the plane out for Christmas.'

Mallory groaned, unable to help herself. 'It's all right,' said Livvy, smiling. 'I've spoken to him on the phone and told him I'm happy here. My stepmother offered to come over to accompany me back but I don't need anyone fussing around me.'

Mallory thought that was exactly what she needed, but as she was never going to win a mother-of-the-year award, it wasn't really up to her to criticise.

'Have you got any more puzzles for me? I want to help discover who killed Ms Wells.'

Mallory made a face. 'Absolutely not, given the amount of trouble I've got into already. I should never have involved you in the first place, and I'd at least like to stay here until the end of term.'

'Why?' asked Livvy, putting aside her book.

'Do you know where I usually live?'

Livvy shook her head.

'In a caravan, and given the weather, I'm not exactly looking forward to going back. I'm in enough trouble for getting you involved in what's happening here already.'

'So there are no more puzzles? Do you know the identity of the person who killed Ms Wells?'

'Who said she was killed?' asked Mallory, her voice sharp.

'I heard two police officers talking outside my room. They said she'd been strangled.'

'For fuck's sake,' said Mallory, temporarily forgetting her role as teacher. 'I'm sorry you had to hear it that way. I don't think you're going to be able to help me solve the murder of Freya Wells. It's too large for you.'

Livvy smiled. Although her skin had the paleness of someone who hasn't seen fresh air for a while, there was no dullness in her intelligent eyes.

'The thing with big puzzles is that there are often smaller ones which lead to them.'

'I know. Look.' Mallory sat down on Livvy's bed. 'I've been asked, well no, I've been told by both Dr Rhys and my boss DI Evans that I'm not to speak to you.'

'Harri? I met him a few days ago when he came to see me.'

'What?' Mallory was fuming. So it was all right for him to pump the girl for information but not her. 'What was he asking you about?'

'He wanted to know who I'd spoken to about solving the puzzles with you. I told him that I'd said nothing, not even to my friendship group.'

'We now think that your attacker discovered that the book we found was put there by Ms Wells.' Mallory put her finger to her lips. 'I can't tell you more, but you're not to blame yourself for the attack. Nothing you did brought this on.'

Livvy was regarding her, with her bright eyes shining with tears. The girl had been blaming herself.

'OK, Livvy. I have a puzzle for you. The guard outside your door is going to remain there because, although the killer of Ms Wells knows we've discovered the punishment book, you might still be in danger.'

'So you're saying Ms Wells was a member of the Solstice Sisterhood?'

'Almost certainly. Have you been looking them up?'

'The internet is full of stuff about them and it sounds completely gross. I can't believe Ms Wells would get involved in a group like that. She was so... I dunno... light-hearted.'

'Did you notice her hand shook sometimes? I think there was a lot your teacher was repressing.'

'I saw she had the shakes sometimes. I thought it might be a drink thing.'

'Livvy!' Mallory almost laughed. 'Why did you think it might be down to alcohol?'

'My grandmother on my mother's side was an alcoholic and her hands shook.'

'Well, fair enough, but I'm wondering if there might have been something else going on with Freya. A tremor can be a sign of extreme stress, for example.'

'I never spotted anything else, and she was always kind to me. Have you seen Ms Owen?'

Mallory shook her head. 'I need to speak to Jem shortly.'

'You've got to see if she can tell you anything about the sisterhood. It's there that you'll find the solution to the puzzle. Have you traced the original members? I mean the ones who were arrested.'

Mallory smiled. 'You're interested in a career in policing, are you?'

Livvy flushed. 'Sorry.'

'No don't be. Harri is interviewing the members that are still in Wales, but we're pretty sure none of them are at this school. He does, however, think that there's an unknown woman from the sisterhood who we haven't yet identified.'

'An X?'

'Exactly.'

'Like a maths puzzle.'

'Not really. I mean, in order to find X, we need to at least have some of the other variables. All we know is that she will have been female, aged between, say, twenty to fifty at the time to be still working now.'

'Does your boss think she was in charge?'

'He's sure of it.'

'So not twenty then. You can start reducing some of the variables, which will lead you to a list of suspects.'

Mallory rolled her eyes at Livvy. 'Easier said than done, but you might be able to help.'

'Go on.'

'I want you to think about people who go unobserved in a place like this. Harri and I are at a disadvantage because we don't know the culture of Penbryn Hall. You do. I could ask Dr Rhys but she's too much on the inside. She's vetted all the staff, and from the way she acts, I'm pretty sure that she views people in tranches – the teaching staff, the caterers, the contractors. I need someone who can think outside the box.'

'You don't think Dr Rhys could be X, do you?'

The thought had crossed Mallory's mind and it was interesting that it was Livvy's first suggestion. Lowri certainly had the brains and the personality to be the power behind a strange sect, but ten years ago she had been the newly appointed head teacher of Penbryn Hall. Before that she had been deputy, and was a former pupil of the school. Her career was traceable and without blemish right up to the killing of Pippa, who had met Lowri at the interview without any drama. If she had been pulling the strings of the sisterhood back in 2015, she'd been combining it with a high-flying career at the school. She also admitted to only meeting Angharad Prytherch once.

'I'm pretty sure it's not Dr Rhys, but I'd still appreciate you not mentioning any of this to her.'

'Tell no one.'

'Exactly. Look, maybe I've made a mistake—'

Livvy swung her legs around. 'No way, Ms Dawson. You're not going to stop me working with you. What shall I do? Write a list.'

'No. Definitely don't write anything down. I'm going to come and see you tomorrow and you update me then. If something needs to be written down, I'll do it.'

'Someone hidden in plain sight?' Livvy pulled on a cardigan over her pyjamas and shivered. 'Like a police officer.' She spotted Mallory's expression. 'Only kidding.'

33

Mallory waited until she left Livvy's room before leaning against the wall and breathing deeply. Livvy's comment had been light-hearted, but Mallory had once worked with a bent copper and it wasn't something she wanted to think about. She wondered if any of her colleagues were going through a similar thought process, deciding trouble had only properly come to the school after Mallory's arrival. The uniformed officer outside Livvy's door was typing something into an iPad.

'Everything all right?' she asked the officer, who looked up. She had close-cropped hair and an open gaze.

'Everything's fine, ma'am.'

Mallory felt herself flush at 'ma'am'.

'Has anyone been asking to see Livvy?'

'Not on my shift, and I've instructions to tell DI Evans the minute anyone does.'

'You didn't check my credentials with anyone,' said Mallory. 'How do you know my motives were benign?'

The officer looked down at her iPad. 'DI Evans said you'd likely be nosing around. His words not mine, ma'am. He said to let you through, but make a note of how many times you visit.'

'I see.' Damn Harri, thought Mallory. 'Has he left similar instructions as to whether or not I'm allowed to visit Jem Owen?'

The officer shrugged. 'You'll have to check with the liaison officer who's supporting her.'

Jem and Freya's small apartment was at the top of the purpose-built teachers' accommodation block. Mallory had been unsurprised at the quality of the architecture of the boarding house. Constructed of spruce-clad steel on a steel frame, it looked contemporary, yet blended into the rural setting. The door on the fourth floor was opened by a family liaison officer, who nodded when Mallory showed her ID.

'She's been asking for you constantly. Thank you for coming over, but I'll sit with you while you chat, if you don't mind.'

'How is she?' asked Mallory, pausing at the door.

'Not good. Still in shock, I'd say, and gets very agitated. Do you know why she wants to speak to you?'

'Let's find out, shall we?'

Jem sprang to her feet as Mallory entered the room and crossed over to her. 'Is there any news?'

'I don't have any updates for you – they will come through—' Mallory glanced across at the FLO.

'My name's Ali.'

'They'll come through Ali here. I got a message from Rose that you wanted to see me, though.'

Jem grasped Mallory's arm. 'It's about that book. The punishment book that DI Evans showed me.'

'I know which one you mean. What about it?'

'You need to know why I kept quiet. I thought she was harming herself, you see. I saw the marks. There were cuts on her hands and on her thighs. They are classic indications of self-harm and I tried to get her help.'

'And the marks on her chest? I saw teardrop scars but they're unlike any other I've seen before.'

'She said… she said…' Jem's face crumpled. 'She told me that she held a lighted candle against her skin.'

'Jesus.' Mallory saw in her mind the teardrops on the page, the shape mirroring the marks she'd seen on Freya's chest. 'Did she say why she was doing that?'

'I couldn't get anything out of her. She said it made her feel pure and brought her into the light. I thought she was seriously fucked up.'

'Did this start before you got married?'

'She's had scars ever since we first got together three years ago.' Jem rubbed a hand across her face.

'Three years?' That wasn't good. 'When you read the punishment book, did you still think Freya was harming herself?'

'I don't know. I began to think someone was maybe blackmailing her. It seemed so codified.'

'Didn't you ask her about the Solstice Sisterhood? The name was there on the front of the book.'

'I… I asked, but I didn't get an answer.'

Mallory glanced at Ali, who was trying to persuade Jem to sit down. 'What about Freya's tremor? Did she ever explain the cause of it?'

Jem shook her head and allowed herself to be led back to the sofa. 'I thought it was just one of those things, something she'd always had.'

Mallory reflected, not for the first time, how love made fools of us all. 'Was Freya particularly close to anyone here apart from yourself?'

Jem scowled, her eyes flashing with anger. 'I've already been asked that.'

'And I'm asking you again,' said Mallory.

'She liked Emiah, the librarian,' Jem said after a pause. 'But they weren't lovers or anything. Did she say anything to you?'

'Me? Why would Freya say anything to me?'

'Because she talked about you a lot from the moment we met you. I got jealous, to be honest, but she kept saying you didn't fit in here.'

'That's certainly true. Is that why you've asked to see me? Do you think Freya knew I wasn't in fact a teacher?'

Jem shrugged. 'She was wary of you and I couldn't understand why. Now I think maybe someone else had already worked it out, your real profession, I mean.'

'Who? Emiah?'

Jem ran her hands through her cropped hair. 'I don't know.'

'I'm sure you've already been asked this, Jem, but I'm going to put the question to you again. Was it you who inflicted those wounds on Freya?'

Jem didn't react the way Mallory had expected. She froze and gave Mallory a hard stare. 'No. Otherwise I'd be dead, because I'm going to kill whoever murdered my wife. They now have me to reckon with.'

—

Back in the main school building, Mallory bumped into Jonathan, who glanced at the floor, clearly not wanting to talk to her. He'd been unsure about the value of her presence at the school, and it looked like he was blaming her for Freya's death.

'Could I have a quick word with you?'

Jonathan stopped. 'Are you asking as an investigator or teacher?'

Insulted by his tone, Mallory folded her arms. 'Both. I need to talk to you about the Solstice Sisterhood.'

Jonathan glanced up the corridor to check no one was listening. 'I'm glad Lowri finally thought it fit to tell me about the possible connection of the sisterhood to this school, but there's no point asking me about them. They wouldn't have a man in their midst.'

'I need to talk to you about the general principles of group control. You told me you had trained as a psychologist when we met in my room. You'll have more insight into this kind of thing than me.'

Jonathan, in fact, had an interesting background, as she'd scanned his personnel file, which was now accessible by the investigation team. He'd come to teaching in his late twenties after a PhD at Bristol and three years practising as a psychologist. Perhaps the front end of clinical practice hadn't been for him, but he must have gained insights into group behaviour during his studies and work.

Jonathan sighed and nodded. 'I can spare you five minutes max. I'm needed to help with the students who are leaving immediately. Some parents don't want their children spending another night at the school.'

He took her to his office, which, unlike the last time Mallory had visited, was in disarray. Eirin was there, attempting to bring some order to the pile of papers balanced precariously at the end of the desk. She smiled wanly when she saw Mallory.

'Jonathan's marking is piling up, I'm afraid. I thought I'd try to restore order.'

Jonathan scowled at her. 'Leave it, Eirin. Some of these pupils might never be coming back. I'll sort it out when things are a bit quieter. Where's Lowri?'

'She's making herself available for diplomatic calls. We might yet save the school, but she needs to use all her powers of persuasion.'

'What about the press?' asked Mallory.

'At the gates, I'm afraid.' Eirin was composed, although her eyes strayed to the window. 'There's a TV van, too.'

'Damn,' said Mallory. 'I can call Harri to increase security. They might be tempted to stray onto school land.'

'It's already done. We're employing a private security firm who'll be arriving shortly. I have to go now, sorry.'

Jonathan watched as she left. 'She's frighteningly competent, isn't she? God knows what she's doing here tucked away in West Wales.'

'The same as all of us. Trying to find her place in life.'

Jonathan glanced at her in surprise. 'Is that true of you too?'

'Of course. What about you?'

He shrugged. 'I was deputy head at the comprehensive I mentioned to you, and making a name for myself despite the pressures. Then the deputy head position here came up and I was surprised to get the job. I think Arabella, or Angharad as she became known, wanted a male in the post.'

Mallory frowned. 'Do you know why that might be?'

'I don't, sorry, and it's just an impression. I later found out that all the other applicants had been women.'

'And you've not kept in touch with her?' asked Mallory.

Jonathan's eyes widened. 'Of course not. I'm not even sure if she's in the country.'

'Fair enough.' Mallory smiled. 'You prefer teaching to clinical work?'

'I do. I did consider applying for university posts, but academia in this country is on its knees, and of course I had issues in the state school system. It's only schools like Penbryn Hall that are thriving.'

Mallory fixed her face. School fees for boarders were over £40,000 a year, although many students received some form of scholarship, usually supported by former pupils at the school. Still, it was an institution only for those who knew how to access funding – whether from their own coffers or others'.

Jonathan sat heavily in his chair. 'So how can I help you with the sisterhood?'

'Had you heard of them before the incidents at the school?'

'Not at all. I mean, I've heard of religious sects which often pop up around the countryside. The dynamics of a group often require control and submission, so physical isolation is good.'

'This one started in a city, though. Cardiff.'

Jonathan shrugged. 'To form a nucleus you have to persuade people to come to you. Cities are good for that.'

'I wonder what made them leave the city. I mean, you can remain anonymous. I didn't know my neighbours in London. I could have passed them in the street without recognising them.'

'They were likely to be expanding, or at least wanted to. I believe there were only six members, which is small for this kind of group.'

'How do cults usually recruit members?'

'Word of mouth, adverts in like-minded publications, online infiltration. I'm talking off the top of my head, as it really isn't my area of expertise.'

'You'll know more than me.'

Jonathan picked up a paper from the top of the pile nearest to him and glanced at it. 'I can probably help you with group dynamics. My study of it has been helpful in my school jobs. Groups can be a great support, but also completely toxic.'

'Are there any toxic groups here?'

'I haven't noticed any this year, but occasionally student friendship groups turn sour.'

'What about among the staff?'

Jonathan smiled slightly. 'Funnily enough, any friendships that form tend to be between two people. Adults can be a bit more wary, especially when they're in a situation a long way from the ordinary world. I haven't seen evidence of problematic groups here.'

'So you don't think the sisterhood is having a resurgence here?'

'Christ, of course not.' He stopped. 'Do you?'

'I think Freya was killed because she knew the identity of someone here who was a member of the sisterhood who probably recruited her to its cause. There were clues – her tremor, which suggested severe strain, her fascination with me, but refusal to engage when I tried to talk to her. The strain must have been almost unbearable when she knew that Livvy had been attacked to protect that identity. Perhaps at that point she was determined to tell Jem who that person was. It's the same member of staff Pippa also recognised.'

'Who?'

How the fuck should I know? Mallory wanted to say. 'I don't know. Not you, then?'

'Of course it's not me. Surely male teachers are above suspicion.'

'No, they're not. How do I know that the group isn't being controlled by a male presence? Is that completely impossible?'

Jonathan exhaled. 'No, it isn't.'

'Tell me.' Mallory leant forward. 'I know or can imagine some of the dynamics of group control, but what about these punishment rites? How do they get members to submit to punishment?'

'The same methods I've already mentioned. Coercion, control, maybe enticement. I mean, it's not my thing, but some people might be attracted by punishment. At a more extreme level there are plenty of people involved in the S and M scene.'

Mallory wrinkled her nose. 'You think there might be a sexual element to the group?'

'You know what, I don't think so. It's possible it's a fetishist club, but I'm not convinced. What little I've read about them is that punishment is a form of purification. Whoever came up with the concept was looking at the religious connection with discipline. Think of the Desert Fathers or the Inquisition. Pain was seen as part of rooting out heresy.'

'Right.' Mallory had no idea what he was talking about, but it made her thankful her own mother had decidedly secular views. She'd been spared all that religious claptrap, and her son showed no interest either.

Jonathan was picking at the lapels of his jacket. He must be worried about his own position, now the school had been plunged into controversy. 'You think there might be something happening in the school? I had assumed we were talking about someone historically involved in the cult.'

'I don't know, but probably.' Mallory wasn't able to tell him about the marks she'd seen on Freya.

'This is terrible. What am I looking for?'

'I thought you could tell me. Signs of physical punishment, but they're likely to be hidden. Maybe unusual dynamics between staff, now there's a murder taken place. Any remaining teachers involved must be appalled by what happened and fearful for their own safety. You need to look for signs of existing tensions beyond the usual worry about what staff might be feeling about their future.'

'What does Lowri say about all this?'

'I haven't spoken to her since Freya's death. There's a killer at the school, which is her main problem. I guess that supersedes any issue about cult members operating on the premises. It's a police matter.'

'You don't think…' Jonathan stopped. Mallory knew exactly what he was thinking, his suspicions echoing Livvy's. Lowri had all the attributes of a cult leader – dynamic, charismatic, authoritarian, even if she was at pains to hide it. Lowri would make a very good cult leader, but why would she call in police to help discover what was happening at the school?

'I don't know,' said Mallory. 'But interesting you thought it possible.'

34

Harri was in a foul mood. The meeting that morning with Steph hadn't gone well, and she was seeking extra resources from South Wales Police and possibly further afield. This enraged Harri, as he was sure that if the killing hadn't taken place at Penbryn Hall, his team would have been left to do their work without the threat of being sidelined on their home patch. At least Steph agreed that the Solstice Sisterhood was the best lead on the killing and he was to make tracking down the remainder of the group a priority.

The hunt for the whereabouts of Angharad Prytherch was still underway, and they were now up against the run-up to Christmas where even embassy staff were slow. The member who'd been named Rhiannon had been located in Llandeilo, but when Harri rang the mobile number he'd been given to make an appointment to see her, the phone rang out unanswered. He'd need to make a trip down there to see if he could catch her at her property, but there was always the possibility she'd gone away for Christmas. Really he should send officers to speak to her, but he wanted to be there himself. He knew the right questions to ask and when not to take what was said at face value. Micromanaging, Siân would have called it, but it was Harri's style to be out there doing the legwork alongside his team.

In desperation, Harri decided to make contact first with Carmel Byrne, formerly known as Kigva, whose address and phone number had been received from Newcastle colleagues. Interestingly, she was the only one of the sisters who had a criminal record. In 2018, three years after the sisterhood wound up, she had stolen money from her employers, a large firm of solicitors, and had been prosecuted. The amount wasn't large, just over two thousand pounds, which had involved her invoicing a client for reactive PR work – something about a property dispute – that was never undertaken. The fraud had only come to light when the man who'd paid the invoice had mentioned it at a subsequent meeting with the solicitor. A minor misdemeanour perhaps, but Harri wondered if it was motivated by lack of money, or whether it was a power game to prove she could. Perhaps a burgeoning criminal career had been nipped in the bud.

Kigva answered on the first ring. Her soft Irish burr was now mingled with Geordie and she sounded more vulnerable than the smart-suited woman Harri remembered. Kigva most definitely hadn't been wearing the clogs made by Ceridwen.

'Christ, it's not to do with the conviction, is it? That was spent three years ago.'

Interesting, thought Harri, that she hadn't immediately thought of her time in Wales.

'I'm from Dyfed Powys constabulary and I want to talk to you about your time with the Solstice Sisterhood. We have already spoken to each other. I was one of the officers who interviewed you back in 2015.' There was a long silence, and Harri worried that Kigva had hung up. 'Are you still there?'

'Well, that's a blast from the past that I wasn't expecting. What's happened now?'

'I'm investigating the death of a teacher in Penbryn Hall, West Wales.'

'Penbryn? I saw that on the news. That's one loose connection you're making with the Solstice Sisterhood. Angharad was only briefly head teacher there.'

'There might be other connections apart from Angharad, but I do need to speak to her. Are you in touch?'

There was a snort of laughter down the line. 'We are not. I couldn't wait to get away from those women. God knows why I ever went there in the first place.'

'There must have been something that attracted you.' Harri was feeling thirsty and took a swig of cold tea. He wondered what his blood sugars were up to, but thirst was not a good sign.

'Yeah, the money.' Kigva laughed again. 'It's always been my downfall. I answered a job advert for a live-in post at the farmhouse and bingo, next minute I'm one of the gang.'

'Who interviewed you?'

'Angharad, of course. She was in charge of recruitment and gave me the lowdown on the sisterhood. Funnily enough, the group reminded me a little of the sects you get popping up in Ireland, except they were into Welsh mythology. It seemed a little left field, but I thought why not?'

'When were you named Kigva?'

'Straight away. Angharad asked if I minded in the interview. I thought it an affectation, but it made no difference to me.'

Harri thought this was an interesting approach to recruiting new members. Offering them a paid-up job and, presumably, gradually assimilating them into the group. 'So you were known as Kigva during your time there. What did you think of the other women?'

'You know, for a movement living in such close proximity, we didn't really have that much to do with each other. We had breakfast separately – I can't face much in the morning, so I'd just go into the kitchen to brew some coffee and chat with Rhiannon. The others I hardly saw in the day, but at night, we'd have dinner together and talk about plans for the sisterhood.'

'How long were you with them?'

'About seven months, from February to August, when all the trouble started with that girl who claimed she was beaten.'

'Bethan Rossi. You said in your statement that you had seen some of the women chastising each other. Were you hit?'

'No I bloody well wasn't. I was there to do a job. I acted as Communication Manager for the sisterhood and I was the public face of the community, not that that amounted to much.'

'I believe you accompanied Luned to hospital when she had an infected wound. Didn't that raise any concerns with you?'

'I told you, I was doing a job.'

'The sisterhood paid you a good salary?'

'Too damn right. I wouldn't have done it for nothing.'

'And where did the money come from?' It was possible Angharad had been financing the group, but Harri wanted Kigva to confirm the source of her salary.

'I didn't care, as long as I was getting paid.'

'Were the others receiving a salary?'

'I doubt it. Branwen said she'd been originally employed to set up the kitchen garden in their former home, but I'm pretty sure by the time we were in West Wales I was the only one getting paid.'

'There was a spare room at the farmhouse. Who used to stay there?'

'No one. It was a large house and we had one bedroom too many.'

'Are you sure? Two of the sisters – Luned and Branwen – shared. Why not give them a bedroom each?'

'No idea. Perhaps they preferred it that way. There's no accounting for taste, especially when it came to the sisterhood, although I thought Branwen's affections lay elsewhere.'

'Come on, Kigva. Who was the other member? Who made the decision to wind up the order after the police raid?'

'Angharad did.'

'Are you absolutely sure about that?'

There was silence, then a sigh. 'I don't know. The thing is, I saw evidence of punishment on Angharad's hands. Like the others, she favoured long skirts and tops, but you can't really hide your hands. I don't know who was administering the chastisement, but I can't imagine she'd have let any of us hit her.'

'You think it was someone else. When could this have happened?'

'At night. Someone did use that room occasionally, but it was late at night when they came, and I think they only slept for an hour or so.'

'Would any of the others know the identity of the person apart from Angharad?'

'I doubt it. It's Angharad you need to speak to.'

Damn, thought Harri. Where the bloody hell was that woman? 'One more thing. I need to know what goes on during Winter Solstice celebrations.'

'Solstice? These are the oldest celebrations in the world, when our ancestors would have rejoiced in the changing of the seasons. Winter is when we celebrate light in darkness and the coming of days of warmth.'

Harri bit back his irritation. There was nothing there she couldn't have got from Wikipedia.

'Yes, but what did you do? Celebrate by burning a yule log?'

'I told you, I was with the sisterhood from February to August. How the fuck should I know what they did at midwinter?'

'But it was at the heart of your name.'

'I can tell you what we did during the Summer Solstice. We ate too much food and decorated the farmhouse with garlands of flowers. That much help to you?' Her voice was tart.

'Not really,' said Harri, desperate to cut the call. 'Thanks for your help.' He didn't bother to hide his sarcasm.

35

Mallory had gathered the remnants of her lower sixth class into one of the little rooms off the library. Emiah was busy preparing for the end of term and had been called out for a meeting with the deputy, and the large library space was empty. The events of the last couple of weeks meant students were desperate to get away and parents only too happy to oblige. She had seen two cars with diplomatic plates arrive along with security staff to pick up the students from European royalty, and other families who had also arrived with bodyguards. The vast majority of the arrivals, however, were ordinary parents worried about their offspring. The few Mallory had met had appeared to want to get away as soon as possible, and some, possibly many, might not return the following term. Lowri would need all her powers of persuasion to restore Penbryn Hall's once-powerful reputation.

The departure of the students did little to quell Mallory's unease about the solstice, which was now only a day away. While the school would be depleted, there would still be students and staff to be protected. Harri had so far been unable to discover what might happen during celebrations, but that did nothing to allay Mallory's fears. Despite the upheaval, the festival atmosphere had become a little hysterical, students still on a high about leaving early. Even staff appeared to welcome the break, and Mallory was left with the impression only she could feel the danger building. Now her cover was blown, she'd decided to openly question the remaining students to use what little time she had left to guess where the danger lay.

There were four students left in her class – Isabella, Molly, Hannah and Livvy, whose head still bore the evidence of her attack. Isabella was swaddled in layers of clothes, despite the heat from the library room. She was probably suffering from shock, and layers of warmth helped. Molly had her rucksack next to her as her father was due to pick her up that morning but had phoned to say he was stuck in traffic on the M4. Hannah had been a quiet student in class, and Mallory felt she'd hardly got to know her, but was impressed by the way she kept glancing towards Livvy to check all was well. Livvy was, well, Livvy. Cool, focused, but her face still pale.

'I know you've all had the opportunity to speak to one of the school counsellors as part of the investigation into Ms Wells's death. How are you all feeling about it?'

'It's just unreal,' said Molly. 'As if we're taking part in a classic murder mystery. You know, girls' school, small pool of suspects. I keep expecting Hercule Poirot to walk in any time.'

'She's Hercule Poirot,' said Isabella, pointing at Mallory without rancour. 'She's a police officer.'

'That's not quite true,' said Mallory. 'I'm a civilian investigator, but I am a former officer.'

'You're not a maths teacher, though,' continued Isabella, most definitely on the attack.

'No, I'm not, but did you notice?' Mallory caught Livvy's eye, but she just smirked at her.

Isabella shook her head.

'Do you think the school will continue next term?' asked Hannah. 'I like it here and I want to come back.'

'That's certainly the plan, but a police investigation needs to take place, and the best place for you all to be is away while that happens. None of you is a suspect, so it's a case of making sure you're in the best place. It made sense to shut the school early.'

'Do they think one of the other teachers killed Ms Wells?' asked Molly. 'I heard she was strangled.'

'Who told you that?' asked Mallory, hoping it wasn't another indiscreet officer. A press conference had been called the previous evening, a Steph and Lowri double-hander with Harri nowhere to be seen. Freya's death had been confirmed as suspicious, but no other details had been given.

'We all know, miss,' said Hannah. 'Everyone's talking about it. Was it one of the teachers?'

Mallory hesitated. 'We're not sure, but staff have been asked to stay on to help with inquiries.'

'Do you want us to tell you who we think did it?' asked Molly.

Mallory was shocked. She'd guessed that the girls would have spoken about the crime among themselves, but hadn't expected them to focus on a suspect. 'Go on,' she said.

'We think it might be Ms Jenkins.'

It took a moment for Mallory to identify their suspect. 'Emiah? Why do you say that?'

Molly looked at the others and decided to act as spokesperson. 'Hannah saw her arguing with Ms Wells about a week ago and she looked upset.'

'Who did? Freya Wells?'

Hannah nodded. 'They both did actually, but Ms Wells was crying.'

'Have you passed this information on to the investigators?' asked Mallory, and she received another nod. Harri hadn't mentioned it to Mallory, which suggested either he hadn't got round to that piece of information or was following up on the revelation, especially given Jem had said Freya and Emiah were friendly. Mallory, aware of four students waiting for a response, smiled. 'I'm sure it's all being checked up, but please don't speculate any further. It can make it harder for an inquiry to sift what is fact and what's conjecture.'

'What's it like, being in the police?' asked Isabella. 'Do you get to solve lots of murders?'

'I was a detective in London and there were more violent crimes there. But I've been involved in some cases in Wales, too.' Mallory paused, choosing her words carefully. 'This is really important, and I'm going to ask you something that may give away more than I should. Do you understand what I mean?'

The group nodded. 'You mean we'll discover something by the nature of the question you ask?' said Hannah.

'Exactly, so I'm going to ask you not to mention our conversation to anyone, especially a teacher. If anyone asks, tell them I was giving a maths lesson in a cosier environment, given the circumstances. OK?'

Everyone nodded, and Mallory saw curiosity in everyone's face. 'So my question is, have you heard of any secret groups that exist within the school? It could involve students only, staff only or a mixture of both.'

Mallory knew she was seriously overstepping the mark here, but the chance would be lost once these girls left for the holidays.

'This is a school,' said Molly. 'There are secret groups that exist all the time. You're going to need to be more specific.'

'OK. I'm specifically thinking of among staff and maybe pupils, although I think it more likely to be just staff.'

'Then we probably wouldn't know,' said Livvy, speaking for the first time. 'Teachers guard their private lives because there's not much privacy here. They don't talk to students usually about their partners or families, for example.'

Livvy knew about the punishment book, so must have guessed the direction of Mallory's questioning, but kept her eyes lowered.

'Have you seen or heard about a teacher being in distress?'

'Only Ms Evans,' said Isabella.

'Pippa?' said Mallory. 'I'd heard she was fine in the classroom.'

'This wasn't in lessons. I saw her follow someone into the chapel one day and when she came out, it was as if she was running away. Like she was frightened.'

This wouldn't have come up in the interview, and Mallory now saw how much of a mistake it was not to question the pupils about Pippa's death. 'Who was she following into church?'

'I don't know. I just saw the back of their coat. It was a dark navy blue. The only thing was that when Ms Evans came out, she was clutching a feather.'

'A feather?' All Mallory could think of were white feathers that had been given to conscientious objectors in the First World War. This surely couldn't have been the symbolism she was searching for. 'And Pippa, I mean Ms Evans, was upset?'

Isabella curled her lip. 'I told you she was frightened. That's why I remember the feather. She was like a bird desperate to escape from a cage.'

—

After class, Livvy lingered behind, wanting to speak to Mallory.

'I've been thinking about the feather,' she said.

Mallory pulled the door shut and sat down next to her student. 'Go on.'

'Feathers have a significance throughout history. They're often associated with the divine – angels, for example. But they often represent freedom, both spiritual and mental.'

'How do you know all this?' asked Mallory, exasperated. 'It's got nothing to do with your maths talent.'

'I read a lot. But the thing is, it doesn't sound like the feather represented freedom to Ms Evans.'

'Pippa was scared,' said Mallory.

'Exactly. So what I'm trying to say is that the feather represents something much more specific. It was associated with the person you're looking for. The killer of Ms Wells.'

'OK.' Mallory scratched her arm. 'Do you know of any teachers or staff that have an association with feathers?'

'Well, I did once see Ms Jenkins with a pot on her desk.'

'Emiah?' Mallory got up and opened the door, checking the library was still empty. She hurried over to the computer, but apart from a pile of books hastily returned by departing students, there was nothing there.

Livvy stood next to Mallory, pointing at the table. 'There were about five of them in a small pot. I thought they might have been owl – the colour and length was about right. I was going to ask Ms Jenkins about them, but she seemed angry when she saw me looking at them.'

'Did she?' Mallory led her away from the desk towards the library entrance. 'Do me a favour and don't mention our conversation. I'll speak to Emiah myself.'

36

That afternoon, Mallory was summoned by Harri for a catch-up and, as she drove out of the school grounds, she felt her spirits lift. Her time at Penbryn Hall had been an eye-opener beyond stretching her professional capacities. It made her realise that the world of wealth and privilege didn't suit her. She'd have hardly called herself left wing, but she was constantly dismayed by the assumptions of both staff and students. There was an ordinary world outside that they'd insulated themselves from that Mallory was desperate to return to. One good thing that had come out from her stay at Penbryn Hall was her conviction that it was time to put down roots of sorts. She'd never been entirely sure whether she'd stay in Wales, but perhaps now was the time to commit herself to her new life with a long-term rental and a regular income.

At least she didn't have to worry about what to do for Christmas. Harri had invited her and Toby to lunch and, given she knew his sister Fran and the kids, it should make for a relaxing day. Toby would also be pleased to escape from the caravan for his visit. While he'd loved the leisure park and nearby beach in the summer heat, his early October visit in the dreary weather hadn't gone well. She might just check them both into hotel rooms in Carmarthen when he visited and make looking for somewhere more permanent a priority in the new year.

Mallory's phone buzzed as she was nearing Carmarthen and she answered on the hands-free.

'It's Harri. Can we change the location of the meeting? I've been trying to arrange an interview with Rhiannon Edwards, one of the original sisters, but she's proving hard to contact. I want to head over there after seeing you.'

'Want me to come with you? I quite fancy meeting one of the sisterhood in person.' There was a short silence. 'Keeping them for yourself? Don't be so coy. If I meet one of them, I might have a better idea of the type of woman I'm looking for in Penbryn Hall.'

'There isn't a type,' said Harri, clearly cross. 'That's the whole point. They were a completely disparate group of women.'

'Of course they're a bloody type,' Mallory shouted down the phone at him. 'It's the type who are seduced by someone in power. The type who lets them inflict punishment on you. Think I'd let someone do that to me?'

'Um… Mallory.'

'Don't "Mallory" me. I wouldn't let anyone touch me with a bargepole, so I'm not their type, am I? Neither was Bethan, by the sound of it, given she fled the house the minute she was whipped, and not without putting up a fight, too. And bloody good for her.'

'Let's wait until we meet. There's a pub in Llandeilo that serves good food. Join me there for something to eat and you can let me know how you're getting on.'

—

It wasn't until she'd finished her fish pie and glass of white wine that Mallory realised firstly how hungry she was and also how much she'd missed Harri. He was eating his pie and mash with relish, although Mallory was pretty sure diabetics weren't supposed to eat so many potatoes. Over their meal, she updated him on the argument between Freya and Emiah, and Isabella's curious story of seeing Pippa flee from the chapel holding a feather. It was the second story that got his attention.

'A feather. Did she say what type of feather?'

'She didn't, but Livvy also spotted a vase of feathers on Emiah's desk that she thought might belong to an owl.'

'I think it might solve the sisterhood name of the woman we're trying to track down. Do you know the story of Blodeuwedd?'

Mallory shook her head. 'From the Mabinogion, right?'

'Exactly. It's one of my favourite stories. She's a woman made of oak, broom and meadowsweet flowers. However, she killed her husband to be with her lover and, as revenge, she was turned into an owl, never to show her face in daylight again.'

'Like our missing sister.'

'Yes, exactly. I should really have made the connection. The feather might have significance, too. I remember seeing one in the drawer of the empty bedroom at the farmhouse in Carmarthenshire, but I didn't think anything of it at the time.'

Mallory frowned, thinking of Livvy and her quest for patterns. 'The feather might be some kind of calling card, then? Blodeuwedd reminding the sisters of her presence even when she's not there.'

Harri shrugged. 'Possibly.'

'OK, we know the sisterhood name of the woman. Do you think it might be Emiah? She's my prime suspect, especially given she clearly doesn't like me. She's one of these people who always seems to be around. I thought that librarians squirrelled themselves away, but she's very visible, plus she had some kind of altercation with Freya before her death, according to my students. I presume she's already been interviewed. Did she mention that in her statement?'

'Not that I'm aware of, but even the innocent might think twice about mentioning that to a murder team.' Harri pushed his plate away and looked at his phone. 'Just checking my blood sugars. Jesus, they've gone up to 14.2.' He showed her the figure on his phone.

'It's all those spuds. The problem with our X, or missing sister, being Emiah is that Lowri says that the librarian was the only person Pippa actually spoke to, and we're looking for someone she lived in fear of.'

'You do need to speak to her about the feathers, though. Tell me what she says.'

'Do you know, I was wondering about Jem Owen, Freya's wife. She was at the school during the brief period when Angharad Prytherch was head teacher, so she's a possibility. She might be lying about her wife's injuries. I put it to her that she might have caused Freya's injuries and she was pretty convincing in her outrage.'

'She looked pretty devastated to me, too,' said Harri, 'but you might have stumbled on her after she'd just strangled her wife.'

'Have forensics come up with anything in relation to the strangulation marks on the body?'

'Wool fibres were present on the skin rather than someone else's cells, which meant her assailant was wearing gloves, which is no surprise given the weather. And before you ask, Jem didn't have gloves on when you found her, unless she disposed of them somewhere.'

Mallory groaned, looking at her watch. 'Look, did you find out anything else about the solstice celebrations from the members you spoke to? I feel the clock is ticking and I'm no nearer what might happen tomorrow.'

Harri shook his head. 'Nothing of any great interest. They certainly seemed to enjoy their food at the sisterhood. I expect when I see Rhiannon this afternoon, I'll get more of the same. I really don't think you need to worry about it.'

'I just can't rid myself of the thought that Freya's killer, if she's the person behind the sisterhood, is going to do something dramatic to celebrate the solstice.'

'Then thank God the school is nearly empty.' He finished his pint. 'Still want to see Rhiannon with me?'

Mallory reached for her coat. 'Most definitely.'

37

It was clear when Harri and Mallory knocked on the door of the grey stone bungalow next to the imposing chapel that Rhiannon was astounded at their visit. She was a faded-looking woman with pale grey hair and light eyes wearing stone-washed jeans with a fisherman's jumper. She glanced at their ID in dismay, putting on her glasses which hung from a chain around her neck to get a better look at them.

'What have I done?' she appealed to Mallory as she held the door fast against her body.

Mallory glanced at Harri and adopted a reassuring smile. 'I'm sorry, we need to speak to you about an incident you were involved with some years ago.'

A light of comprehension came into Rhiannon's eyes. 'Oh God. You'd better come in. Do you mind dogs?'

'I love them,' said Harri, catching Mallory's eye. He knew she was less than keen on the animals, and it was naturally her that the cockapoo came barrelling towards when Rhiannon let them into the hall. Mallory ignored the dog and looked around at the space. It had a homely feel, and there were children's crayoned pictures tacked next to the mirror.

'Do you have grandchildren?' asked Mallory. It was funny, but she'd got fixed in her mind that the members of the sisterhood were single women, leaving convention behind them. This bungalow wasn't dissimilar to her own mother's, right down to the hanging plant in front of the window.

'Three,' said Rhiannon. 'My daughter doesn't live far away, so I see them regularly. Making up for lost time, you could call it. I didn't see much of her during my solstice years.'

The smell of cooking wafted towards them, something oniony which turned Mallory's stomach. The fish pie had been rich and she was feeling slightly queasy after eating so little in the past few weeks. Rhiannon brought them to the kitchen and turned down the oven.

'Coq au vin,' she said. 'It'll wait. It's the joy of living by yourself that you eat whenever you want.'

'Were the regimented meals difficult for you when you were at the sisterhood?' asked Harri.

'Everything was difficult for me in the sisterhood.'

They sat on high chairs around the breakfast bar. Rhiannon lived by herself and yet here she was, making a complex meal for one. Mallory was about to beat herself up about her own poor domestic arrangements until she saw the cardboard wrapping of a Marks and Spencer ready meal next to the bread bin. Maybe she should just pay for a better class of junk food. Rhiannon had been the cook in the Solstice Sisterhood, but the kitchen wasn't one of a foodie. There was a toaster and kettle on the counter along with a jar containing a few kitchen implements. It was too clean, too tidy to be the preserve of a dedicated cook.

'We need to talk to you about life in the Solstice Sisterhood,' said Harri. 'There are a few of you left in Wales and we're paying everyone a visit.'

'Who's still here?' asked Rhiannon, her voice flat.

'Branwen and one of your former helpers, Bethan Rossi. We also think Angharad might be in the area because Branwen says she saw her once in Swansea. Have you seen any of them?'

Rhiannon grimaced. 'None, but I steer clear of Rossi's in Carmarthen. That was the restaurant run by the girl's family, wasn't it?'

'It was. Bethan is still there.'

'She was a nice girl, and she ran away. I admired that.'

'She gave you a black eye, if I recall.'

'No, that was Angharad. Bethan shoved me out of the way after Angharad whipped her and I banged my head against a kitchen cupboard. It was Angharad who had the black eye. She probably enjoyed getting it.'

'You were aware of the system of punishments going on in the sisterhood, then?'

Mallory watched the woman and wondered if she was abuser or abused. The statements of the six members of the sisterhood had been split in half. Three had denied the accusations that any physical assaults took place – Luned, Branwen and Rhiannon. The other three – Angharad, Ceridwen and Kigva – had said that mild corrective punishment was at the heart of the sisterhood as a cleansing and healing tool. Rhiannon, so swift in her denial back in 2015, hesitated.

'I received some punishments. It was hard to get things right all of the time.' Rhiannon pulled up the sleeve of her jumper to the elbow and turned her arm so they could see the soft flesh of her forearm. The pale skin was pitted with eight purple teardrops of scar tissue.

'Dear God,' said Harri. 'How did you get those?'

'Angharad held a lighted candle against the skin each time I made a mistake in the kitchen, usually involving a cooking mishap. It was her favourite form of punishment for me and my punishment book reflects it.'

'You've still kept it?' asked Mallory.

Rhiannon shook her head. 'I threw it on the fire years ago.'

'What I'm struggling to understand,' said Mallory, 'is how you joined a group and accepted the punishment?'

Rhiannon put her elbows on the counter and held her head in her hands. 'If you ask all six of us, you'd get very different answers. Angharad, for example, loved the whole ideology of the sisterhood. Living a basic lifestyle, reading Welsh myths and correcting any mistakes.'

'I haven't met any of the others,' said Mallory, softly. 'It's you I'm interested in. Why did you join?'

'I was lonely. My daughter had left home and I was looking for something in my life. I met Angharad at a women's choir in Cardiff and we got talking. She'd just left Penbryn Hall and wanted to stay in Wales rather than return to the States. She talked about the Mabinogion and how she wanted to start a community where like-minded people lived together.'

'You definitely got the impression it was Angharad who was forming the plans for the group.'

'Of course.' There had been a moment of hesitation before her reply and Mallory saw Harri had noticed it too.

'The reason I ask,' said Harri, 'is that in 2015 we interviewed six of you.'

Rhiannon's expression became watchful. 'What of it?'

'I got the impression there was another who was missing. A seventh member, perhaps one who had a more senior position in the group.'

'I don't know anything about that,' she said.

'Are you sure?' asked Harri. 'It's important, Rhiannon. A woman has been murdered at Penbryn Hall, and before that, a girl who once worked with you died. Pippa Evans. So you remember her?'

'Pippa is dead? How?'

'She died in suspicious circumstances, but we think she saw someone at Penbryn Hall she recognised from her former days. Was it you?'

'Me? I've never been near that place. Why are you pestering me about this?'

'Because the second death was definitely no accident and the victim had marks on her chest like your ones. It means the Solstice Sisterhood is in existence again. It's come back to life.'

'It can't,' Rhiannon whispered. 'We all left.'

'No,' said Harri. 'There's someone else. Not Angharad, but another. Who?'

Rhiannon picked up a tea towel and began to sob into it, her arms shaking as Freya's had done. 'I have no idea what you're talking about.'

Harri looked across at Mallory and shook his head. Rhiannon was clearly a victim and possibly knew little more than she'd already told them. Mallory was dismayed to realise how much Rhiannon reminded her of Freya, now lying dead in an autopsy room in Aberystwyth. Something about their frailty and passivity. How many more victims would the sisterhood take before they discovered the identity of its founder?

38

After their interview with Rhiannon, Harri was desperate to get back to the station. Siân had texted him to say there was a possible lead for the whereabouts of Angharad, and he wanted to follow it up as a priority.

'Everyone else is hinting at or prevaricating over the possibility of another woman in the sisterhood. Angharad will know for definite the identity of the woman I'm calling Blodeuwedd.'

'She might not tell you,' said Mallory, stamping her feet against the cold. 'The currency of the sisterhood is secrecy.'

'Trust me, Angharad always knew when the game was up. She'll tell us.'

The drive back to Penbryn Hall took Mallory an age in the dark. Cars were either driving too fast or too slowly, and she spent twenty minutes trailing a tractor, which sprayed her small car with some foul-smelling gloop. The school was still a hive of activity when she finally arrived. The reporters were congregating at the entrance and she waved at Eirin, who was handing out hot drinks from a tray under the watchful eye of a private security firm. Once through the gates, Mallory saw that the odd student was still being collected, while a ring of light illumin-ated the white-overalled members of the forensics team still working at the spot where Freya's body had been discovered.

It was twenty-four hours until the solstice and Mallory felt sick to the stomach with worry. There was no one apart from Harri she could confide in. Everyone here was preoccupied with departing students and their own end-of-term plans. In the main building, Mallory was reluctant to return to her room and contemplated what to do with herself while she waited for something, *anything*, to happen. The school was eerily quiet without students and the little noise that was made, footsteps on wood and muted conversations, was amplified by the silence. There was none of the laughter or cries of enthusiasm that had disorientated her when she'd first arrived. How quickly she'd gotten used to the hubbub of people around her, and much as she hated to admit it, she'd also begun to enjoy the classroom work. There was nothing like bright teenagers to keep you on your toes. Not a bit like policing, where most of the criminals were downright stupid.

She bumped into Eirin as she emerged from the garden, carrying the empty tray. 'That's the press watered, if not fed. It helps with PR, according to Lowri, and God knows we need all the help we can get.'

'How is Lowri?' asked Mallory. 'I wouldn't mind a quick chat with her if possible. You know tomorrow is solstice night?'

'You think something might happen then? Surely not, with all the police that are on site.'

'I don't know.'

'I'll tell you what.' Eirin looked at her watch. 'Keep an eye on your emails and I'll ask Lowri to see you either tonight or first thing in the morning. You can tell her your concerns then.'

'She's not said anything to you, then.'

Eirin shook her head. 'Nothing at all.'

Mallory climbed the stairs, passing a pair of male teaching colleagues, who averted their eyes when they saw her, likely viewing her as a traitor for her deceit. And yet her motives had been good, and she could have told Lowri that first day that any investigation revealed festering wounds and toxic secrets. If pressed, she might have even warned that people could get hurt, but she'd left it to Harri and the superintendent to make that clear if they thought fit.

The thought of what was in the offing on this solstice night continued to gnaw away at her. The tension was unbearable, and as she paced the room, Mallory thought she needed to do something to occupy her time. Harri's phone was switched off and she couldn't get through to Siân either. She was desperate to know what the lead on Angharad was and how long she'd have to wait to learn the identity of the seventh sisterhood member.

Checking her emails, Eirin had scheduled a meeting with Lowri at nine that evening. There was also an email from Harri, who had sent through his notes from the interviews of Branwen, Bethan and Kigva. He'd made a point of highlighting the passages that related to solstice rites and none of it was very illuminating. The comments of Kigva were what Toby would call a word salad, a bunch of meaningless phrases, particularly useless given that Kigva hadn't had a winter with the sisterhood. She'd been drafted in by Angharad, almost certainly at Blodeuwedd's request. However, she had confirmed that the centre of the Summer Solstice celebrations was fire, and the other three had stressed the prominence of light as part of Alban Arthan, as the Welsh called the Winter Solstice. Or *some* of the Welsh, as Harri had stressed. As good an investigator as he was, he didn't like his language taken and repurposed for criminal means.

So perhaps she was looking for the makings of a fire beyond the woodshed and meagre kindling under the tarpaulin. Christ, there was a mini forest out there, so there was no shortage of fuel, but she'd need an accelerant and some kind of bonfire. This was something Mallory could usefully look for, and she didn't care right this very minute who Blodeuwedd actually was. She just had to address the potential action of the mystery woman and worry about identification later.

The weather app on Mallory's phone said there was a yellow warning of wind coming the following day, which was all she needed if there was a potential fire issue. It wouldn't help the forensic team either. Mallory put on her quilted jacket and her ribbed hat and armed herself with the heavy torch she kept in her car. The woods were the best bet, and Mallory took a breath and began to follow the path Pippa had taken weeks earlier to her death. She shone her torch between the tree trunks but saw nothing that looked like the beginnings of a bonfire.

In the distance, she could hear two women talking. She recognised Emiah and another lower female voice she couldn't place. They stopped abruptly as they heard her approach and one of them slipped off into the darkness. Emiah pulled the hood of her coat over her head, as if just remembering it was a freezing night.

'What are you doing here?'

'I could ask the same of you,' Mallory retorted. 'Who were you talking to?'

'That's none of your business.'

'I think you'll find it is. I want to know who you were talking to and what about.'

'And I'm not telling you,' shouted Emiah.

'I also want to talk to you about the feathers that you keep on your desk. Were they yours or did someone give them to you?'

Emiah took a step forward. 'You're messing with things far darker than you're aware of.'

The menace in her voice was unmistakable, and Mallory's blood froze. She shone the torch at the woman's face. Emiah winced in the glare of the beam and raised an arm to shield her eyes from damage. The sleeves of her coat were loose fitting and slid down to reveal an expanse of white arm. And there Mallory saw the now-familiar teardrops.

'Emiah,' she whispered. 'For God's sake.'

Emiah pulled down her sleeves and her lips curled in a snarl.

'Keep away from me.' Emiah shoved Mallory hard. Mallory's leg, the one that had taken an age to heal, bucked and she was unable to save herself from falling to the floor with a thud. As her head made contact with the hard ground, she panicked that she would lose consciousness. She managed to crawl on all fours to a nearby tree and use it to hoist herself up. Stumbling, she followed Emiah back to the school building, ignoring the white heat of pain in her head. As she crashed out of the woods, she lurched again, and reached out to steady herself, but found herself caught by Jonathan, reassuring in his solidity.

'God, I've never been so glad to see you,' puffed Mallory.

'What's wrong. Is someone pursuing you?'

Mallory's legs buckled again. 'The other way round. I'm chasing after Emiah. Have you seen her?'

'She didn't come out this way. What's the matter?'

Mallory began to shiver. 'I'm fine. She pushed me, but she was just trying to get away. We need to find her as a matter of urgency. I think she's another member of the sisterhood.'

Jonathan and Mallory began in the library, which had been closed for the evening but left unlocked.

'That's odd,' said Jonathan. 'Emiah usually locks up.'

Mallory switched on all the lights and searched the room. 'She's not here. We need to split up and carry on looking for her. We need to find out who she was talking to. It was a woman with a low-pitched voice.'

'Jem?' asked Jonathan.

'I don't know. Maybe. Jem was certainly suspicious of Emiah. It could have been her.' She stopped and looked at her watch. 'Damn, I've got a meeting with Lowri. Look, will you carry on searching for Emiah? When you find her, don't let her out of your sight.'

Eirin smiled as Mallory entered her office. 'Lowri's just on the phone at the moment, but she'll be with you shortly. Is everything all right?' Eirin's smile dropped as she took in Mallory's trousers.

'I had a bit of a set-to with Emiah. Jonathan's looking for her now.'

'What happ—' Eirin broke off as the door opened. Lowri stood on the threshold, immaculately dressed as usual, only the slight smudge of her eye make-up an indicator of the pressure she was under.

'You wanted to see me,' she said to Mallory, her manner cold. 'I have to tell you I'm getting regular updates from Steph, so unless there's something urgent, you'd be better going through your chain of command.'

Mallory nearly lost it. She was missing Toby, Harri, even her caravan. Emiah was a victim and possibly perpetrator and Lowri had the gall to cite chain of command to her. She'd clearly been watching too many detective dramas on TV.

'Fine. If you won't talk to me, I'll go and speak to a member of the press standing outside. They'll listen, especially when I offer them the news for nothing.'

'You wouldn't do that. That's your job over.'

'You know what, I don't think I like my work anymore. I was doing you a favour coming here and I've had almost no support while you sit there and complete your damage-limitation exercises. The job can get stuffed. I'm perfectly capable of earning elsewhere.'

This wasn't strictly true, as Mallory had found to her disappointment, but being a civilian investigator at least gave her some freedoms, and walking away without worrying about her pension or promotion prospects was one of them.

Mallory turned to go.

'Wait a minute. Tell me what's happened.' Lowri glanced at Eirin. 'You can say anything in front of Eirin. What do you know?'

Mallory recounted her meeting with Emiah as Lowri folded her arms.

'I've known Emiah for years. She's far too sensible to be dragged into something like this. What do you think, Eirin?'

Lowri's secretary took her glasses off and placed them on the table. 'I don't know.'

'Come on, you must have an opinion. Tell me as a friend if not as your boss.'

Eirin looked pained. 'I just don't know. I don't know Emiah as well as you. We've never been close. I just can't help feeling…'

'What?' asked Mallory and Lowri in unison.

'That something terrible is about to happen.'

Thank God, thought Mallory, that I'm not the only one who can feel it.

'Then we mount a search for Emiah,' said Lowri, turning to Mallory. 'Are there any members of your team here who can help us?'

'I can get something put out on the radio.'

'No,' said Lowri. 'I've been told by the security team that the press will listen in to radios. I'll call the site manager now and get the word out among the guards that they need to look for Emiah. Perhaps you could do the same with your colleagues?'

'All right,' said Mallory. 'With so many looking, one of us must discover her whereabouts.'

Mallory tried everywhere, but Emiah had been at Penbryn Hall too long and knew all its hiding places. Her panic began to mount, which made it hard to think objectively. As she was rootling around in an outbuilding, Livvy walked in on her with a torch in her hand.

'Livvy! What the hell are you doing here? Where's your escort?'

'Probably looking for me,' said Livvy, switching on the light. 'Why are you looking in here?'

Mallory sighed. There was no point keeping the search from the girl. If Emiah wasn't found soon, she would be reported missing by Lowri and everyone would be on the lookout for the missing librarian. 'I'm trying to find Emiah, I mean Ms Jenkins. She's gone missing and we need to find her as soon as possible.'

'Did she kill Ms Wells?'

'We're not sure, but we think she's connected to the sisterhood. I saw her tonight talking to someone, and her arms had marks that might correspond with a punishment by the Solstice Sisterhood.'

'What marks?'

Mallory hesitated. She had a duty of care towards Livvy and yet the girl's intellect might be the thing she needed to unravel what was going on. 'There were burn marks, which we also found on Ms Wells's body.'

'Burn marks?' The girl was outraged. 'Someone burnt Ms Wells?'

'I'm afraid so, and it seems this represents the teardrops in the punishment book. Emiah is clearly also involved, but I'm not sure in what capacity. Do you know where she might be?'

'No, but I can help you look. Is it connected to the feathers I saw on her desk?'

'Almost certainly.' Mallory told Livvy about Harri's theory that her sisterhood name was Blodeuwedd.

Livvy pulled at her lip. 'The feathers are important. Can I look with you while I think about the feathers?'

Mallory shook her head. 'I need to take you back to your house. It's safer there. I'm sure we'll find Emiah this evening.'

But by the time Mallory collapsed into bed at ten past one in the morning, Emiah had still not been found.

39

Harri was up at the crack of dawn for a long drive to Porthmadog, stopping only to pick up Siân from her flat. As he'd hoped, it was the American consulate who'd tracked down the whereabouts of Angharad, who was still officially known as Arabella Prytherch. They definitely weren't closing for Christmas, the official he spoke to told him. It had been a case of finding the right person to speak to, and he was it.

Harri had telephoned Steph with the news and she'd made the decision to ask the North Wales police force for help with the interview. Two officers were already with Angharad and she was to be interviewed under caution. Steph wanted her escorted to the local police station, but Harri persuaded her that interviewing Angharad at her home would likely result in a more compliant witness.

'If she doesn't play ball, I want her arrested for obstruction,' Steph huffed down the line.

For God's sake, thought Harri, Angharad's solicitor would have a field day if it came to that. Silence wasn't the same thing as obstruction and Steph well knew this. As he turned into the track that led to the farmhouse where Angharad now lived, he could see that Kigva's comments had been correct. Angharad had gone up in the world. While the track was typical of any rural farm road, once beyond the trees, a white house came into view.

Although only two storeys, it was a huge place, ranch style with two top-of-the-range Land Rovers stationed near the entrance. In contrast, the police Peugeot 208 looked tiny parked alongside them.

'Nice pile,' said Siân.

As they exited Harri's car, the front door opened and an officer let them into the house, his face flushed. Harri got the impression this was as exciting as their week would get.

'How is she?' asked Harri.

The officer took their coats. 'Composed. I think our visit wasn't a complete surprise, like she was already expecting us.'

'That makes sense, given the news coverage of Freya Wells's death. Would you wait outside while Siân and I interview Ms Prytherch? We want privacy, but make sure she doesn't bolt.'

'No problem, although I think that's unlikely, given her manner. Her husband's away for the week, so you'll be uninterrupted.'

'Has she called him to say you're here?'

'Definitely not. She's been sitting watching TV since we arrived. She's cool as a cucumber.'

'That figures.' They walked into the living room, Harri's eyes on the woman perched on the edge of the sofa. 'Hello, Angharad.'

Angharad, formerly Arabella Prytherch, smiled at Harri's use of her adopted name. Harri remembered her as an attractive forty-something woman who'd presented herself as the de facto head of the order. She had a high-maintenance look about her that Harri hadn't noticed at their earlier meeting, but her face was almost gaunt. What was the phrase his daughter had used the other evening?

Ozempic face. Angharad looked much thinner than he remembered, but it didn't suit her.

'Tracked me down, have you? I thought I was difficult to find. I remember you, DS Harri Evans.'

'It's DI now.'

'Congratulations. Can I ask what gave me away?' Angharad had not lost any of the abrasive manner that had so wound up Lowri a decade earlier.

'You renewed your US passport three years ago and the consulate gave us your address. It took some time to go through the appropriate channels, but we got there in the end. If you'd moved in the interim it might have slowed us down, but we'd still have a trail to follow.'

Angharad folded her arms and turned off the television. 'I suppose you'd better sit down.'

'No thanks. Time is of the essence and those at Penbryn Hall are in danger. I just want a name from you. You know why I'm here, I suppose.'

'I do. I had hoped when I left Penbryn Hall in 2012 that it would be the end of my association with the school. It wasn't a happy time. I find Welsh high society both provincial and snobby at the same time.'

'You applied for the role,' said Harri, ignoring the rise in blood pressure her comments were creating. 'Had you not visited the country before? You have a Welsh last name.'

'I'd been to Cardiff twice when I was a child. To hear my parents speak, Wales was the promised land, the place of their ancestors that was much mourned. I fell for all that to begin with and I immersed myself in Welsh culture, but I found reality to be much different.'

'You're still here, though.'

247

Angharad smiled. 'I am. I've found love with a Welshman and it looks like here I'll be staying.'

Harri looked around the room, noting the expensive-looking cream sofas and thick velvet curtains.

'He's doing well, for a farmer.'

Angharad's expression hardened. 'Keep Huw out of this. He knows about my past and he doesn't care. He's focused on the land – his livestock and the cheeses he produces. I don't want him involved.'

'No reason to talk to him at all.' Harri could feel his legs getting hot, but he was determined not to sit down. 'I simply want the name of the seventh member of the group that I failed to speak to after the assault on Bethan Rossi.'

'Bethan?' Angharad's expression darkened. 'She was nothing but a drama queen. I gave her a light tap on the hand, nothing more, and I got hit in the face for my troubles.'

'I've seen the scars, Angharad. They weren't caused by a tap on the hand, but an assault using a riding whip.'

'Nonsense.'

'I want to know who came up with the idea of the Solstice Sisterhood. The reason why members were named after the Mabinogion and why punishment was at the heart of your ideology.'

'Christ, you've come all this way for that? I told you when we last spoke, we were a community. We developed our ethos together and everything was consensual, including minor corrective punishment. As for the Mabinogion, why not? It contains both Christian and pre-Christian beliefs, which fit very well with our own way of thinking.'

'How soon did you change your name to Angharad after you left Penbryn Hall?'

Angharad hesitated, pretending to consider the question. 'Within months, I'd say. After I realised that the trustees were about to boot me out because they didn't like the way I ran the school, I rented a house near Roath Park in Cardiff and began to consider setting up a community.'

'And how long had this idea been brewing? While you were head?'

'Not especially. I know what this is about. A teacher has died at the school, hasn't she? I saw it all over the news, but it's nothing to do with me. I've never heard of the woman.'

'And yet here you are, unsurprised at our presence. Tell me about Cardiff. Who was there? Remember, I only met the community when you moved to West Wales.'

'There was Rhiannon and Luned, who I met through two different choirs. Rhiannon was the cook, if you remember. Luned was unfortunately frail, but she lived at Greenham Common in the early Eighties and so embraced communal living.'

'And punishment. I remember the hospital visit. Who else?'

'I recruited a gardener, Branwen, and then Ceridwen joined us after I placed an advert in the *Spiritual Times*. Kigva came along a little later, once we'd moved to Ceredigion. I recruited her through an online advert.' Angharad smiled. 'There we are. That's the six of us.'

Harri was beginning to sway on his feet, but it was too late to sit down now. Siân continued to stand slightly behind him, happy to let him lead. He said, 'Let's go back to Cardiff, when there were five of you. You were helped in the house by a girl called Pippa Evans.'

'I remember. Why do you mention her?'

'Pippa died in tragic circumstances recently, but not before she'd seen, we think, someone from those Cardiff days.'

'Who? Was it Branwen? She's still in Wales – I saw her one day in Swansea and she scurried into a shop when she saw me. That was fine. The feeling was mutual and I had nothing to say to her.'

'She didn't see Branwen. Pippa was working at Penbryn Hall when she died.'

Angharad stared at him, trying to make sense of his words. 'Died, how?'

'She took her own life, but not before we think she saw someone from her sisterhood days. Was it you?'

'Of course not. You think I'd go back with Lowri Rhys in charge? She couldn't stand me. I saw it in her face the first time we met. Then I discovered she'd gone for the post herself which explained everything.'

Harri wasn't going to be diverted by reference to Lowri. 'If it wasn't you, who else might she have seen?'

'I don't know. I refuse to talk about this any further.'

'I think you do know. My colleague and I have specifically asked each member of the sisterhood who worked in the Cardiff house if they've been to Penbryn Hall recently and the answer has been no. So who did Pippa see?'

Angharad chewed her lip. She was probably thinking about all she'd acquired since leaving the sisterhood. She had a comfortable life with a husband who was often away, by the sounds of it. Harri also knew what it was like in rural communities. Once Angharad's name was in the paper, she'd get no peace here.

'I believe you and someone else came up with the idea of the Solstice Sisterhood. Someone you worked with while you were there, who, like you, is proud of their Welsh heritage and has woven Mabinogion tales into their way of life. I think she visited you regularly in Cardiff at night to see how the community was progressing and to check you were all living the life you had concocted.'

Angharad remained silent, looking to Siân for reassurance, although Harri was sure she'd find none.

'This woman, let's call her Blodeuwedd, is still working in Penbryn Hall, but I've no idea why she inspires such fear in former members of the group. You of all people would know her name.'

'Ask the others.'

'They don't know, although both, in their own ways, confirmed the presence of another group member, but they didn't have a name for me.'

'But you think I have.'

'If we conducted a search of you, we'd find evidence of beatings too. Who would have dished them out to you? Kigva?'

'Don't make me laugh.'

'Ceridwen, then. Do you know she's living in a community in Australia?'

'No, and I don't care. And it wasn't Ceridwen. This is all nonsense. The sisterhood ended when the order broke up. What if there was a seventh member? It's all history.'

'Don't be ridiculous. People are still dying. The sisterhood has been resurrected and I need a name, Angharad. It's all over, but on this Solstice day, I need to make sure the deaths have finished.'

Angharad slammed her fist on the arm of her chair. 'I knew you were trouble the moment I saw you back in 2015.'

'The name, please.'

Angharad took a breath and told him.

40

'This is the end of the sisterhood.'

Angharad stood with her hands on her hips and glanced around the farmhouse. The layout had worked better here than the terrace in Roath, where it had been a major task to keep visits by Blodeuwedd secret. She had usually come at night and had occasionally stayed over, sometimes sharing Angharad's bed, sometimes not. Angharad could still remember Pippa's expression when she'd happened on them late one night when she'd returned to the house to pick up the watch she'd removed to do the dishes. Everyone else had been in bed, just her and Blodeuwedd left to their pleasures until Pippa had caught them. But Blodeuwedd knew how to instil compliance and fear. She'd grabbed the girl and whispered in her ear and that had been the last they'd seen of her.

Shame, but it would never have lasted. Pippa was destined for university, but Angharad wondered how often her thoughts strayed back to the house in Cardiff. The move to West Wales had been more of a success, as they had been nearer to Penbryn Hall, so overnight stays had been kept to a minimum. Angharad marvelled that they had pulled it off, but it couldn't last. They'd chosen badly with Bethan Rossi. Angharad's hands strayed to the swollen eyelid that was impossible to camouflage.

'Does it hurt?' asked Blodeuwedd.

'Of course. I don't mind.'

She saw Blodeuwedd smile, of course. From the moment they'd met, they'd known what made each other tick. There was a faint sheen of sweat on her brow, probably from the cleaning and clearing she'd been undertaking.

'Don't worry about me,' she told Blodeuwedd. 'I have an over-friendly farmer who's been offering to take me in since we met at the Carmarthenshire show. He thinks I've been corrupted by the others. He won't need much persuading to be my knight in shining armour.'

She saw Blodeuwedd was surprised by the news. Perhaps it was an American thing, a legacy of the pioneer days. She'd shrugged on a new name and role as easily as she was now shedding the life she'd chosen. There would be a new chapter for her and she would flourish. Of the others, Branwen would also be fine. She had the solidity of generations of agricultural workers and would be able to find employment elsewhere. Ceridwen wouldn't stay in Wales, Angharad knew. Of all the sisters, it was she who embraced the punishment rituals the most, but couldn't see the point of the names from Welsh mythology. Angharad had heard she was headed for Australia, and as far as she was concerned, the further away, the better.

Rhiannon had been the last to leave, fussing over the packing, and Angharad had used the payphone in the village to delay Blodeuwedd's arrival. Rhiannon was a worry – nervy and temperamental, she was as far removed from a traditional cook as you could imagine. There was nothing Angharad could do except hope she kept her head down and forgot about what had gone on inside the sisterhood. Kigva was also a worry for different reasons. She could be persuaded to do anything for money, even spill the beans on the sisterhood if necessary. Fortunately, Luned would soon depart this world for the next and would never be a problem.

Blodeuwedd came to stand next to her and Angharad gazed out over the garden Branwen had so lovingly tended. Blodeuwedd took some money out of her bag and handed it to Angharad. 'That's for anything that needs tidying up before we hand back the house to the lettings agency. Make sure all evidence of our activities is removed.'

Angharad took the money and put it into her bag. The name on the lease was Angharad's, and she would be handing the keys back in the morning to the managing agents. 'Will you stay where you are?' Angharad asked.

'Of course. My superpower is that I pass unnoticed. Don't worry, the sisterhood is merely resting. I have every intention of resurrecting it when the time is right.'

'Not inside the school, surely. If you involve the students, you'll be exposed and sacked.'

Blodeuwedd shook her head. 'Not the students. Too risky. But Emiah Jenkins is showing interest in the sisterhood. I saw her reading an article about your arrest and she was more interested than repelled. Emiah is definitely on my radar.'

Angharad kept her expression neutral. So, the sisterhood would carry on, but without her. It was time to split. She realised Huw had a good business going at the farm, and if she was very careful, nothing, not even her past at Penbryn Hall, would ever come out. It was time to assume a new life. There were lots of different types of submission, after all.

Blodeuwedd picked up her coat and said, 'Well, I'll be going. Goodbye, Arabella.'

'Goodbye, Eirin,' Angharad replied.

41

'Eirin?' Mallory stopped still in her tracks as she listened to Harri's update, the wind whipping up around her. He'd rung her on his mobile just as she was about to embark on another search of the grounds. She'd decided to jettison her obsession with wood or other fuel and now was looking for signs of accelerant. The coach house with the school bus and car was to be her first port of call, but she wondered if she was just getting obsessed with fire. There was no actual evidence that the woman they'd been calling Blodeuwedd since hearing about the feather was planning a fire. Now, finally, Blodeuwedd had a name.

'Are you sure it's Eirin?'

'That's the name that was just given to me by Angharad Prytherch. They dreamt up the idea of the sisterhood together when they were colleagues, but they realised the community could only work outside the school. Angharad was tasked to bring in new recruits while Eirin helped finance the operation from her job at Penbryn Hall.'

'But why? I mean, Eirin's a poet, but she made reference to Philip Larkin, not Welsh verse. Also, she's a secretary. I mean, she'll get a decent salary, but we're not talking megabucks. Oh no.' Mallory thought back to their conversation in her room.

'What is it?'

'We talked about earnings when she gave me tea and cake. She said she was saving up to retire and write poetry. I've been an idiot.'

'No, Eirin's been very clever.'

'I'm still trying to get my head around it,' said Mallory. 'She's just so, I don't know, friendly. She stays in the background, a model of efficiency and discretion.'

'Which is exactly who we were looking for. If it helps you understand Eirin's motivations, I think there was a sexual element to the relationship between her and Angharad.'

Mallory picked up the exasperation in his tone. Bloody men. She bet he was certain, had he been in situ, he'd have marked Eirin as a prime suspect. In his dreams. 'You didn't spot her either, so don't think my instinct is skewed. She was very good at operating under the radar. Shit, I've just remembered that Eirin was present last night when I told Lowri what had happened with Emiah. She knows we're closing in on her.'

'Siân and I will be with you in about an hour and a half, but you need to start looking for Eirin now. Have you managed to track down Emiah?'

'Nope, and now I'm beginning to think she might have come to harm, given her car's still here, according to security. What shall I do if I find Eirin?'

'I'm sending two cars to you now and they should be with you in under ten minutes. I've tried Lowri's phone but it's not being answered, which might be bad news. If you see Eirin before they get there, you're going to have to act like nothing's wrong. You have no powers of arrest, remember.'

'I remember.'

'Mallory,' Harri warned. 'Don't do anything stupid.'

As she cut the call, she knew she wouldn't be able to stand still while she waited for the cars. She hoped to God they came with their sirens off as that would give them a fighting chance of catching Eirin unawares. She thought back to breakfast. Eirin had been there, Mallory thought, but she couldn't be a hundred per cent sure as she'd been busy scouring the room for Emiah. Damn, she'd have to make some excuse to see Lowri just to check Eirin's whereabouts. Mallory abandoned her plans to look for evidence of fire accelerant and crossed to the admin wing. Glad to get out of the wind, she felt the heat wash over her as she entered the house. She shrugged off her padded jacket and hung it on a nearby peg, and tried to look as nonchalant as possible as she headed to see Lowri. As she passed Jonathan's room, however, she saw the head teacher sitting in the chair opposite him, talking intently. Mallory attempted to pass, but was spotted by Jonathan.

'Is everything OK?' he said.

'Fine. I was just going to have a quick word with Eirin about something. Don't mind me.'

'She's not there,' said Lowri, twisting in her seat. 'She got an urgent text about ten minutes ago and has to sort something out.'

'Urgent text from who?'

Lowri frowned at Mallory's tone. 'She didn't mention who the sender was. She just said she'd need to take some time off for an hour or so.'

'Does she drive?'

'Of course, but she never said she was leaving the site.' Lowri stood. 'Is there something I should know?'

'DI Evans has been trying to contact you. I suggest you give him a call as I don't think I'm authorised to tell you. Do you know the make of Eirin's car?'

'I do,' said Jonathan. 'It's a four-wheel-drive Mini Clubman in a pillar box red colour. Security will have the registration. Why?'

'Not now,' said Mallory. She ran out of the building, racing towards the staff car park to the right of the entrance while searching for the red Mini. She saw it immediately and pulled fruitlessly at the locked door. 'Damn.'

In the distance, between the bare oak trees, she could see two patrol cars heading along the straight road. Thank God their sirens weren't on, but Mallory had the sinking feeling their quarry had bolted. She waited for the vehicles to pass the throng of press and waved the first vehicle into the car park.

'You need to check who this car here belongs to – it'll be quicker than going through security. If it's in the name of Eirin Carew, then we know she's still on site.'

'We were told by the boss to be discreet.'

'It's a bit late for that now. There's a strong possibility that someone has tipped her off.' It could have been Emiah who had texted Eirin for help, perhaps to let her know where she was hiding out, but the speed of Eirin's departure suggested that Angharad, for all her protestations of a new life, had decided to give her friend one final gift. Mallory scanned the huge building in front of her. Even at two o'clock, the threat of darkness was near and the student boarding houses were silhouetted against the pale sky.

'What time is the storm due to arrive?'

'In the next hour, but it's already blowy along the road,' said one of the patrol officers. 'It won't take much for the trees to come down, so we need to get searching now before it gets dark. Where do you suggest we start? She may be heading away from the school on foot.'

'I doubt it, but I agree the roads need patrolling. We can't do much if she's making her way through the forest until we get backup. The priority, though, is to make the school secure as soon as possible. The final students will be leaving tomorrow morning.'

Reinforcements came quicker than Mallory had expected. Five cars and a van arrived and soon the school was awash with the figures in their dark blue uniforms searching methodically through the buildings and grounds. Mallory finally got to check out the coach house. The green school bus was there alongside a battered-looking Peugeot. She looked for cans of petrol or other fuel, but everything looked in its place. Even the small amount of two-stroke oil for the garden strimmers was carefully labelled in a cabinet. Mallory was surprised by a noise behind her and wheeled around to see Lowri looking around her, for once at a loss what to do.

'I've spoken to DI Evans and Superintendent Morris. I blame myself. I can't believe this has been happening under my nose. How long do you think my staff have been enduring these assaults by Eirin?'

Mallory went over to the fuel cupboard and tugged at it. 'If Jem's account is correct, a couple of years at least, for Freya.'

'But why? Freya I can understand a little more. She was nervy and vulnerable, but an excellent teacher. I kept an eye on her when she first arrived, as I do with all my staff, but she settled in so well.'

'Did you notice she was especially pally with Eirin?'

'I knew that Eirin entertained her in her rooms, but I had no idea that she was in fact recruiting for the sisterhood.'

'She's probably been keeping her eye out for likely candidates since the sisterhood broke up on the outside in 2015. Freya's vulnerability would have been an attraction. But it's funny – Emiah never struck me as the vulnerable type.'

'She's not,' said Lowri, glancing around the coach house. 'Whatever her motivation, I doubt Eirin had the upper hand. Christ, I saw that Emiah was acting more and more oddly. Do you think she tipped off Eirin that Pippa was looking into the sisterhood?'

'Possibly. There was some kind of confrontation, but don't blame yourself. We're all feeling the weight of guilt at the moment – me, Harri, Steph, Jem. Transgressors excel at making others feel guilty. Did Eirin have access to this cabinet?'

'Not directly, but Eirin could find the key easily enough. You think she might be hoarding fuel?'

'It's a possibility. There are trained officers here now looking for Eirin. I'm better off looking for what might come in the hours until we find her. Do you have any ideas?'

'I know nothing about the sisterhood beyond what I've read in the papers. The worst thing is, while I have put the school into lockdown once more – the process made significantly easier by the fact we have only a handful of students left – it's Eirin who usually helps me with this. She's insinuated herself into the heart of this school.'

'Then she'll know what to expect.' Mallory saw a uniformed officer beckon her. 'I need to go.'

The bearded officer spoke to her in a low voice. 'We've found Emiah Jenkins. DI Evans says he wants you to talk to her. He's about forty-five minutes away now.'

If Eirin had killed Freya to preserve the secret of the revived sisterhood, she must have realised that it was all over when Emiah forcibly pushed Mallory to evade her questions. Emiah was discovered during a search of the staff accommodation, sheltering with Rose, who looked bewildered at Emiah's story.

'Jesus Christ, Mallory. She came to me last night saying she was terrified of what might happen to her. You've no idea what she's told me about what's been going on here. That's what I don't understand. I teach theology and RE, so you'd have thought I might have been at least approached to join the sisterhood.'

'Eirin is very careful who she picks. I think you should count yourself lucky.'

'I've seen the marks on her arms. I count myself *very* lucky. Are you going to speak to her? She says she doesn't know where Eirin is.'

'That's probably true. Yes, I need to talk to her.'

Rose's room was along the bottom of the corridor leading to Mallory's, but was twice the size, with a small room off the bedroom, where Emiah was sitting in a chair, her legs drawn up to her chest.

'How are you?' asked Mallory, taking the seat next to her, aware that only recently she'd been on the receiving end of this woman's anger.

'All right. I suppose I'm under arrest.'

'Not for the moment, unless there's something you want to tell us. We know you were a member of the Solstice Sisterhood. I saw the marks on your arms yesterday and they're similar to the ones I saw on Freya and also someone called Rhiannon, who was a member in the sisterhood's previous incarnation.'

Emiah pulled her sleeves down and folded her arms. 'I'm not answering any questions.'

'It's all over,' said Mallory. 'We're looking for Eirin and it's only a matter of time before she's discovered. How long has this been going on, Emiah?'

The librarian shrugged. 'A few years.'

'Not since 2012, when Dr Prytherch was here?'

'No. I know what happened in 2015 when all the group were arrested. When I casually said to Eirin that there was nothing wrong with women living together in a community, she mentioned that she and Freya were reviving the sisterhood.'

'Did she tell you how it started?'

'Eirin was into Welsh mythology and loved the idea of creating a group of like-minded women that celebrated the maternal divine.'

Mallory stopped herself from rolling her eyes. 'And the punishments?'

'I don't know.'

Mallory wondered if they'd ever know. Perhaps just an extreme form of control that cults often embraced. 'Was it just you three, or are there other teachers involved in the sisterhood?'

Emiah buried her head in her arms. 'Just us. Eirin used to say it was never about numbers. She wanted to reconnect to her ancestors and to nature, and she could only recruit women who felt the same as her. I was glad, as it meant we were chosen. You'll never understand the draw of a supportive community when everything in this school is so corporate.'

'Tell me about Pippa. I was under the impression you were friendly, or at least helped to cover for Pippa's research into the sisterhood. Did you tell Eirin what she was up to?'

'Of course,' mumbled Emiah. 'I was bound to the sisterhood, so it was my duty, and Eirin said she'd deal with it.'

'She hadn't recognised Pippa before then?'

'She hadn't seen her. Pippa crept around the school like a shadow. Everyone was talking about it. If she'd just taught her classes and joined everyone for dinner, no one would have noticed a thing. Instead, she started all this.' Emiah waved her arms around. 'The school's ruined.'

'I notice you call Eirin by her real name. Didn't you have Mabinogion names for yourselves?'

Emiah shook her head. 'Too easy to slip up in a school.'

'What about the feathers, then?'

'I... I was asked to display them by Eirin.'

'And Freya was recruited before you? When did the punishments start?'

'Gradually. You know the Solstice Sisterhood is about more than chastisement.'

'Sure,' said Mallory. She needed to get a move on because it was now dark outside and the steady tread of boots and shoes outside told her Eirin had still not been found. 'What were you and Freya arguing about before she died? One of my students overheard you.'

Emiah drew her legs tighter to her chest. 'After Pippa's death, Freya had said she was going to confess all to Jem and together they would go to Lowri. I told her it would be all over for her as a teacher and Jem would lose her position, too.'

And you, thought Mallory. You'd go too. 'When Freya died, you must have known Eirin was responsible. Why did you protect a killer?'

'I… I was scared.'

'Listen,' said Mallory, leaning closer to the woman. 'I know you've already been asked this, but do you have any idea where Eirin is? It's important we find her. She could still be in the school – if so, where might she be hiding?'

'I don't know. I promise, I don't know.'

'Has she said anything about what she might be doing tonight? Come on, Emiah. You're called the Solstice Sisterhood. You must have had plans for tonight, even if it was just a special meal.'

'I… I don't know. We used to go to her room in previous years. We'd read poetry, eat things foraged from the grounds, throw things on the fire. Is that what you mean?'

'No, it's not.' Mallory stood up and began to put on her beanie hat and gloves. Her coat was still on the hook downstairs, which she'd need to retrieve. She was desperate to get away from Emiah's self-pity, and getting outside into the thick of things would help. The wind was beginning to rattle the windows, and she could see one of the tall firs bending in the breeze.

'What are you going to do when you find Eirin?' asked Emiah.

'Stop whatever destruction she's got planned.'

42

Harri was desperate to get to Penbryn Hall and, in the end, let Siân take over the driving after finding he was too agitated to handle the country roads. She drove swiftly south, ignoring the gusts of wind that began to buffet the car while Harri responded to updates on the phone – Eirin's bolt, Emiah's discovery and the worsening weather at the school. Mallory sounded breathless as she combed the school for Eirin, and by the time they arrived, Harri's nerves were shredded. He was more confident than Mallory that they'd find Eirin somewhere on the premises, but less sure what destruction she'd leave in her wake.

He found Mallory searching the teachers' rooms in a foul mood. She'd wanted to join in the search of the school grounds, but the coordinator hadn't wanted a civilian involved, even one contracted to the police. Instead, Mallory was focusing her energy on searching rooms already looked through. In Harri's view, that was fair enough. He'd worked on investigations where a first sift had failed to spot anything, only for a second or third search to find a crucial piece of evidence. Harri, looking for Mallory, pushed open a few doors in the staff wing. He was interested to see that, while most were in the process of packing for the Christmas break, a few were completely clearing their rooms. It suggested that any reassurances

Lowri gave about the school reopening after the holidays weren't shared by her staff.

'Any news?' Mallory asked him when he finally found her rooting through a cupboard.

'Nothing of any import. If she's here, we'll find her.'

'I know, but when? If it was any other night I'd agree with you.' Mallory looked pale against the rich colours of the wallpaper.

'Where are the teachers while their rooms are being searched?' asked Harri.

'Mainly in the staff room, although I've left Emiah with Rose in her room as I don't want her infecting the others with her own brand of weirdness. Everyone is claiming they've no idea of Eirin's whereabouts, but God knows if they're telling the truth.'

'What are we expecting, Mallory? Hit me with the worst.' Harri sat down on the room's chair and scratched his head.

'What I've managed to discover about the Solstice Sisterhood is that they closely align themselves to druidism. The literature suggests that one of their beliefs is that darkness isn't necessarily associated with evil, which is an invention of Christianity and other world religions. For druidism, darkness represents a time to connect to yourself, like meditation, a time for rest and quiet. Druids like to reclaim the dark from Western industrialised societies' attempts to drive it away through artificial light.'

Harri was angry now. He was as Welsh as Eirin Carew and he didn't like the misappropriation of the ancient druids of Wales, ancestors of the bards, by people with their own agendas. This was the twenty-first century, and he remembered his grandparents' tales of their childhoods living in abject poverty in a rural farmhouse with no running water or electricity. What was wrong with a house heated by gas fires and lit by table lamps bought in John Lewis? For him, it represented progress, and he wanted to live in a forward-looking Wales, not one which harked back to days when survival to adulthood was uncertain.

'Are you OK?' Mallory was looking concerned, her hands in her pockets.

'Don't worry about me. I'm about to climb on my soapbox. Tell me, how many people are left in the school?'

'There are four students until four p.m. when two of them are being driven to Aberystwyth to catch an evening train to Birmingham to catch late-night flights. That leaves two, including Livvy, who are being collected in the morning.'

'I suspect it'll all be over by then,' said Harri. 'Where are the girls now?'

'All four are together in the library. There's a police constable with them, and they were playing Monopoly when I checked on them. The door is bolted from the inside and PC Collins knows to only answer to you or me.'

'Make sure the bolt doesn't leave them trapped.'

'There's a fire door on the other side which can only be opened from the inside. Another constable is making regular sweeps of the building to ensure it's not blocked.'

Harri wondered whether it would be better to remove the girls from the school, but Aberystwyth station was a good half hour's drive away and they were already getting reports of trees down in the high winds.

'What about staff?'

'About thirty in total. Some of the teachers and auxil-iary workers have already left following their interviews, no contractors are on site except security and we're really down to skeleton personnel, such as caterers and cleaners.'

'Thirty is still more than I'd like. There's a warning system in place, you say?'

'There's an alert system for everyone's phones. The problem is that one of the administrators was—'

'Don't tell me, Eirin?'

'Exactly. So Dr Rhys has sent a message instructing staff to ignore any communications from either the WhatsApp group or text messages. In case of any emergency, the school bells will ring continuously and everyone is to congregate by the fountain.' Mallory saw his expression. 'The fountain has been switched off and checked for anything untoward. It's out in the open, no trees or other structures nearby.'

Harri groaned. 'Your anxiety is infectious, Mallory. Do we really want everyone out in the open with a killer at large?'

'It's the best I could do, Harri,' said Mallory. 'This is a school and we have to have some kind of emergency procedure in place.'

There was a knock at the door and Siân stepped inside. She was dressed for an arctic winter, and sweat dripped off her brows in the heat of the building.

'Forensics have arrived to remove Eirin's car. Are you OK with that?'

Harri stood, feeling a wash of embarrassment that she'd caught him with Mallory. 'She won't be needing it, will she? Any taxis been to the school?' Harri was clinging to the hope that Eirin would take her warped spirituality somewhere else. Hopefully well away from his patch. Siân, however, was shaking her head.

'Sorry, my guess is she's gone to ground somewhere here.'

'Christ. Well, she's very good at hiding without leaving a trace. Keep looking.'

'Care to join us, sir?' She coloured slightly. 'I mean, you were very good at spotting her presence before.'

Harri saw from the corner of his eye that Mallory was smiling slightly. It would save him from moping about this building waiting for something to happen.

'Why not? You show me where you've been looking and make sure the emergency services are on standby.'

'Fair enough,' said Mallory. 'I think I'll go and check on the girls.'

—

It was the first time that Harri had seen the house almost empty. Although Mallory had been complaining about the heat, in fact that was the only luxurious thing about the building. The rest of the rooms had that utilitarian feel common to all schools, despite lacking the scored desks and chipped paint of his own comprehensive. It confirmed his view that Lowri knew how to balance refinement and practicality, and yet she'd been blind to what had been happening under her nose. Perhaps that was a bit unfair. She'd come to him, or rather Steph, to say she thought Pippa's death was suspicious, but she'd no idea what a nest of vipers she was uncovering.

'You all right, boss?'

Siân was unawed by the school, and Harri suspected she disapproved of private education. He shook himself, concentrating on what Siân wanted from him. 'In the farmhouse, Eirin had a room that she lived in like a hermit. Her motto could have been "leave no trace" because when I walked into that bedroom it was only instinct that suggested to me someone had been staying there.'

'Do you want to see her actual room before we go outside?'

'Sure.'

Siân led him to the back of the house and up a flight of stairs behind a door that suggested access to servants' quarters. Harri wondered if the downgrade in status had amused or infuriated Eirin. Once on the narrow corridor, Harri saw that the wing was roomy enough, with five doors leading off the landing. Siân led him to a room at the end and opened the door. The fragrance was one of grass and lemon, and for a moment, Harri was assailed by the memory of the room in the sisterhood house. Here, though, the scent was stronger. Eirin had taken possession of this space with her paintings and rugs, and looking at the chest of drawers, he could see toiletries, a crime novel with a bookmark peeping out of its pages and a glass pitcher filled with an amber-coloured liquid. Harri lifted the stopper and sniffed.

'Brandy,' he commented, remembering the alcohol used to accompany the pills Pippa had taken to end her life.

Inside the wardrobe was a row of dark-coloured clothes – wool jackets and dresses. This was more like Eirin, selecting clothes to fade into the background. Irritated, Harri shut the door.

'We won't find anything here. She knew this room might be searched, and what we see here is what she's happy to let us discover. Are all the other rooms in this wing occupied?'

'Yes, and allocated to non-teaching staff. Do you want to take a look? They've all been searched.'

'Not really. We keep looking.'

Harri wondered why he was so sure that Eirin would have another lair. It was partly her personality, as she was a woman always with a plan B, but there was something else as well. The need to split her role of secretary from that of her wider mission. Forcing her warped philosophy on others.

They went down the stairs together, Harri thinking hard. 'Are there any rooms unallocated to either teachers or staff?'

Siân stopped mid-flight. 'I don't know. I've got from the administrator a list of all staff and their accommodation, but I didn't ask about empty rooms.'

'Then we go there now,' said Harri.

The administrator wasn't at her desk, and looking round, Harri thought there was a general air of disorder that he hadn't spotted on earlier visits. They could hear the sound of heels tapping on the parquet floor and a woman with cropped grey hair came into view. Her face was reddened from the outdoors and she shrugged off a heavy navy overcoat and hung it on a hook behind the door.

'Sorry, I've just had to check on the shed behind the house. It's a wild night out there. I had a message from Dr Rhys to ensure the building was empty and secured. Do you know what this is about?' She stopped as if aware the words were pouring out of her. 'You *are* police, aren't you?'

'We are.' They showed her their ID. 'Did Dr Rhys say why she was focusing on the stable block?'

'It's where the wood's kept. She's checking all the fire procedures. What are we expecting?'

'I don't know.' So now Lowri was worried about the midwinter celebrations. 'We need a plan of the house that includes rooms that aren't being used.'

'But this school is constantly pushed for space. There's nowhere lying empty. I've already confirmed this with the searchers.'

Harri remembered the outline of the school with its brooding presence. At the top of the Edwardian building was a row of tiny windows, not the sash kind he'd seen in Eirin's room. 'What about the attic?'

'The *attic*? That's empty. The ceilings are too low to use as classrooms, and even in Edwardian times the staff—'

'For fuck's sake.' He ignored the look of outrage on the woman's face. 'Has the floor been searched?' he asked Siân.

'I don't know.'

'It's kept locked,' said the administrator. 'There are two doors at either wing of the house. The same key fits both.'

'Then can we have the keys?' asked Harri with studied patience.

The administrator went over to a tall metal cupboard and handed the key to Siân, refusing to acknowledge Harri's presence. Perhaps he'd overreacted, because the keys were here, weren't they? 'You go up through the back staircase and there's a door either side that says "Linen Cupboard". It's been put there to stop students exploring the attic. It was one of the dares a few years back.'

Harri decided it wasn't the time to say that, given the intelligence of the girls, he was pretty sure they'd already worked that out.

'Which side should we go to?' asked Siân as they hurried up the stairs.

'It doesn't matter if it's empty. We just need to search the rooms and close it off. Did you see the doors when we were in the back wing?'

'No, but I'm now wondering if we should have looked ourselves. I hate relying on others' searches.' They passed Eirin's room once more and Harri had another glance round the empty space. While he was contemplating the ceramic vase of feathers on the chest of drawers, he heard Siân shout.

'Here.' Siân was putting in the key and turning it fruitlessly. 'Maybe she's given us the wrong one.'

Harry looked at the tag. 'It says attic. It suggests the locks have been changed.'

'Then she's probably there. I'll call down for support. We need both entrances covered.'

'Phone down and stay here. I'll make my way to the other side of the house to keep an eye on that wing. We need an enforcer to break down both doors as soon as possible.'

'Wait.' Siân grabbed his arm. 'Can't you smell something?'

'No. What is it?'

Siân sniffed the air. 'I can smell fire.'

43

'Have you handed over the personnel files for Eirin Carew?' Mallory asked Jonathan, as she barged into his office. He had on a thick Barbour jacket and tweed cap, sporting a pair of designer wellingtons. He looked like he was going out for a country stroll rather than assisting in the hunt for a killer.

'I've given everything to DI Lewis. The paper files have gone missing and God knows how long they've been absent for.'

'It'll be a recent theft, given Lowri was looking through all staff files after Pippa's death. What have you got on computer?'

'The bare minimum, but at least it's something. I've sent it all over to Siân to look at.'

Interesting that it had gone from DI Lewis to Siân within seconds. Harri's colleague had a fan. 'Is there anything on there that could give us a clue to where she's hiding out?'

'Nothing. I've got details of her references, which were impeccable. She worked for a financier, and was recruited by Lowri herself.'

'How is Lowri?'

'I'd say she was distraught but doing her best to hide it. She'll be beating herself up that she recruited Eirin in the first place. Look, I'd like to be outside searching for her.'

'All right. I'm going to check on the students before I join you.' On impulse, Mallory walked the three doors to Lowri's room. The empty desk usually occupied by her secretary was in stark contrast to the chaos Eirin had left behind. Lowri's door was shut and, for a moment, Mallory wondered whether to knock, but the 'chain of command' comment still rankled. Instead, she went to the library and was let in by PC Collins. Mallory had met her a couple of times on previous cases and had been struck by her air of calm capability. She was also in her early twenties, so an ideal choice to watch over the remaining Penbryn Hall pupils.

'How's everything?' asked Mallory, seeing that two of the students had now departed the school and it was just Livvy and a younger girl left.

'Fine,' said June Collins. 'This room is secure. It's a good choice as we can get into the school easily, but there's a double fire door to the right, which is being checked regularly. Any problems, we can go outside.'

'Has anyone tried to get in?'

'No one, and there are notices on the main door that the room is shut. This is Inez, by the way. You know Livvy.'

The girls were playing cards and had cans of fizzy drinks and crisps next to them. It was a scene similar to the one in Mallory's caravan over the summer, and she reflected that teenagers were all essentially the same, easily distracted by a card game and crap food. It was getting wilder outside, but the library curtains had been drawn, giving the room a cosy feel despite its size. Livvy paused her turn, her hand suspended over the cards she was about to turn over.

'What's happened? We can hear lots of feet going up and down outside the door. June here won't tell us anything.'

Mallory looked at Inez, a student in the lower school who was staring at Mallory in wide-eyed apprehension, and shook her head. 'Nothing you need worry about, Livvy. We need to keep you both safe while we undertake some searches. This is the best place for you.'

'If we're in danger, maybe we should leave now.' Livvy threw down her cards. 'Everyone else has gone, and my dad says I might not be coming back to school next term.'

'Mine says that too,' confirmed Inez.

Mallory glanced at June, who was gathering up the cards and shuffling them ready for a new game. 'You'll be in more danger on the roads. There are trees down in both directions.'

'The local farmers will help clear it,' said Livvy. 'They always do. We've been out to watch the clear-up a few times.'

'I hope so, but, for the moment, you're safest here.'

'Who are you looking for? I know Ms Jenkins has been found, so it's not her. Inez and I have the right to know,' asked Livvy. Mallory noticed Inez was taking her cue from Livvy and allowing her to speak for both of them. It was the first time she'd seen Livvy take the role of spokesperson.

She considered. It was no point keeping the girls in the dark, especially as the whole school was being searched. 'We're looking for Dr Rhys's secretary, Eirin.'

'Eirin!' Livvy's mouth opened. 'Is there something wrong with her?'

Something very wrong, thought Mallory. 'You don't know where she might be, do you?'

Livvy, however, was tracing the scar on the back of her head with her fingers. 'Was it her I saw by the rose bush before she attacked me?' Her voice rose. 'Is it *her* who killed Ms Wells?'

'I don't think we should be talking—'

'I'm not a baby,' said Inez. Mallory gave June a despairing look. She shrugged.

'We think it might have been,' said Mallory. 'We need to find her first to formally interview her.'

'It's solstice night,' said Livvy. 'It's important for her.'

'Maybe she's driven away somewhere,' said Inez. 'If I was running from the police, I wouldn't stay here.'

'She can't go anywhere,' said Livvy. 'She's got no petrol in her car.'

Mallory frowned. 'How do you know that? How do you know the car's empty of petrol?'

'I saw her drain it this morning. She had this hose thing and a bucket. I was with my friends, who left this morning. She didn't look happy to see us, and said she'd put the wrong type of fuel in—'

Mallory grabbed the pair, taking them both by surprise. 'We need to get out of here.'

'What?' June Collins looked as if she was going to tackle Mallory to the ground, given that she had strict instructions from Harri that the girls weren't to leave the room, no matter who tried to remove them. Mallory was desperately formulating a quick way to relate her fears when their ears were assailed by a deafening clanging.

'That's the fire alarm,' said Inez. 'They don't usually test it at this time.'

'Where's the emergency exit?' shouted Mallory above the din.

'There.' Mallory's panic had finally conveyed itself to her colleague, and June ran to the double fire door, flinging it open.

'Be careful. Eirin might be out there. Can you get your coats on, girls? Wrap everything you can around you – I'm going to take you to safety.'

As Livvy and Inez pulled their warm things on, Mallory looked out through the door. In a fire, you were told to leave everything behind but it was a freezing blowy night and she wasn't sure how quickly she'd be able to get them to shelter. Mallory didn't think the girls were the target of Eirin, now her identity had been revealed, but they could easily become another of her unwitting victims.

'The coast is clear, I think,' hollered June. 'If we follow the path, it will take us round the side of the building to the front lawn.'

'You hold on to Livvy and I'll take Inez. We go to the fire point, but when we arrive, I want you to hold on to each girl and don't let go.' Mallory was joined by the girls, wrapped up in their thick coats with their hats down to their noses, who were taking Mallory's frantic directions in their stride. 'Ready?'

'Yes, miss,' said Inez. Mallory took hold of her arm and saw June guide Livvy out of the room. A blast of icy wind hit them immediately, and Mallory pushed forward to get them away from the room where the bell continued to clang. The four hurried along the path as the wind began to gust plumes of smoke into the night sky. The main building must have been alight, but Mallory couldn't see the source of the fire.

'Just keep going,' she shouted, hoping she wasn't leading them into a trap.

'Look, miss.' Livvy pointed skywards, and Mallory saw the top floor was a crescent of orange.

'Keep moving. Don't run.' They turned the corner and saw people streaming out of the building, hurrying towards the fountain, most turning round to catch glimpses of the flames pouring out of the cracked windows of the upper floor. As they neared the fountain, Mallory saw Jem and Rose huddled together.

'Where are the fire engines?'

'Coming,' said Jonathan, hurrying over to Mallory. 'They'll move the fallen trees, but it'll slow things down. I'm going to take the students to a patrol car away from the fire. There's one parked at the entrance. Thank you, Mallory, for bringing them out.'

'Go with them,' she said to June. Even now, she couldn't bring herself to trust anyone from the school. 'Do you know where Harri is?' Mallory stared in dismay at the burning building.

'I'm here.' Mallory wheeled around in relief as he coughed into a handkerchief. He pulled her close to him. 'I was just coming to look for you. The fire's in the attic. If the fire engines get here soon, we might save the building. What the— Is that Eirin?'

Mallory pulled herself from his arms and wheeled round, and followed the direction of his gaze.

'Oh my God.'

44

It was the darkest night, where the earth beneath them was furthest away from the sun. For Mallory, in past years, it had meant a time when she could look forward to lighter evenings, even if she had the execrable months of January and February to get through. Mallory thought, with a pang of guilt, of Toby, who she was seeing at Christmas Eve. She would pick him up at Carmarthen, and then on to Harri's house, staying in the hotel she'd booked until Boxing Day, a feast of food, television and board games. That was Mallory's focus, not this strange day in the heart of darkness.

For the woman standing in front of them, however, solstice represented something spiritual and cleansing. It was the night when Eirin's ancestors came together and stood side by side with her, and she was revelling in her twisted power. Part of Mallory could understand the pull of the natural world around her. As a Met detective, she'd paid scant attention to the seasons, and the turn of the year had been marked by holiday shift patterns and birthdays. It was only since moving to West Wales that she had seen how the seasons ebbed and flowed, and how each month brought its own beauty. Eirin, however, had warped this harnessing of nature into a religion of control and domin-ance. What was even more remarkable was she had done it from behind the scenes. Her power had been exerted through others, who had bent at her will.

Mallory had known there would be fire, and it would culminate on this night. She'd kept an eye out for bonfires and containers of fuel, but had underestimated the scale of her adversary's plans. Eirin stood in front of the building – once the home of the Cadwallader family, and for over seventy years a prestigious school – as it burnt and crackled behind her. What was the novel that ended with an all-encompassing fire? It came to her in a flash – Daphne du Maurier's *Rebecca*. Well, this was no Manderley, but Eirin had the monstrousness of Mrs Danvers. Somewhere behind Mallory, in the crowd of people being marshalled away by the fire commander, was Lowri, watching as her life's work turned to cinders. Mallory could only guess at the tumult she must be feeling. Meanwhile, Eirin stood with a flaming torch in her hand, the type Mallory had only ever seen in films or pageants.

'We need to reason with her,' Mallory said to Harri. The fact that she now had Eirin in her sights had done nothing to lessen the terror of the night. There was still the capacity for someone to get hurt. 'I don't like the way she's just standing there as if she's commanding the flames. The families of Eirin's victims need to get some answers – can't we pull her away from the building?'

Harri stamped his feet against the cold. 'You know I feel the same as you do, but my orders are to stay put. We're now under the command of the Fire Service's watch manager.'

'Has everyone been accounted for?'

'It's too early to say, but the fire started in the attic, which was empty. I hit a fire alarm switch on the way down, so people had plenty of time to get out.

Don't forget that flames shoot upwards, which means the building has lost its roof, but its progress downwards should be slow.'

'But the wind,' wailed Mallory. 'The whole building will go.'

Harri shrugged. 'Maybe. Christ, look at everyone milling around. I thought this was a well-run school. People should be at their assembly point, but it seems they've forgotten all procedure in the face of this.'

Mallory couldn't blame them, and she hoped to God that everyone had got out of the building once the alarm had been sounded. It had been a stroke of genius from Lowri to finish term early so students could depart, with only Livvy and Inez to worry about. She could see the pair sitting in one of the patrol cars by the gate, Livvy in the front passenger seat watching the flames. Beyond the entrance, camera flashes suggested the press were having a field day, and she guessed it might be live on the news.

Mallory was aware that Harri was like a coiled spring next to her. They had much in common. Both liked to take charge and hated the feeling of powerlessness a situation like this brought.

'She's a danger to herself,' murmured Harri. 'I'm going to ask for permission to talk to her.'

He strode off into the night, making his way to the white-helmeted figure, the person in charge of the fire scene. Mallory couldn't keep her eyes off Eirin. The wind, whipping up the flames, changed direction, and Mallory caught the whiff of petrol. Petrol? It should have all burnt off in the attic. In a daze, she moved forward, feeling the heat of the blaze against her face.

'Mallory, what the hell are you doing?' she heard Siân shout. She carried on, refusing to listen to her colleague.

Two fire engines were in front of her, stationed outside the wings of the house. They were attempting to douse the flames with arcs of water, some of the spray landing on Mallory as she moved forward. She could feel the power of the woman standing in front of her. Sparks flew at Mallory and, for a moment, Mallory thought that Eirin had ignited herself, but instead she raised the torch in her hand like an Olympian. All around her were feathers, long and snake-like on the grass. She was Blodeuwedd to the end.

'All power to my ancestors,' she said. 'This is the night where they talk down through the generations and guide my soul.'

What absolute claptrap, thought Mallory, furious as she inched forward. Anger was beginning to replace her fear. The Solstice Sisterhood had never done it for her, and here was the reason why. Someone was at her side, and Mallory thought it was Harri, but it was another woman who also wanted explanations. Lowri.

'Get back,' shouted Mallory.

'You're not supposed to be here too. We've got precious little time to reason with Eirin.'

'You speak to her,' said Mallory. 'Tell her to put the torch down. She'll listen to you. I don't believe you didn't know about Eirin,' she said to Lowri. 'There's nothing in this school that you're not aware of.'

Lowri turned to Mallory and shouted her reply, trying to make herself heard as the roar of the flames got nearer. 'I knew something was off, nothing more. When I went to Steph Morris to ask for help, all I wanted was to discover what had induced Pippa to kill herself. I should have let sleeping dogs lie. As soon as Harri brought you into the room, I knew you were trouble. I can scent a rogue personality at a thousand paces.'

Rogue personality? Mallory quite liked that, and she was also gratified to see that whatever power Lowri had over the women, the school and anyone else she focused on, it did nothing to Mallory.

'I need you to go back,' she shouted at Lowri. 'It's too dangerous for civilians to be here.'

'It's my school.'

Mallory turned to see Harri running to them. For Chrisakes. Harri grabbed both of them by the arm and swung them round, surprising Mallory with his strength. Lowri was the first to break away but was grabbed by a uniformed officer and dragged back to join the other watchers. Another officer stood uncertainly by Mallory and, responding to a nod from Harri, clamped his hand around her wrist.

'Harri!' she screamed, furious that she wasn't going to get explanations from Eirin. 'Please let me talk to Eirin first. She's a danger to herself.'

'I've permission to talk to Eirin, but only me. No civilians, and that includes you.'

Mallory tensed to get away from the restraint, but took one look at the six-footer who'd tightened his grip on her, and she relaxed. Bloody men. She allowed herself to be steered back towards the main group, craning her neck to watch as Harri reached Eirin.

'I can smell petrol still. That's not right. It should have burnt up if it was just in the attic. She might be covered in fuel,' she shouted, her voice lost in the wind. 'Please, Harri!' She felt like sobbing, and was surprised at how vulnerable this made her feel. It felt as if every step Harri took, he was moving closer to his doom.

Siân came to her and put an arm around her shoulders, ignoring the officer still clamped to her other side.

'You'll have to trust Harri,' she whispered in Mallory's ear.

They both watched as he reached Eirin, standing a foot or so away. His strategy was a mistake, Mallory saw immediately. Agitated, Eirin was waving the torch, the flame aloft above her head, a human beacon. It would be a disaster if one of the sparks caught wherever she had placed the petrol. Mallory saw something else reflected in the fire and lights from the engines – the metal glinting dangerously.

'What's she holding in her other hand?' she asked Siân.

'I think it's a long-bladed knife,' said Siân. 'Are armed response here, yet?'

'On their way I hope,' said Mallory, despairing of Harri's fate. If only she could get to him.

They watched as Eirin swung the blade towards Harri, looking in the flamelight like an ancient gladiator. Harri was defenceless, and Mallory saw in horror that he clutched his cheek.

'She's wounded him.' Mallory pushed forward, but both Siân and the officer held tight to her.

'Let go of me!'

A huge gust of wind swept across them and sparks shot from Eirin's torch. There was a white shoot of flame and she was engulfed, her screams loud across the valley. 'Harri move,' Mallory screamed.

'Fuck this,' said Siân and shot off. Mallory, taking advantage of the officer's slip in concentration, plunged ahead after her, desperate to reach Harri. Eirin was on the ground, rolling in the damp grass to extinguish the flames. Siân was younger and fitter and reached Harri first.

'He's got a face wound. Find something to staunch the bleeding.'

Mallory shrugged off her puffa jacket, pulled her T-shirt over her head and pressed it against Harri's cheek, watching as blood seeped into the white cotton.

'Put your bloody coat back on, woman,' Harri said. 'I'm fine.' And fainted.

'Hold on, Harri,' screamed Mallory. She turned him on his side as paramedics joined them and took over. Only then did she allow herself to look at the woman whose screams had stopped abruptly. Siân and two paramedics were tending to Eirin. Mallory watched for a moment until Siân turned and shook her head. The end, and with it, the end of answers to how this all began.

As Harri was stretchered towards the waiting ambulance, Mallory joined the group for a moment and stared at the remains of the leader of the Solstice Sisterhood. Martyrs had been burnt at the stake, but she doubted any of them went to their deaths voluntarily. Eirin must have known the outcome of holding a flame so near her body. Martyr? The woman was a killer and bloody sociopath, and nearly responsible for the death of Harri. Mallory wouldn't mourn her.

45

'The thing is,' said Mallory, 'it's usually me who ends up in mortal danger. We've kind of got into that habit – I'm about to die and you rescue me. I didn't actually expect to watch Eirin try to kill you.'

'She had a bloody good go.'

Mallory was sitting on Harri's hospital bed. On the board above his head, there were instructions written in various forms of code that she couldn't decipher but was pretty sure Livvy would have solved in one go. One word she did spot was 'diabetes', and she now regretted bringing in the bag of fruit for Harri. It had seemed a good idea at the time, but she was fairly certain the grapes and bananas would be packed full of sugar. She had arrived as Ellie, Harri's daughter, was leaving, accompanied by her aunt. A hurried consultation with Fran had confirmed Mallory and Toby were still invited for Christmas lunch, with Harri due to be discharged that afternoon.

Mallory saw that Harri was fully dressed. He wasn't a man to sit around in his pyjamas, and he was wearing some kind of tracksuit bottoms with a top, the zipper fastened up to under his chin. As usual, the top didn't match the bottom, but looked better than she'd expected, despite the gash across his face. He noticed her looking at the scar.

'Shame my kids aren't younger. I could have revisited my pirate impression.'

Mallory turned her head so he wouldn't see the emotion there. She had learnt the hard way that scars took time to heal, both physically and mentally. Harri claimed to have got through his career so far with only minor physical injuries, and he'd find this wound, so prominent on his face, a difficult adjustment.

'Was everyone safe after the fire?' he asked. 'My last memory is of the heat and crackle of the flames. I've asked the doctors here, but no one is able to tell me anything.'

'Everyone is fine, except Eirin,' she said. 'But I think it was the end of the road for her. There's only so long you can stay in the shadows, and we finished what Pippa started. We discovered the seventh member of the Solstice Sisterhood.'

Harri touched the pucker on his face and winced. 'I've asked for a second post-mortem for Pippa, given everything that's happened. I put the wheels in motion when Freya died, but it means an exhumation of Pippa's remains, which Steph might not go for. There's going to be some serious attempts to suppress the more lurid elements of this case.'

'Lurid?' said Mallory. 'We've got a punishment cult operating in a girls' school, which has burnt to the ground. Try suppressing that.'

'Steph and Lowri between them are going to have a bloody good go. However, I'm going to be pushing for that new autopsy.'

'So you don't think Pippa took her own life?'

'I do not. What I think happened was that when she first saw Eirin at the Cardiff house administering punishment to Angharad, it had a big impact on her mental health – her mother admitted as much to me – but she'd learnt to live with it.' Harri leant forward. 'Can you pass me that glass of water?'

Mallory reached over and placed it in his unsteady hand, remembering Freya's tremor.

'I understand Pippa was frightened when she saw Eirin, and we now know she was making plans to leave. Once she was away from Penbryn Hall, she could have resumed teaching and put the past behind her once more. But then Emiah told Eirin about the new teacher's strange behaviour. Do you think she recognised Pippa?'

'I'm sure of it, and probably before Pippa even arrived.' Harri set the glass of water carefully on the table. 'Don't forget, Eirin took charge of all Lowri's correspondence. She'll have seen the paperwork come in for a new teacher called Philippa Evans with a Cardiff address. There's no way an able PA like Eirin would forget a name. She probably knew who Pippa was before she arrived.'

'And there was no way of avoiding Pippa once she was here. I'm surprised she recognised Eirin so quickly.'

'Eirin has a very distinctive look. Pippa must have been frozen with fear when she saw the old leader of the Cardiff house.'

Mallory thought for a moment of her predecessor, who she'd never met but had thought about often over the past two weeks. 'Do you think Pippa was prepared to expose her, even though she was planning to leave?'

'I'm not sure. I think Pippa was just desperate to get away, but Eirin didn't know that. She was very clever. The easiest way to poison someone is to get them to overdose on a drug they are already taking. Unfortunately, citalopram has been proven to induce suicidal thoughts, so Eirin thought she had struck lucky by the fact that Pippa was ingesting a drug that could lead to her taking her own life. Administering an overdose of the drug in Pippa's evening drink and combining it with the toxic effects of alcohol induced a lethal seizure, with her dying of exposure.'

'I still don't understand why Pippa wasn't more on her guard. She was frightened of seeing Eirin, and she must have known that, as Lowri's secretary, she had in effect access to the whole school. If I'd been in her position, I'd have just left and not waited for another position to become available.'

'She had nowhere else to go unless it was to her mother's, and I can tell you from the interview that they weren't close. She was going to leave, but needed to wait for an opening.'

'I wish I knew what she saw in Cardiff.' Mallory had conjured up plenty of images, but all that remained imprinted in her mind were the marks she'd seen on Freya's body.

'We'll never know for sure, but my guess would be Eirin punishing Angharad was probably pretty extreme. I've only ever considered Angharad as the punisher, but when I met her, something seemed off in what she was wearing. She kept pulling down her sleeves and adjusting the neckline of her jumper. God knows what explanation she's given her husband for the marks on her skin, but I suspect the only person she'd have allowed to do that to her was the leader of the group, Eirin.'

'And where does the Mabinogion come in?'

Harri sighed. 'Some people just take what they want and run with it. When you get a chance, Mallory, read the stories yourself. Claim some of the mythology of your adopted country for yourself and don't associate it with the sisterhood.'

'I'm trying. I borrowed a book from the library, but I suspect it's just ash now.' Mallory wasn't sorry, preferring books a little lighter than bloody battles and family rifts, but, given the way Harri looked, she'd do it just to make him happy. Maybe.

'How's Lowri?' Harri asked.

Mallory rolled her eyes. 'Fine. The Lowris of this world always are. She's already making plans to scout for alternative locations for the school. She says she'll keep the name – the former students are making it a condition of their fundraising efforts – but she was thinking of somewhere towards the Welsh Marches. Monmouthshire, for example.'

'Out of our patch, then,' said Harri, with satisfaction.

'Think the sisterhood might have a resurrection one day through one of the old members, or perhaps a teacher we haven't yet identified?'

Harri shrugged. 'Branwen and Rhiannon have finished with the group, I'm sure. I'm less positive about Angharad and Kigva. They got some satisfaction with the control element, but I also think they've made new lives for themselves.'

Mallory reached over and took one of Harri's grapes. Popping it in her mouth, she winced at its sweetness. 'There could be teachers in the school we haven't identified that were being targeted by Eirin, despite Emiah saying it was just the three of them. You know what happens with criminal activity, you end up playing whack-a-mole with it. As soon as you've erased one form, another pops up.'

'As long as it's in Monmouthshire, I don't care.'

'Sure.' She didn't believe him for a minute, and knew Harri would be keeping a close eye on the women he'd reacquainted himself with in the course of the investigation. 'So,' she said, taking hold of Harri's hand. 'You've got me for Christmas and I'll be bringing Toby over when he comes down.'

Harri groaned. 'I've never felt less festive. Can't we just pretend Christmas isn't happening?'

'Don't be a spoilsport. However, I had a chat with Fran. Toby goes back to his dad's on the twenty-ninth, and Fran's got nothing planned for the New Year.'

Harri closed his eyes. 'Don't organise a party. I've got no energy.'

'And I've got no friends. I've found a hotel in Ireland. We could get the ferry over from Fishguard and drive there for a few nights. Fran will stay with the kids. It'll be just the two of us.'

Harri groaned. 'I'm not sure I can cope with the thought of a ferry.'

'All right. Come and stay with me in my caravan.'

'For the love of God, Mallory, will you please find somewhere else to live?'

Mallory laughed. 'In the new year, I'll start looking. After our holiday.'

Harri closed his eyes. 'Anywhere but Monmouthshire. I never want to hear the name of the Solstice Sisterhood again.'

Acknowledgements

Thank you to my agent Kirsty McLachlan at Morgan Green Creatives for her constant support and to my Canelo editors Louise Cullen and Alicia Pountney for their work on this book. Also thanks to Kate Shepherd. Tony Butler helps with his forensic look at my writing which is much appreciated as is the support of Judith Butler to whom this book is dedicated.

Thanks to promoters of my books especially the brilliant Niki and Karen at Gwisgo Books in Aberaeron, Karen Meek, my fellow authors – Sheila Bugler, Julie Ann Corrigan, Jeanette Hewitt, Rachel Lynch, Vicky Newham, Marion Todd and Michael Wood – and Crime Cymru pals including Bev Jones, Alis Hawkins, Gail Williams, Phil Rowlands and Philip Gwynne Jones. Chloe Tilson at Waterstones in Aberystwyth is a huge support of Welsh crime fiction (and other genres) and we're very lucky to have her in West Wales.

Thanks to all my family who read and recommend my books, especially Dad who sends them far and wide, and to my husband, Andy. Finally, thanks to all my readers, especially those who chat on my Saturday morning Facebook posts. We have a lovely community talking about books, if you want to join in at: https://www.facebook.com/SarahWardCrime

Do you love crime fiction and are always on the lookout for brilliant authors?

Canelo Crime is home to some of the most exciting novels around. Thousands of readers are already enjoying our compulsive stories. Are you ready to find your new favourite writer?

Find out more and sign up to our newsletter at canelocrime.com